Praise for **FREE the BEAR**

"Free the Bear is a fascinating and richly detailed glimpse into a near future that might be upon us sooner than we realize. The novel is full of complex, well-rounded characters, from the Chinese martial artist and Zen student who initiates the secession to the quirky cast of youthful gamers who are its non-violent army. The evocation of the Independent Free Republic of California (IFROC) makes the speculative scenario realistic and absorbing. Free the Bear! is both provocative and a great fun read!"

– **Stephen Billias**, author of *The American Book of the Dead* and *Quest for the 36*

"CD Spensley's Free the Bear is an especially timely work of speculative fiction for the age of Trump. A novel of ideas – the creation of a self-aware Artificial Intelligence from glowing tropical fish and human neurons; a rebellion of a million gamers and one philosopher; a twenty year plot to withhold key science from the Federal government; the dream of a genuinely peaceful succession of California from the Union – all dreams on the cusp of reality until triggered by the national emergency created by the election of Donald Trump. Free the Bear is a rousing adventure story and a cautionary tale of the unintended consequences of utopian dreams."

– **Michael Alenyikov**, author of the award-winning novel, *Ivan and Misha*

"An AI's exponential growth, brilliant minds steeped in both science and spirituality, and the Bay Area's frustrated youth – these are the seeds of California's independence. Free the Bear is a fun and smart look not only at how it could happen, but also at how the movement creates its own myths along the way."

– **Jeff Liss**, author of *The Second Pact*

"Wildly ingenious, Free the Bear follows in the hallowed footsteps of Ernest Callenbach's 40-year old Ecotopia, but in the new breakaway nation posited by CD Spensley's fictional West Coast exit-plan, it's tech geeks who run the show. Might we have here a revenge of the coders and gamers scenario...or is this update on the utopian/dystopian genre a cautionary exposé of idealism gone astray? Either way, this rocking anti-gov- and sci-fi-flavored adventure could not be more timely, as real secessionist movements rear up across the globe and the US Feds threaten Blue State values. This engrossing novel regales the imagination with thought-provoking what-ifs."

– **Mindela Ruby**, author of the novel *Mosh It Up*

"Believable science, fast pacing, an Ender's-Game-styled teen gamer-gang, and a tank of fish so smart it hurts. What's not to love?

This fun, sharply plotted romp through the California zeitgeist is a fever dream where the nightmare of our current political fate finds an escape for the enlightened.

CD Spensley has done their homework and the well paced, character driven tale hits all the right notes; near future AI technology, a corrupt federal government, the political long game the right wingers specialize in, the Marin County dirt biker mentality of ride hard and take no prisoners (but if you do take prisoners house them in a Lake Tahoe resort they're loath to leave)."

– **P. Honan Keeley**, author of *Strong Box*

FREE the BEAR

CD SPENSLEY

FREE the BEAR by CD Spensley
http://www.freethebearbook.com
© 2017 CD Spensley – All rights reserved.

No portion of this book may be reproduced in any form without written permission from the authors and publisher, except as permitted by U.S. copyright law.

For permissions contact:
info@freethebearbook.com
Cover by DC Spensley
ISBN: 9781549914010

CONTENTS

Prologue   Pg 1

Chapter One   Pg 7

Chapter Two   Pg 15

Chapter Three   Pg 23

Chapter Four   Pg 28

Chapter Five   Pg 46

Chapter Six   Pg 55

Chapter Seven   Pg 60

Chapter Eight   Pg 64

Chapter Nine   Pg 67

Chapter Ten   Pg 74

Chapter Eleven   Pg 86

Chapter Twelve	Pg 96
Chapter Thirteen	Pg 104
Chapter Fourteen	Pg 118
Chapter Fifteen	Pg 123
Chapter Sixteen	Pg 141
Chapter Seventeen	Pg 153
Chapter Eighteen	Pg 161
Chapter Nineteen	Pg 166
Chapter Twenty	Pg 178
Chapter Twenty-One	Pg 182
Chapter Twenty-Two	Pg 193
Chapter Twenty-Three	Pg 209
Acknowledgements	Pg 221

PROLOGUE

Pound, pound, pound.

"Order, order. As chairman of the United States Senate Committee on Appropriations, I hereby bring this emergency meeting of the California Noncompliance Subcommittee to order."

Keeping a grip on his wooden gavel, the Chairman, R-Mississippi, sits down at the head of the sprawling conference table. On the right side of the table are seated six senators: R-Kentucky, R-Alabama, R-Tennessee, R-South Carolina, R-Arkansas, and R-Oklahoma. Absent from the table's left side are any members of the Democratic Party, where normally on subcommittees they would sit in parity with their Republican colleagues. Also missing is a ranking member of the Democratic Party, normally present at all subcommittees. Most unusual is the gentleman seated at the far end of the table – the current White House Chief Strategist.

Suddenly from the other side of the massive door to this historical room erupts a series of loud pounding, then a woman's voice, muffled by the three inches of ancient oak:

"As a senior senator and member of the Appropriations Committee I demand that you open this door and let us in!"

The men in the room murmur and face the Chairman. More pounding is heard from the other side of the door, followed this time by a muffled male voice:

"It is unconstitutional to convene while deliberately excluding seated Appropriations Committee members! This will not stand!"

The Chairman rolls his eyes and motions to the armed federal officer to open the door.

The senior senator, D-California, leads the way, followed by the junior senator, D-Maryland. It is just the two of them, and they take their seats on the table's left. The Senior Senator declares: "This is unconscionable and outrageous. What is the purpose of this meeting?"

"Madam Senator, please desist with the dramatics. I have just opened the meeting to discuss the matter of California, where the governor now stands in direct defiance of Federal mandates."

A voice drawls from the back right side of the table: "Who does this goddamn Moonbeam think he is? I thought we were done with this pinhead hippy in the 1970s. How'd he get the nerve to defy the Government of the United States of America?"

The Senior Senator from California, the only woman in the room, gasps loudly, while the Junior Senator from Maryland openly shouts: "I can't believe this is happening! You can't do this!"

"We can," the Chairman, says, "and we will. And any more outbursts from you or your matriarch here and you'll be ejected for obstructing a government proceeding and subject to fine and/or imprisonment."

The Senior Senator stands up in objection.

The Chairman pounds his gavel. "Parliamentary order will be observed in this chamber! Order right this minute!"

The Senior Senator, in defiance, remains standing. She outstretches her hands, as if to quiet the room:

"Gentlemen and Fellow Senators, we have worked together for years. What could possibly be so important to convene while the Senate is on break for our historic Independence Day, and without inviting your colleagues across the aisle? This is highly irregular and probably illegal."

The Chairman now stands.

"We have a legal quorum, Madam Senator, and I assure you that nobody wants to be here on their holiday. If you had been able to keep a lid on your goddamn governor, we would have no reason to forgo time with our families to straighten out this mess."

"Keep a lid on my governor? Mess? The only mess here is one Republicans have created by not rebuffing this unqualified and dangerous oligarch before he was electe.

In response, the White House Chief Stra_ end of the table, leaps out of his chair:

"Don't push your luck here, Madam Senator. _ recriminations will become problematic for you un_ current administration. We don't take these kinds of t_ lightly. This is not your old Uncle Tom presidency. Those da_ are over."

The Junior Senator, his face flushed with fury and disbelief, leaps up and points to the Strategist.

"What gives you the right to be in here from the Executive branch? What about procedure or law? What about separation of powers? I will not stand for this illegal meeting. I will not yield the floor until you all see reason and cease with this parody of governance!"

The Chairman motions to a uniformed officer nearby. "Will the federal officer please escort the Junior Senator from Maryland out of this chamber. As chair of this committee I am appalled by this behavior and will not stand for it one more second."

The federal officer quietly but forcefully walks over behind the Junior Senator.

"Hell, there is so much wrong with this I don't know where to begin! You can expect the Senate Judiciary Committee to have my full report, and I will go to the press, whatever the consequences."

He glances over at his fellow Democrat, who nods in approval. The Junior Senator is escorted out and the door closes on the chamber. Those standing reluctantly take their seats.

"Now that we have that bit of foolishness out of the way," the Chairman chuckles, "we can finally proceed. I need to reiterate that we are here to decide on a fitting response to California's escalating belligerence. As you know, recently all Federal funding for programs in the state was suspended because of this 'sanctuary city-state' and other nonsense."

He glances over at the Senior Senator, but she's not falling r the bait.

"To add insult to injury, Brown announced on Friday that his state will suspend all tax and other revenue owed to the Federal Government. This is both unwise and illegal. He's quite an idiot."

"Well," the Senior Senator responds in an even tone, "as you know, California is a donor state, meaning it pays more in federal taxes than all the aid it receives from the federal government. And I think it is revealing that the chairman presiding over this meeting comes from a state that receives, in the form of federal grants and other assistance, nearly ten times what it pays the federal government."

The Chairman chuckles again. "Be that as it may, Madam Senator, what your governor is doing is illegal, and worse, treasonous. You'll be lucky if the President doesn't order Federal Marshals and National Guard to crawl all over Sacramento and make sure your state pays its fair share."

"What?!" the Senior Senator exclaims. "Have you sunk so low as to resort to threats of violence on American citizens on our own soil? What, is this a military dictatorship now?"

Suddenly the door to the chamber opens, startling the Chairman and eliciting looks from everyone in the room. The White House Strategist stands up, just as President Trump enters the room. Two secret servicemen follow, who walk around the room briskly checking for threats and take up station at the entrance.

"Welcome Mr. President" the Chairman says, starting to stand, along with everyone else, including the Senior Senator.

"Sit, sit," the President says, plopping himself down in the seat that should be holding the Democratic Ranking Member of the Appropriations Committee.

"Mr. Chief Strategist, Senators, and Madam Senator, I hope you are making progress on the matter of California's little…" the President uses his index fingers to mime scare quotes: "…problem."

A few chuckles come from the right side of the table.

The President smiles, pleased with the approval. "I sure

would like to fire the bastard. He's never been a good governor. A complete disaster! A very, very, very crooked screwball!"

The President looks around for more chuckles, more approval, and the men on the right side accommodate.

The President, egged on now, pounds his fist on the table. "Mr. Chairman, I want you to make this hurt! I want you to punish California and fine them until they bleed." He flashes one of his famous grins, then gushes sickeningly sweet: "Can you do that for me, Mr. Chairman?"

A secret serviceman whispers into the President's ear, and the President nods.

"Okay, I have a meeting with my lawyers now. The ACLU thinks they can rattle my chain, but I have a very, very big chain, so I don't see it happening. Get this done now! I want these idiots from California to feel the pain!"

President Trump pushes back his chair and walks out of the room, before anyone has much of a chance to rise. The Senior Senator from California stares in open-mouthed disbelief. The Chairman looks around the table.

"You heard the President, let's get this done before dinnertime!" He then gestures to the man at the end of the table. "Mr. Chief Strategist, please proceed."

"Thank you, Mr. Chairman."

The man from the Executive branch stands up to better address everyone in the chamber:

"Senators, until the President's recent appointment to the Supreme Court, it has not been possible to impose large, and in this case, fitting fines, on any individual state because of protections from the 8th Amendment to the Constitution forbidding 'cruel and unusual punishment' – the measure of which is whether these fines are so grossly excessive as to amount to deprivation of property without due process of law. Our people at the Supreme Court, however, have surgically overturned the precedent, as it applies to the states, while preserving the protections for individuals and corporations."

All the men nod, while the Senior Senator focuses off in the distance, her face white as a sheet. The Strategist leans back on his heels defiantly.

"So you see, the road ahead to punish California is cleared. All that remains is for the Senate to set the fine to the suitable level, keeping in mind the President's wishes expressed just now. I believe the phrase he used was 'fine them until they bleed.' After which we fast-track the order through the House, which is already standing by to do exactly that."

The Chairman leans in on the table. "Okay, thank you."

The Strategist sits down.

The Chairman addresses the men on his right. "As you know, the committee has already deliberated this. Who will make a motion that the fine for California's failure to comply with Federal mandates regarding immigration, drug enforcement, and many other crucial national security measures – compounded now by their withholding of much needed Federal tax revenue – is hereby fixed at 1.5 trillion dollars."

This motion is forwarded and seconded. All eyes fix on the Senior Senator from California.

The Chairman calls the vote: "All in favor say *aye*."

"Aye," say the men in the chamber.

"All opposed say *nay*."

The Senior Senator from California stands, faces the Chairman, and says firmly and solemnly: "Nay".

The Chairman responds with a loud laugh. "Well, the ayes have it."

The Senior Senator from California walks directly out of the chamber.

CHAPTER ONE

I was the last to leave the bunker that bloody night. All the kids, in shock, ended up in a group huddle, saying they were going to quit, even Courtney. Then still in a huddle, they stumbled out of the bunker, with a dazed but determined Courtney leading. I didn't follow her, or them. Believe me, I didn't want to stay in there either with a dead soldier, but I felt I needed to separate myself and wait until they were gone. When I was sure of that, I ran outside. I had no idea what I would do next, but I ran with purpose.

Passing the next bunker, I noticed a teen's mountain bike propped up against the wall. Following my instincts, for once, I grabbed the bicycle, swung a leg over the crossbar, and began careening down the fire road. As a tall man, my legs were definitely out of proportion and bowed like some circus clown act, but by gripping the handlebars tightly I managed to keep the front tire from wobbling under my weight and throwing me off the side of the mountain. I was pretty sure I had left the bunker without detection, and without being followed. By land, anyway. You could never tell who was observing from above.

At the bottom I reached the saltwater lagoon and veered left, onto the dirt trail along the water's edge. The gibbous moon illuminated a squadron of brown pelicans bobbing on the water. I tried to consciously weigh what I was doing. Was I in shock, responding to some fight or flight impulse? Was I acting irrationally and sabotaging my role as an objective chronicler?

Across a short spit of sand, the ocean breakers pounded the shoreline, threatening to raise the stakes even higher. Should I stop and weigh the options? But instead, I pushed forward, pedaling even faster, digging into it. I reached the old army road, and when that ended, the fire road with its steep Marin County incline. I switched on the electric motor. Within minutes I was passing a hundred year old bunker left untouched by IFROC, the Independent Free Republic of California, which had been left open for tourists to climb around on and read the faded U.S. Park Service plaques about the military history of the area. IFROC wanted Californians to remember the extraordinary efforts directed towards building a coastal defense for a California that had never been invaded. Not by the Japanese, not by the Russians. No, it had been left to the Americans to attack their own West Coast.

And I had just witnessed it.

At this point I knew I could still turn around and no one would be the wiser. I could remain the impassive, objective chronicler – the academic historian who had agreed to record an exceptional movement in history – but I kept going. Something told me I would never forgive my cowardice if I didn't put being a human first. Nanook of the North all over again. And then there was the obvious breakdown of command that all of us had witnessed between Courtney and Sabatini – even before the Fed soldier's incursion into the bunker and his gruesome murder by Sabatini.

I shivered uncontrollably as these images flashed back to me. I was now climbing the imposing Coyote Ridge, second only in height to the rugged and invisibly fortified Mount Tamalpais. My journey from here was longer than I liked. From the IFROC bunkers to Green Gulch it was probably six miles as a crow would fly, but it was nearly twice as far by fire road. And across terrain where I would be more exposed.

Feathery tops of wild fennel towered over the rutted fire road. Placing my feet on the footrests, I let the bike do its work, climbing steadily, gravel sputtering off the back tire. The fennel gave way to creosote bush, then sticky monkey brush.

FREE the BEAR!

On top of the ridge, I stopped to get my bearings. The moon was gone and the sky to the east, over the Berkeley Hills, was turning light. I pictured myself displayed on hundreds of IFROC monitors.

What did it mean that Virgil hadn't responded to the kids' urgent messages from the bunker? And why hadn't CAL answered my own calls for help?

I scanned the fallow fields of Green Gulch below. If I continued overland, the sensors would detect an intruder and set off a general alarm. Yet if I approached by the mountain road, only CAL's hidden cameras would detect my presence, which is what I wanted. I veered toward the mountain road, just hoping CAL would let me through.

Twenty minutes later I braked at a sharp curve where the mountain road met the faintest tracks of a four-wheeled vehicle in the grass. A giant eucalyptus tree stood sentry. I straddled the under-sized bike between my legs and posed for the cameras that were certainly hidden somewhere up in the branches. In the olden days – the early 1990s when I'd first visited Green Gulch – instead of hidden cameras, a beautifully hand-carved, wooden sign had swung from the massive tree, inviting visitors to venture down the asphalt lane that wound through the tenacious grove of eucalyptus, bringing them to the bottom of the gulch, where live oaks shaded the rustic buildings housing the world-famous Zen Buddhist center. Since IFROC, the welcome sign was gone, as was the asphalt. All the oak trees in the gulch had disappeared, having been wiped out by the '98-'07 Sudden Oak Disease.

Satisfied that my image had been recorded, I wheeled the bike behind the tree, taking my time to hide it beneath the bark and dried leaves. It was better to allow as much time as possible for CAL to inform Virgil.

I had no idea how I would be greeted. I hadn't come to Green Gulch since the secession had started seven months ago. And I was more than breaking the Council ban. I was about to defy, after twenty years as official chronicler of this revolution, a professional oath of objectivity. I was actively participating in history unfolding.

Again, it occurred to me that I might be in shock. Before tonight I had never seen such graphic violence. Sure, in movies and games, but not what it really looked like, with unbearable blood and gore. I walked down the hill through the trees, knowing my decision had more consequences than I could keep in my mind at once. I was no master of chess like Clement, who was a true genius. Or like CAL, who was Clement's work of genius.

It was the season when monarch butterflies were supposed to start migrating back to Northern California from Mexico, but I hadn't seen any yet. Not one set of fluttering wings that might alter the course of events. The leaves crackled under my feet, producing the pungent odor of eucalyptus, and I allowed myself a moment of calm nostalgia. I missed the times I hiked in the woods here, and the days spent working silently in the fields. And the simple meals, followed by pithy conversations about zazen with the monks. It was indeed contradictory that a revolutionary council should have been born – well, if not born, then propagated – in a Zen Buddhist center. It was equally contradictory that being a Quaker, a pacifist, I should become involved in chronicling a conflict to which I was morally opposed. Yes, the IFROC secession was supposed to be entirely non-lethal. But did anyone, including myself, ever truly believe that a separation from the United States, the most militarized country in the world, would not turn to a bloody war? That Northern California, along with western parts of Oregon and Washington, could challenge the Federal Government and not sustain horrible casualties?

Two generations of IFROC leaders believed it was possible and made it happen. But was this miraculous moment in time about to come undone?

As a much younger person, coming of age in The San Francisco Bay Area, I fully embraced what some called the California Ideology – the idea that the human race would accelerate its evolution through technology. And when I was introduced to the idea of Calexit early on (long before the

Russians adopted the term for their own nationalist purposes, and long before Brexit) it made a lot of sense to me. I could envision technology providing the tools for a new kind of revolution, and I could foresee Calexit as a model for how a corrupt, outdated, and malignant superpower could be broken up into smaller, less dangerous nation-states – without the loss of human life! At twenty-seven, struggling to finish my doctorate in history at UC Berkeley, unable to focus and succumbing to existential angst, I leapt at the chance to act as the official chronicler of the Independent Free Republic of California, better known as IFROC.

And here I was, directly influencing the storyline. Something I had promised others I would not do. The gamers had accomplished amazing advancements for the revolution, but Louie Sabatini had become the bully on the playground. And now he had spilled the first blood, killing a Fed soldier. The leaders had to know.

Leaving the protection of the eucalyptus, I stepped into the early morning sun and the dusty smell of manzanita and sage. The dry heat of Indian summer bore down on me. I reached the bottom of the gulch where tall grasses now camouflaged the half-dozen abandoned-looking buildings. When approaching the Japanese tea house, I hesitated, knowing what was hidden inside. The risk of entering, of revealing IFROC's greatest ally, was too great. I continued walking and stepped onto a redwood deck.

This is not a personal issue between Sabatini and me, I told myself.

The deck creaked below my feet. I walked to the edge and scanned the brush.

Or were these kinds of decisions always personal?

A short distance away I spotted the telltale steam. At the plume's base, I could make out Virgil's jet-black hair catching the glint of the sun. I stomped my feet on the deck and saw the commander raise his head towards the sound. Virgil was extremely nearsighted. I waited for him to grab his glasses and to see it was clearly me.

I jumped from the deck and walked along the footpath through the French broom, the rangy shrub brought from the Mediterranean during the last century for erosion control. Where once languid oak trees had stood, and before that, thousand-year-old redwoods, this invasive bush, with its twisted, hairy branches, filled the gulch and surrounded the hot tub, where it thrived off the steam. Its presence only added to the run-down, abandoned feeling of the place, which was the idea. When the secession was completed, however, Virgil said he was going to restore the center to its original beauty of redwoods, ferns, lupine, and calla lilies. He had observed this in his dreams, he said.

The redwood hot tub was sunk in the ground, surrounded by a soft, thick moss. Virgil nodded in my direction, then removed his glasses and closed his eyes. Beyond his head, a life-sized Buddha sat in zazen: its legs crossed, fingers resting on knees, overgrown clumps of thyme and marjoram lapping at its feet. I slipped out of my clothes and lowered myself into the tub. Closing my eyes, I focused on the sharp sting of the hot water, on Virgil's deep breathing, and on the silence beyond. Green Gulch of 2017 was vastly different from Green Gulch of 1993, when Virgil first invited me to visit. Gone were the monks and the cultivated fields, yet a sense of timelessness still lingered over the place.

"You were instructed not to come here," Virgil said, breaking the silence.

I kept my eyes closed. I wanted to indulge myself with a few more moments of timelessness. There had been so precious little time to relax, let alone meditate, over the past seven months. And yes, I had been resentful at times. Why was I the only one at the front line, suffering the tedium of the kids in the bunker, watching the secession unfold from the insidious disconnect of their computer screens, while the rest of The Council sat around in their steaming hot tubs?

I opened my eyes. Just above our heads, a monarch butterfly hovered before flying off. At last, I thought, a change in the initial conditions that might alter everything. Virgil had taught me that much about chaos theory.

"You know that Sabatini killed a Fed," I said.

I expected a reaction. But the artful warrior revealed nothing.

"In front of all the kids," I added.

Still nothing.

"The kids are quitting, Virgil. Even Courtney. They're gamers, Virgil. They no longer want to play."

And then it was over. The twenty-two year role as chronicler, as objective observer, finally died with these words. Yet the words kept erupting: "You must have known about the killing, Virgil. The surveillance cameras, the alarms. You must have received their frantic messages. Why didn't you respond?"

A turkey buzzard soared overhead, a raven chuckled in a nearby tree.

"I waited as long as I could, Virgil. I didn't want to have to do this!"

Virgil opened his eyes now.

"I just didn't know what else to do," I whined.

Virgil stared through me, and I felt the recurring weight of being around people whose minds flashed differently and came to rest on notions that offered no roadmap for others to follow.

"You came here and disobeyed direct instructions," Virgil said. "You put yourself and the secession at risk, over a personal matter."

How did he know about my hatred towards Sabatini?

"You came here because you're a pacifist," Virgil continued, along a different and unexpected vein. "I cannot find fault in you, only in myself. You told me that you did not believe in war for any cause. And now you want to quit. Now that blood has been spilled."

"No," I replied quickly. "I mean, I don't know. That's not what I was really thinking. My concern is for IFROC and for its success."

I moved closer to Virgil and lowered my voice. "It's the kids who are going to quit. It was a fantastic computer game to them, the best they'd ever played, but now Sabatini has made it a bloody war. And the kids don't want anything to do with that. Not because they're pacifists like me, Virgil. But because they are gamers, not soldiers."

Virgil nodded and closed his eyes again. Maybe it was his time to face truths. I wondered where he would go. Somewhere inside, of course. As a warrior. As a seeker.

For the first time, Virgil looked older than his age of fifty-one. His hair was still jet black and thick, parted straight down the middle – "balancing his face and suiting his temperament," as I had written many years ago. Yet the happy creases around his eyes had grown deeper and more numerous. His jowls had the puffiness of inactivity, especially for a dedicated martial artist. No doubt decades of preparation for the secession had taken their toll. Certainly the sacrifice of giving up the life of a seeker to become the leader of a revolution used up a man more quickly. Virgil had always been much older than the people he surrounded himself with, although you used to not be able to tell. A vision of thick, strong arms came to mind. Gorilla-sized muscles pulling his one hundred and sixty pounds up a three hundred foot redwood tree.

"What are we going to do?" I asked.

"The next action," said Virgil. "We just have to understand what that is."

Virgil then closed his eyes and disappeared from the present.

CHAPTER TWO

Jesus Christ, I hate this! May as well chop the goddamn thing down...

The winter of 1993 was an El Niño year and it was still raining late into May. I hung fifty feet up in a climbing harness, while the ancient redwood tree dripped on me incessantly, even though it hadn't rained for hours. I cursed ever meeting these Earth First! activists. I placed my foot in the climbing loop, flung my body forward, and stood up, all the while fighting off a serious leg cramp. With my left hand I slid the hand knot up as high as it would go, sat back down, and prepared myself to start all over again, moving up the tree in excruciating increments.

The compact Chinese man with the gorilla arms was almost to the platform near the top of the tree, although the two of us had started from the bottom at the same time.

My foot slipped out of a loop and my harness dropped several feet.

"Fuck!"

The man with the gorilla arms peered down. "Everything okay down there?"

A kid with blond dreadlocks shouted from below: "Yeah, dude. What's with the fucking language?"

I looked down at the handful of kids at the base of the tree, who were laughing, some beating on hand drums. One shook a tambourine at me in a mock salute.

"Hang in there, dude!"

At twenty-five, I was probably a decade older than some of

these kids, and I was never very hip. I grew up in Berkeley and considered myself a liberal, even a progressive liberal, but these kids came from a different die. Most of them had probably dropped out of high school. Their education was saving redwoods, combating local authorities, and following Jerry.

I looked up at the gorilla man, who was closer to my age, maybe even older.

"Any suggestions on how to get up this tree faster?"

"Try smaller steps. And don't push the hand knot up so high."

"Smaller? You've got to be kidding me."

"Rely on the leverage."

I was skeptical but I gave it a try and found it was good advice. Still, I felt like an idiot for coming out here. I was all for supporting the cause – stopping the destruction of another grove of old-growth redwoods, after the U.S. Forest Service had auctioned off the lumber rights to some corporate zip-o-log company – but I was annoyed at myself for not having done my homework first. I'd met some members of Earth First! at a death penalty protest at San Quentin, moments after the Supreme Court had denied a final stay for a Tibetan monk, who was refusing his last dinner before death by lethal injection. At the time it had seemed like a good idea to escape to the redwoods. If I couldn't save people, maybe I could at least save some trees by donating some cash for the unique opportunity of spending the night on an eight-by-eight platform, three hundred feet up in an ancient redwood. I'd envisioned something like a Sierra Club outing, with friendly, organized leaders. Instead, I was met at the trailhead by a gruff Forest Service ranger, who wouldn't let me out of my car.

"Sir, what are your plans?"

"Isn't this public land?" I asked.

"Belongs to the National Forest."

"That's what I thought."

I knew my rights. I didn't have to explain myself to this quasi-cop. I used to consider park rangers to be the good guys, more interested in protecting natural resources than corporate claims. And I hadn't come all this way to stir up trouble for myself or for the tree-sitters. Obviously the kids were delaying a logging operation, which was illegal, and they were occupying land that was temporarily closed to the public, even if the four-mile hike to get to their location was unrestricted.

"Okay, sir." The ranger capitulated, moving away from my door. "There's been some trouble up here over logging issues. I just want to advise you to be careful on your hike. Have a nice day."

I watched the man jump into his mint colored pickup and drive off in a cloud of dust.

"Is that working better?"

The Chinese man was now directly above me.

"Yes, I think so."

Within a few minutes I was alongside him.

"Thank you," I said.

"No problem."

He extended his hand. It was thick, like a paw.

"Virgil."

"Durant," I replied. "Why did you stop?"

"I was waiting for you."

We were swinging over a 100-foot drop, yet Virgil seemed as relaxed as a tree sloth.

"Well, very kind of you to wait. I'm afraid I'm out of shape. Too much time on the computer."

"Are you a programmer?"

"No, a graduate student."

"What field?"

"History."

"Ah. Will Durant."

Not everybody was familiar with my namesake, the historian who transformed the art of chronicling in the 20th century. Will Durant was also responsible for popularizing the history of ideas, an accomplishment that I admired more than some of my traditional professors at Berkeley found healthy.

"Yes, my father named me after him."

"Got a problem up there?" one of the kids shouted.

"Just enjoying the view," Virgil shouted back. Then to me: "Shall we?"

"Do I have a choice?"

I cringed at the whine in my voice, left over from my earlier negative attitude, which didn't seem to fit now with this new companion and the expanding situation.

Virgil laughed. "Only you would know."

He took off up the tree, and I reluctantly followed. Within twenty minutes we had both arrived at the first platform, or rather, directly beneath it.

"Interesting," I uttered.

"Yes, very," Virgil agreed.

We looked down for the kids. But conveniently, they had disappeared from the base of the tree, having lost interest in the amateur climbers.

"I don't think we can get on the platform without help," I said.

"An adequate security measure," Virgil agreed.

A birdcall came from an adjacent tree. I had noticed how sounds echoed longer up here, but when they finished, it was exceptionally still.

"It's a different world up here," Virgil said, as if expressing my thoughts out loud.

Suddenly other birdcalls began filtering through the forest, louder and sharper. Human, I realized. A figure appeared among the branches, sliding down a rope connected to an adjacent redwood. Switching my focus to the larger ecosystem, I saw now the large web of ropes between the trees, and counted three blue tarps, telltale signs of other platforms. A rosy-cheeked, blond-haired kid, dressed in full camouflage rain gear, arrived in the branches above us.

"I'll help you onto the platform."

A thump overhead, and the boy's face peered down, over the platform's edge.

"I'll push you towards that tree over there. You can kick off it and get a swing going. When you're high enough, I'll grab you."

"What?" I asked.

But the boy was already pushing, and I just managed to put my hands out in time not to smash into the adjacent tree. I pushed off, and swung back to the platform, and after a few rounds of this, I felt the back of my harness being grabbed and pulled onto the platform – like a fish gaffed and brought aboard a ship. I rolled onto the platform on my belly.

"Wow," I said.

"Yes, so can I ask you to step back? I've got to get the other guy."

"Of course."

The platform wasn't much larger than a double-sized bed. I moved against a back railing and watched Virgil, gleeful like a little kid, land on the platform, feet first. Completely humbled, I allowed the boy to unhook my harness. Virgil unhooked his own.

The boy's name was Matt, and he had been living in the trees ever since the auction had been announced four months ago. He said that he wasn't going down until the Feds cancelled the deal or they killed him.

I looked towards Virgil to see what he thought of this information, but I couldn't read much.

Matt showed us the simple amenities on the first platform: a camp stove, several freeze-dried packages for the evening meal, a radio for music, a lantern, a water jug, a chamber pot, two sleeping bags, and two whistles to communicate to the other tree-sitters, in case of trouble. He pointed out a smaller second platform directly above, connected by a short ladder.

"If there are any problems during the night, wait for instruction from the other tree-sitters."

"Problems?" I asked.

The boy shrugged. "You never know. Freddies can show up any time."

"Freddies?"

"The Forest Service. But loggers are worse. They sometimes come out after the bars have closed."

"Great."

The kid then swung off abruptly, disinterested in any further discussion with the tourists, or paying customers, or patrons of a good cause – however he looked at us.

"What do you think?" I asked, as soon as the boy had left. "What do you think we've gotten ourselves into?"

The sky had partially cleared and the lowering sun sent misty rays through the sparse woods.

"I think," Virgil said softly, so quietly that I had to lean toward him to hear, "that it's going to be one beautiful evening to spend in a redwood tree."

I could only nod.

Virgil then announced that he would take the top, smaller platform. And he disappeared at once. To meditate, he said. He would return for dinner.

I took off my shoes and attempted to make myself comfortable. I sat cross-legged and tried to take in the magnificence of the view. But how could one ignore such devastation? The clear-cutting was vast. An obvious maximization of short-term profits for some conglomerate or another. Lumber sent far and wide to make another backyard deck or hot tub. Only deep in the recesses of the gulches were there vestiges of ancient redwoods. These magnificent trees were being auctioned off quietly. Opposition to this travesty was left to a few dozen kids who were brave enough to face off with bulldozers and determined lumbermen. I worried about the Freddies. I didn't want to be confronted by a bunch of drunken loggers, and I hoped this Virgil would back me up if things got confrontational.

When the sky started its evening show of brilliant pink streaks, Virgil suddenly returned. The kids had also appeared again, down below, and they shouted up that they would be leaving for the night. If any of us tree sitters spotted trouble, we could use the whistles. I realized that my platform was the lowest one in all the trees, so in effect, I was the front line of defense. How convenient.

Virgil and I heated up our dinner on the camp stove. Then reluctant to light a lantern and blind our night vision, we ate in darkness to allow our eyes to adjust naturally, eating from the pots of reconstituted chili between us.

"So tell me about your father," Virgil said.

"He was a famous man, a revered historian."

"So you've taken after your father? Choosing the same career?"

"I never considered other options."

"Oh? What would you have preferred?"

The man was full of questions, but his interest seemed genuine.

"Honestly, I don't know. I still think I want to be some kind of historian."

I found myself telling Virgil about how my father was supposed to speak at my commencement ceremonies at UC Berkeley, but I hadn't finished my thesis in time – in fact, I still hadn't finished it.

"My father spoke at the commencement, but I didn't go. I didn't want to embarrass him in front of his colleagues."

I was surprised how easily I was revealing my big shame to this stranger.

"My father passed away last year," I said. "I know I was a disappointment to him."

"What about your mother?"

"She died in a car accident when I was four. I don't remember her very well. It's always been my father and me. I think I'm still mourning my father's death."

Virgil nodded.

"I'm not sure if I can finish my thesis," I continued. "I realize now that I don't care about that particular past anymore. I was never studying Mesopotamia to please myself. To be honest, I'd rather be reading science fiction."

Virgil gave me the high eyebrow. "Arthur C. Clarke, Isaac Asimov, Kim Stanley Robinson."

I chuckled. "Philip K. Dick, Robert Heinlein, Frederick Pohl."

A sliver of moon peeked through the feathery branches in the tree's mid-section, and I remembered the name of the redwood we were occupying: Manna de Luna.

"I'm also a Quaker and a pacifist," I said. "I think history is important so we can learn from our mistakes. I'm concerned about the future and I don't like where we're headed. In so many ways we seemed doomed to just repeating ourselves. To never progress beyond being fighting little monkeys."

"Agreed," Virgil said. "But I see a growing rift between those who feel a greater interconnectedness with humanity and those who don't."

We heard laughter up in the tree above us.

"And the values of our young people are overlooked," Virgil continued. "Values untainted by commerce."

"They're sacrificing a lot to be out here in the wind and rain and danger. I wanted to come here to support that effort," I said.

I stretched my legs and the two of us fell into silence. An owl hooted close by.

"And what are you doing here?" I asked.

Virgil fell into a broad smile, a smile that would always be a part of our friendship.

"I'm a Buddhist," Virgil said. "And I felt like spending the night in a tree."

CHAPTER THREE

I know this is not how my chronicle of events should begin. Because the story of how I became friends with Virgil in no way passes as an objective, historical perspective of the buildup of the Independent Free Republic of California – IFROC – and its subsequent secession from the United States of America, and what some have recently been calling Calexit. My old Berkeley professors would ridicule me for including such personal anecdotes.

Of course, I never did finish my Ph.D.

The point is, up until the moment I went to Green Gulch seeking out Virgil, I was not an active player in the secession itself. I was an observer, a hired hand, a professional historian, a dedicated and objective chronicler of events and intentions. And as much as I would like to continue in that vein – that is, fulfill my obligation to history and to the grand dream of IFROC – I suspect now that I am too personally involved and have become my own character in this drama. Maybe that had come to pass even before I rode the bike down to Green Gulch to confront Virgil.

This story begins in San Francisco, October 1993, when top scientists from around the world convened at the International Conference on Computer and Communications Security, held at the city's downtown Moscone Convention Center. In attendance is Mr. Virgil Sung, a thirty-one year old, third-generation Chinese American, and a self-made expert in Nonlinear Dynamics, better known as chaos theory. Mr. Sung attended the conference on behalf of an unnamed corporation that periodically contracted Mr. Sung for advanced research and development. Sung listened to a presentation on quantum algorithms and their applications to the thermal limitations of computing, given by Dr. Clement Hastings, who now twenty-three, had already earned two doctorates from Stanford. Mr. Hastings, world renowned for his cutting-edge theories on bioinformatics, was also one of the world's top experts on encryption. Following the talk, Mr. Sung reportedly followed Mr. Hastings out of the conference room.

"Haven't we met before?" Virgil asked.

Several paces ahead, and heavily weighted by shoulder bags, the young scientist turned, and through tinted-blue wire frames, examined Virgil.

"Amsterdam, 1991. Software-robotics poster session. We had coffee afterwards."

"Yes," Virgil agreed, clicking his fingers with a crisp pop, and pointing at Clement. "I knew it."

At five-foot-five, Virgil came up to the middle of Clement's chest, but Virgil's physical bearing was so intense that people tended to stand back from him a few feet, which greatly reduced the height contrast.

"Shall we do coffee again?"

Virgil grinned. "Why not?"

The two scientists pressed their way through the main hall, heels clicking against the hard linoleum, heads craned forward in anticipation of escaping the greenish, florescent lighting. Clement took the lead, nodding briskly at various colleagues, while Virgil sometimes slowed, pressing hands with fellow scientists, working the crowd. A few times Virgil allowed himself to be detained longer, and Clement fought off a stab of annoyance. Still, Virgil intrigued him, this reputed autodidact and outlier scientist who commanded respect from even the staunchest academic. Virgil dressed youthfully, in a black, hooded sweatshirt, faded jeans, hightops, his jet-black hair reaching below his shoulders, but he was considered a genius at theory covering numerous fields, including physics, biology, economics, and yes, politics.

Virgil suggested a shortcut through the poster session. "On the way, there's someone I'd like you to meet."

Leading the way now, he sped through the long rows of posters without stopping until they reached a board that featured brightly colored computer renderings of the cross-section of sheep brains. A petite, full-figured Indian woman stood in front. She was wearing a conservative wool pantsuit and her brown hair was clipped tightly into a large bun, giving her a somewhat dour look. But when she saw Virgil her face lit up and suddenly she was very pretty.

"Virgil," she gushed, falling into his open arms.

The two rocked in an embrace that suggested to Clement that they were, or had been at one time, lovers (which was not true). When they broke apart, the woman noticed Clement for the first time and seemed a little embarrassed, taking a step back from Virgil.

"Clement Hastings," Virgil said, "I want you to please meet my dear friend, Dr. Marta Subramanian. The two of us go way back to elementary school."

Marta laughed. "We were playground rivals."

"She used to beat me up. And I warn you, she's stronger than she looks."

Clement shook Marta's hand, disappointed that she didn't look him in the eyes, but somewhere behind him.

"Clement has a Ph.D. in microbiology," Virgil said. "And another in mathematics. Both from your alma mater, Marta." He leaned forward and whispered in her ear, but loudly enough for Clement to hear. "Stanford awarded him both degrees at a remarkably young age."

Clement was surprised to learn that Virgil's radar was this deep into him. The two of them had never discussed these details.

"Really?" Marta replied, shifting her focus directly on Clement, and in fact, so intently that Clement wondered if she was challenging the information.

"I was twenty," he said.

"Yes, very young."

Then or now? he questioned. Marta crossed her arms and her matronly look returned, which made Clement think she meant now.

"Clement just gave a fascinating lecture on his latest work for the Pentagon developing the next generation of encryption algorithms."

Marta nodded distantly, her focus back to the space beyond him. Clement tried not to feel disappointed. Why should he want to impress this woman?

"And Marta has a Ph.D. in neural science from the University of Delhi, as well as a computer science degree from Stanford. She is currently a researcher at UCSF investigating the implantation of microprocessors into lamb brains for behavior modification and to control seizures."

Clement nodded, trying to exhibit what added up to minimal politeness and nothing more. He did note that Virgil had omitted the level of Marta's degree from Stanford, which probably meant she had only obtained a master's degree in computer science from his alma mater, and he was not aware of any distinction for the University of Delhi's department of neural sciences. What could they possibly have in common?

"So," Virgil said, first patting Clement's back and then Marta's. "Shall we go for coffee and see what kind of arcane arguments the three of us can get into?"

To Clement's surprise Marta responded enthusiastically. "Sounds like fun to me!"

Virgil led the way out of the convention hall. A lanky blond-haired lad, a stocky Chinese man, and an even shorter Indian woman made an unlikely trio, but they fell into deep conversation as they jaywalked across a busy intersection, took seats at an outside cafe, and made a variety of complex coffee orders.

"Half-caf, nonfat, double almond, single mocha," Clement told the waiter.

"Such a Valley boy," Virgil chided.

As far as I know – piecing the story together almost twenty-five years later – this was the first time that these three scientists discovered and discussed the connections between their work: a synthesis of biology, computer science, and mathematics. Would I be getting ahead of myself if I said that this first meeting was the primordial stuff from which IFROC would soon be born?

CHAPTER FOUR

Tucked among the golden rolling hills outside of Palo Alto, a nondescript office building with a smoky glass front and low maintenance shrubbery, circa 1993, remained mostly hidden from the road. Inside, beyond the Ficus trees in the reception area, cubicles filled a vast space, along with miles of industrial gray carpeting, white block walls, drop ceiling, low-level fluorescent lights, and not a single window. A pervasive hum from the lights and from the hundred or so workstations was broken only by the sound of keystrokes, the occasional cough and frequently, coming from a particular cubicle back in the far corner, the rattle of crinkling plastic.

Clement rocked in his office chair and tossed the wrapper near the trash basket, but not in. He'd become infatuated with Ginkola a few months ago while pursuing a Japanese grad student (with no success beyond a few giggly nights at the movies). He had no idea why anyone would wrap a tiny juice box in plastic, only to be unwrapped and thrown away, but he'd become quite attached to the containers themselves. Covered with Japanese he couldn't read, in garish shades of pink and green, Clement was amassing them above his head, extending his cubicle wall with an intricately (and algorithmically) stacked pyramid of cardboard. It drove the visiting VIPs batshit, which he enjoyed.

Continuing to rock in the high-backed, executive leather chair he'd stolen from the conference room, Clement noticed an instant message appear on the terminal that sat apart from his bank of other terminals -- his most secure connection. He swiveled his chair towards this monitor and read, in jagged, bright green letters against a gray screen: *Greetings, half-caf boy.*

"What?!" Clement stared at the message in disbelief. He spun his chair back to his main bank of terminals, and typed: *How the f-k?*

Moments later a message returned: *Too much faith in secure protocol?*

Clement threw back his head and laughed out loud.

"Hey!" barked his cubicle neighbor.

"Hey back," Clement growled, amicably enough. "Gink?"

"Sure."

Clement tossed his neighbor a box, over the pyramid. How did Virgil get through such heavy security? Clement opened up the program window for XGP ("extra good protection") and assigned 2.04 megabit encryption – that they'd touched upon last night. He had no idea how Virgil was pulling this off. A deluge of gibberish of characters appeared on screen. Clement punched in a few keystrokes and the message changed to: *Surprised?*

Clement typed: *That you work for you know who? Frankly... yes.*

Minutes later returned more gibberish, then after keystrokes, the message: *Correction. I work for the hackers who keep you know who on his toes. A few bank accounts removed, thank you.*

Virgil, my man!

The phone rang.

"How'd it go last night?"

Clement put his feet up on his desk. "What are you talking about?"

"When I left, you two seemed headed for some deep conversation."

Clement turned his chair against the cubicle walls and lowered his voice: "Yeah, you didn't tell me those microchips she's developed are actually robotic engineers, tinkering around in the little lamb brains."

"Thought I'd let the two of you make that connection on

your own."

"Well, it's fascinating science."

"Sure is, but let's pick up this thread later. Adios, friend. We'll talk again soon."

Moments later another message came through: *Remember, half-caf—never trust the government. And I mean never.*

Virgil's cautionary message was hardly necessary. Of course he didn't know yet about Clement's uncomfortable indenture to one of the more nefarious arms of the Defense Advanced Research Projects Agency, better known as DARPA. Clement had signed a contract for two years, in return for debt forgiveness for his school loans. While Clement was a genius in many fields, his lack of worldliness back then was disastrous. He simply couldn't imagine the government stooping low enough to entrap him into service beyond the agreed upon time period. But for the past year, Director Jenkins (or as Clement had simply nicknamed him: "the director") kept extending his contract, claiming the market rate on loans had gone up. When Clement hired a lawyer to review the contract – something he should have done in the first place – he learned about the fine print, and yes, he was indeed entrapped, at least until the economy changed. Clement didn't like to think about it, and besides he loved his work.

Marta shut off the lights to the lab and was surprised to find it already dark outside, the street lamps casting an eerie beam across her lab bench and her row of microscopes. The beam caught a misplaced Petri dish, and Marta rushed over to determine the contents: a saline blank, simply misplaced during the day. Still, she liked to run a tight ship around her lab and found herself becoming increasingly irritated at the sloppy graduate assistants. Working at a prestigious university had its perks, but the politics, the bureaucracy, and even the students these days felt cumbersome. They all seemed to lack the drive and focus required for high-level research. She looked at her watch. Seven thirty-five. Another thirteen-hour day. She unclipped her hair, and thick, long strands fell to her waist like a mane. She was supposed to meet a male friend later in the evening, but she was already fading and decided to decline. Marta dated occasionally, but she reserved her passion for her research. She hadn't felt inclined towards any long-term entanglements for some time now.

After locking up the lab, she started down the long hallway toward the elevator, counting time as her Dansko clogs tapped against the linoleum. She was aware that at this hour she was probably the only person left in the building, so it startled her to see two, dark-suited men step off the elevator at the far end of the hall and start walking towards her. Suits were not common around the university, but she'd heard word of these men making the rounds among the scientists over the past few days. Officially, they were investigating allegations into the mishandling of several large federal grants, but her colleagues suspected they were part of a fishing expedition, looking for unfunded cutting-edge research being conducted in the labs. The recent explosion of biotech, generated by the greatly expanded cooperation between scientists and innovative entrepreneurs, was making the government increasingly nervous. Politicians feared they were being left out of the loop, and their large corporate sponsors weren't about to tolerate any level of competition from young upstarts. Marta wondered if she could pretend to have forgotten something and duck back into her lab before they reached her, but as if reading her mind, the suits picked up their pace. She picked up her own pace and walked right up to them.

"Can I help you?"

"Doctor Subramanian?

"Yes?"

She noticed both men gazing where her lab jacket pulled tightly against her breasts. *Bastards,* she thought, giving them her widest eyes. "May I help you?"

The man who'd spoken wore dark glasses; the other had a pug face and looked to be the henchman.

"We need a few minutes of your time, doctor."

They flashed their badges: F.B.I.

Just like the movies, Marta thought.
"Shall we step into your laboratory?"
"Sure, if you'd like."

Marta was unclear if she was required to allow them access to her laboratory, but she didn't think so. Berkeley was a state university, but that didn't mean the Feds had automatic authorization on campus. Still, she knew how the Feds worked: if you demanded your rights, you aroused suspicion, which gave them justification to harass you. Marta knew a great deal about this: the Feds had been extorting her father for over two decades. It was well engrained in her to distrust the government.

She led the men back down the hall, her clogs now tapping in rhythm against the shuffle of their shiny dress shoes. She wished somebody else were around. They knew her name, so it was possible that this was connected to her father. She reached the lab door and had a change of mind. Both men were right behind her, so she turned and smoothed her lab jacket over her breasts and watched their eyes follow.

"I haven't got the right key at the moment, and was just about to leave for an appointment." Before they could respond, she added: "So, tomorrow? During working hours?"

"Miss, we are here investigating alleged misuse of Federal funding in or around this laboratory, the glasses man said. "As a matter of procedure we are interviewing Principle Investigators in your division. You are not necessarily under suspicion of any criminal offense. Do you have knowledge of anyone who you suspect of misuse of funds? We can grant you anonymity if you turn over information about any of your colleagues. We give you our personal assurance that all cooperation will be appreciated."

Marta, stunned by this direct approach, was slow to respond.

"Miss, you do realize that we are carefully auditing your work here, don't you?"

"Of course! All Federal contracts are audited." Marta was becoming heated now. "But I would expect a visit by Steven or

Michael, our contract monitors, and during working hours. This is out of the ordinary. The timing and circumstance is inappropriate to say the least!"

Pug face widened his stance.

"Once again, I'm available during working hours," she barked, then spun towards the door, turned the key, and stepped inside. She half-expected them to push their way in behind her, but the men remained motionless. So she closed the door, secured the lock, and held her breath. After a few long seconds, she heard their shoes shuffle back down the hallway. Marta collapsed against the door. She was under suspicion now for sure, but she'd been afraid of letting them in here. All her Federal research was in perfect order, but the most exciting experiments she was conducting with the lamb brains – the reason she worked late and into the evening – were in fact not funded by the Federal government or anyone else. With the results she'd been getting lately, Marta had started thinking about seeking funding from a biotech start-up. Now it looked like going after that avenue was going be too risky, which was hugely disappointing.

Leaving the lights off, she walked over to the window and saw the black, unmarked sedan parked in the fire lane. She'd wished that she'd seen that earlier. She would have called campus police and had them towed. She watched as the two suits exited the building, unlocked the car with a chirp, jumped into the sedan, and drove off. Marta flipped through her Rolodex and dialed.

"Hi, Virgil. Can I come over? I could really use your advice."

Virgil began chopping a mixture of bok choy, celery root, shiitake mushrooms, and ginger. With one swoop of the knife, he pushed the vegetables into a cast iron pot of simmering broth. He stood over the pot, breathing in the steam, testing the aroma. Satisfied, he reached into the nearby cupboard, where he kept his cooking and medicinal herbs in earthen pots, and pulled out a handful of wakame, gathered from the beaches of Mendocino by his hippy friends. He tossed the thick strips of seaweed, along with a pinch of myrtle weed and ginseng, into the broth. Virgil's taste in herbs was as eclectic and Californian as most things about him.

As a native of San Francisco, he'd grown up surfing Ocean Beach, playing bass in punk bands, and dating the girls from the neighborhood, who more often than not were a little too Irish for his parents. But his parents had nothing to worry about. From early childhood, Virgil embraced his ancestral culture, studying Chinese brush calligraphy with his Taoist teachers, then several forms of martial arts, including qigong, and finally Chinese medicine. As a teen, he was already self-administering acupuncture needles in points in his face and hands, and he became renowned for carrying on whole conversations with his friends while looking like a porcupine.

Virgil left the broth to continue developing and walked into the front room of his beachside bungalow. Sparsely furnished, the room was more Japanese in aesthetics than Chinese, with tatami flooring and a low table in the middle of the room with four sitting pillows around it. Virgil faced the glass picture window and took up the yoga position of sirsasana, viewing the pink sunset lighting up the clouds from his upside down position and contemplating what this new arrival of an old friend meant. He hadn't seen Marta in over a decade, yet he was aware of having set something in motion between the two of them that entwined their lives in a way, fittingly, a chaos theorist would never try to predict.

The pungency of the seaweed filtered into the living room. Marta would be arriving soon, so Virgil came out of his position and walked back to the kitchen. Reaching into the cupboard, he selected two hand-built clay bowls made by a friend at Green Gulch. The Zen Buddhist center had been his home away from home since the day he turned fourteen. Virgil would never forget his father's vehement words on that pivotal afternoon:

"Over my dead body!"

His father was a slight man who had a fondness for

accenting his words by pounding on the dining room table. His mother, forever trying to smooth things over between father and son, was serving jasmine tea – a variety her husband was particularly fond of – but he was slamming his fist so hard against the table that she was having difficulty safely landing the teapot.

"No son of mine is going to join a hippy commune!"

"They're Buddhists."

"Bullshit! They're round eyed, aren't they?"

Even at fourteen, Virgil understood the forces of racism to be as strong as any forces in nature.

Virgil stood quietly, kissed his mother on the cheek, and left the room. Then, because Virgil knew he needed to go places beyond his father's limitations, he secretly defied his father by going out to Green Gulch that very same day, and from then on as many days as possible. With the Zen Buddhists, Virgil found a group who understood the kind of mind that he possessed – a mind driven to deconstruct the world and see what was inside. The Green Gulch monks adopted Virgil as a student, and within a decade these same monks were referring to him as the professor, which was not literally true. Virgil never completed his degree at Berkeley, instead securing a number of mentors, some of whom had been his university professors in the physics and mathematics departments; others were from alternative learning centers, like Esalen at Big Sur and Sufi's from Fremont. In no small way, however, the Buddhists at Green Gulch had been Virgil's most important mentors, showing him a way to reconnect with his Chinese culture that was not only palatable but philosophically enticing. They also gave him permission, as an early teen, to question everything, including, and most significantly, the status quo.

Virgil took the two clay bowls into the living room and placed them on the table. He then walked over to the stereo, its various high-end components tucked inside a black lacquered cabinet, and cranked up the volume. Virgil liked all kinds of music, but particularly early Dub artists. Facing the large plate-glass window, where the last vestiges of pink lingered in the sky, Virgil swayed slowly to Augustus Pablo, waiting for the arrival of his old friend.

Clement pounded the return key as he input a string of commands into his computer. Moments later he heard a series of whirring sounds from the fans on his hard drive, then on a hard drive coming from the next cubicle over, and the next cubicle from that. Clement chuckled, gleeful. His monitor read: *All gamers ready to play.*

"Then let the games begin!" Clement declared, to no one but himself. The clock read 23:00, and he was alone in the building.

He opened a fresh Ginkola, throwing the plastic wrap toward the trashcan, missing as usual. He reached for what looked like an abstract rendition of a paperweight, a chaotic wad of wire and metal and electronics, loosely wrapped around two lithium batteries. Clement attached a contact to the batteries and suddenly the fist-sized object changed shape, resembling a parrot. It began repeating: "Play to win, play to win."

"You said it," Clement agreed.

"Play to win, play to –"

Clement disconnected one of the batteries so that the robotic bird's mouth continued moving, but the sound was muted.

He turned his attention to multiple chess games on his computer, and after a series of quick moves, won all the games easily. Clement rarely lost, but when he did he seemed to suffer. He claimed, if asked, that he forfeited games now and again to make sure his information footprint didn't become so well known (which was a questionable response, since Clement always covered up his footprint). In truth, Clement had only lost a handful of games since he'd been ordained the "Scarlet Knight" – and that was during his freshman days in college, when he was eleven.

After a while he input another long string of commands

into his computer and all the borrowed hard drives in the various cubicles shut down simultaneously.

Clement stood up and stretched. The clock on the wall read 01:05. He walked out of his cubicle and turned right. All around the perimeter of the room were laboratories behind thick glass. He stood in front of a glass door marked "Dr. Clement Hastings" and surveyed the dozen or so fish tanks on the lab benches.

"All right, fishies. Let's play."

Returning to his cubicle, he booted up the computer that sat apart from the others. He selected a game of tic-tac-toe, which he played slowly, making numerous, sloppy mistakes. His opponent was even slower in its response. While waiting his turn, Clement played with his robotic animals: a miniature dog, a monkey, a snake, all the size of a fist. He tinkered with them, making the dog walk on its front paws and sound like the monkey, or the monkey move like a snake. Finally, Clement clinched the game of tic-tac-toe, but just barely.

"Not bad, fishies. You're improving."

Clement typed into the computer: Good game. And moments later came a return message: *Thank you for the opportunity to play.*

Clement smiled. When designing the communication program, he'd built in a high level of formal courtesy.

He quickly entered some keystrokes and took the game back several crucial moves. *Let's keep this improvement between you and me, okay?*

Clement then changed his opponent's last moves in the game, so that it appeared to have lost sooner.

Virgil rolled over in bed and looked at his clock: three ten in the morning. He'd woken up suddenly, thinking of Marta. Not only had she not shown up for dinner, but she'd called several hours later, offering no explanation for her delay, saying she'd call right back. Which she never did. He'd left a voicemail but to no avail. Virgil returned to sleep, but when he woke up in the morning he felt certain that Marta was in some sort of trouble. He called her lab right away.

"Virgil, I owe you an explanation. I promise to call you in twenty minutes."

Which she did, from a payphone.

"Something has happened, Virgil. I must be very careful. I'm torn, my friend, because I don't want to get you involved."

"Okay, I'll meet you at Win's at noon."

Win's was a restaurant they both knew well. In Virgil's mind, he was already involved in Marta's life. She had reappeared for a reason, and Virgil was eager to discover what that was.

"Okay," she said.

Clement opened his eyes to bright sunlight. He had been living in his apartment for over two years and hadn't gotten around to buying any shades yet. His mattress and box spring rested on the floor, and when he rose from his bed, he looked as awkward as a baby giraffe trying to stand for the first time. Clement rubbed his eyes and looked at his watch: ten o'clock. Enough sleep, he guessed.

He staggered into the living room and fell into one of his two high-backed La-Z-Boys, the only furniture in the room other than a TV tray between the chairs and a small bookshelf against the wall, crammed with paperbacks. A floor-to-ceiling picture window revealed a spectacular view of the few remaining golden hills around Stanford University, but Clement's chairs were turned away, facing the interior of the apartment, which was nothing more than a stucco box with a kitchenette. The TV tray beside him overflowed with all kinds of science magazines, a wireless video game controller, and the odd Starbucks cup with his name written with a black Sharpie. Clement dug underneath the pile for his remotes. With one, he started the electric teakettle in the kitchen, and the other, woke up his robotic dog, which proceeded to the front door, to retrieve the newspaper lying inside the mail slot, and return to its creator. Clement reached down and unclipped the newspaper from an extension of the armature that could have been a mouth, but resembled more what it really was: precision-machined, spring-steel wafers, built from airline parts and arranged like clock parts, except instead of the gears, the wafers expanded and contracted, simulating muscle.

Good doggie, Clement thought, *but for it to be more than that, I need to integrate biology.*

This struck a familiar chord, since it was precisely what Clement had set his mind to work on for the past year. Most nights before falling asleep Clement programmed his unconscious to work on a particular aspect of the problem, and last night he'd directed his focus towards one of his most basic concepts: the value of adding biological complexity to the creation of algorithms. The Pentagon was interested in end results, in an encryption that couldn't be broken, but Clement was fascinated by a larger concept: developing an algorithm engine more complex than any silicon-based computer technology could ever be. He'd hinted at this the other day during his lecture at the conference, asking if the answer might lie with biology.

Clement opened the newspaper on his lap, but his thoughts remained on something Marta had said after finishing her coffee:

"The day silicon-based computer technology surpasses cellular biology in memory is the day I will return to the field of computer science."

"Interesting," Clement had said.

Clement knew he was onto something huge by crossing the common neon tetra, a well-adapted aquarium fish, with the South American knifefish, or *teleostei gymnotiformes*, which have the ability to detect and emit weak electrical fields – somewhat like nerve cells. Clement had been genetically engineering these fish for two years now, but in the past four months he'd been crossing the fish with human neurons, creating a single neural cluster of ganglia, or as he considered it, algorithmic, superbrain cells. In combination, the fish and these super-brain cells formed a biological processor which Clement called, for lack of a better term, the algorithmic life form, or the AL for short.

Linking it to advanced computer technology, by direct interface to a mainframe, the AL's intelligence had reached a level where it could play tic-tac-toe – poorly, but with steady improvement. What excited Clement the most was how any advancement seemed to be in exponential proportion to the number of brain cells added. In other words, the AL was not a brain in a box, or a super-smart machine, but an expandable neuroprocessor.

Clement sat up suddenly, his recliner snapping shut. The teakettle whistled away, but Clement wasn't hearing it through his thoughts. Marta's work with the lamb brains was entirely relevant. While she was investigating the advancement of technology inside the brain, he was bringing advanced biology to technology. It was obvious that they could help each other.

Best of all, Clement realized that if he could fulfill his government contract in the next year or so – turning over the AL to the government and successfully propelling the Pentagon ten, maybe fifteen years into the future of information security – then he would be free to pursue any field of investigation he wanted. He despised the government for entrapping him so young in exchange for a college education. Like a soldier in boot camp, he hadn't realized how much he'd resent being told what to do by that *asshole director* and his *department of entrapment*.

Clement finally heard the kettle whistling. Passing his overflowing bookshelf, he pulled out a book at random. Maybe he would read some this morning before going to work. A little scifi brain candy, to get the synapses clicking.

Marta moved around her laboratory with the grace of a dancer. She was focused on pipetting, dissecting, transferring liquids from beaker to beaker. Her students came and went throughout the morning, fulfilling their tasks without any direct interactions with the Principal Investigator. They knew better than to interrupt her concentration, although Marta sometimes caught them watching her and had to fight off the distraction. She was required to mentor these kids, and she did her best, but she had never wanted to teach. Her interests lay solely in research, but thus far in her career the opportunities outside academia were practically nonexistent, especially for women scientists.

The phone rang and Marta jumped, her nerves still on edge after last night. She realized it was probably wise to answer it. She was surprised to hear Clement's voice.

"I've been thinking about our research," he said, skipping any formal niceties, not even identifying himself. "The techniques I've developed in genetically engineering the tetras, combined with your expertise in your micro robotic engineering, could lead to an exciting new project."

Before Marta could respond, Clement was off detailing this new joint project, none of which seemed relevant to her own research interests. What struck Marta the most was his audacity. Did he not consider that she might be in the middle of something? The boy genius obviously lacked social skills.

"And I think it would be best if we used your lab for this project."

Marta burst out laughing. "My lab?"

"Why not?" He sounded offended.

"Clement, you know, I have to get back to work. Can we discuss this later?"

"Okay, let's meet for lunch. Today."

What an ego, Marta thought. As if she should already arrange her life around his.

"Sorry. I have lunch plans. In fact, I'm meeting Virgil."

"Great! I'll join you."

She'd recognized her mistake as soon as she'd said it.

"Where are you meeting?" Clement pressed her.

Marta gave him the address of the restaurant because it seemed rude not to do so. Still, she told herself, if she were going to continue to associate with Clement, let alone ever consider working with him, she was going to have to adopt a more aggressive stance – a position she'd been forced to take with many of her male colleagues.

Win's was an old-school, neighborhood Chinese restaurant

in San Francisco, where whole Peking ducks hung upside down in the storefront window, along with stuffed lotus leaves and cured Chinese sausages. Both Marta and Virgil knew the restaurant from childhood, when almost every family in the Sunset District ate at Win's at least a few times a year. She arrived a few minutes early and walked past the exotic delicacies and down a narrow aisle lined with Formica tables. In the back, sitting in the dark where the storefront light no longer reached, she found Virgil and Clement waiting for her at one of the family-style tables. She regretted letting Clement come along. Now she would not be able to explain everything to Virgil.

"So here she is," Virgil said. "The long-lost Marta."

Virgil must have already told Clement about last night. His eyes were twinkling.

"So, what happened?"

Marta looked from Virgil to Clement and back again. Then she began telling them both her story, in a lowered voice.

After she had called Virgil from the laboratory, Marta had waited until she saw the unmarked car leave the parking lot. Then she locked up again and left the building. When she was crossing the parking lot, however, the black sedan suddenly appeared in front of her and the pug-faced man jumped out. She thought about screaming and making a scene, but no one was around. The man told her not to panic, that Director Jenkins has required them to speak with her privately, because it was about her father. They felt certain she would understand.

Clement's face switched from sympathetic to incredulous.

"Director Jenkins," Marta continued, lowering her voice even further, "is a government official who has been threatening, under trumped up charges, to deport my father for years."

"Oh my efffing God," Clement exclaimed. "You're dealing with Jenkins too?" Shaking his head, "I can't fucking believe this."

Virgil motioned to Clement to calm down and thought: *Now this is getting interesting.*

"You know him?" Marta asked.

"Please go on," Virgil insisted, "then we can go into this other coincidence."

Marta continued her story. The pug face man said, if she preferred to speak in a public place, they could follow her to a nearby coffee shop, and Marta agreed. She took the lead in her old Volvo station wagon, realizing she had no choice, now that the agents had mentioned her father and Director Jenkins, his arch enemy.

"The U.S. Government won't give my father a green card, but they allow him to stay, as long as he keeps paying," she told Virgil and Clement. "This Director Jenkins has been extorting him for years. Not large amounts, but enough to keep the pressure on."

"Why?" Clement asked.

Marta hesitated. "It's complicated," she said.

"Who is Director Jenkins? And who are these men working for him. Are they really FBI?" Virgil asked.

Both Marta and Clement started talking at once:

"My colleagues thought they were biotech spies," Marta said. "But now it appears they really are Feds, and working for this Jenkins guy."

Clement jumped in: "I know this Director Jenkins. His department has been manipulating me, extending my contracts for years. I may never be able to pay back the student loans the Feds co-signed. These guys are thugs not spies."

"Yeah, Feds, spies, thugs, little difference." Virgil said. "Besides the obvious graft, the Feds are always looking for insidious ways to co-opt and weaponize research. Our friend Oppenheimer found that out the hard way."

"Absolutely," Marta said.

"Unbelievable," said Clement.

A momentary silence passed as the three scientists recalled their own less-than-savory experiences with the federal government.

"Well, their cover story is always that they're investigating the graft with our research grants," she said. "And they want us to turn over informers."

"Do you know anyone who's cheating?" Clement asked.

"No, but it won't matter to these guys. I'll have to give them a lead or else they'll up the extortion amount on my father."

Virgil and Clement shook their heads.

"After I called you, Virgil, I went directly to my father's house, to check on him. I didn't tell him about what had happened. He's old. He's been through enough."

Marta sighed deeply.

"I'm not sure what I'm going to do."

Clement spun the Lazy Susan around slowly.

"I know."

He picked up the hot chili oil and applied it liberally to his egg roll, then looked up and met Marta's gaze.

"You can work with me."

"What? Won't that send red flags to Jenkins and his cronies?"

"No. They aren't that smart. You should quit the university and come work at my lab instead. I am not under surveillance by these people. My deal is different. Other than my screwed-up contract, I have nearly carte blanche, a fat budget and the best lab Federal money can buy. They watch your state university contracts like hawks, but I have almost complete autonomy."

Marta looked at Virgil. He seemed equally caught off guard, but a smile was forming at the corners of his mouth.

"We'll combine our resources towards the project I've been telling you about," Clement said, his voice picking up speed, as if the ideas were rolling off the top of his tongue and he was becoming increasingly used to them himself. "We'll redesign the experiments with the fish, to speed up their development."

"What fish? And I can't drop my own research," Marta protested.

"You won't need to. I can offer you better lab facilities than any university."

"You could do worse for a lab partner," Virgil said, grinning now.

Clement leaned across the table. "Have I told you we've just obtained a protein splitter? Only the third one in the world."

Clement sat back. He could tell by Marta's look of astonishment that this last detail was going to cinch the deal.

I understand the question has been asked over and over: Could this have been the first meeting of IFROC? In fact, this was the second time the three scientists had met, yet it must be acknowledged that over Chinese food at Win's by the beach was the first time Marta and Clement had discussed joining forces over scientific research. Furthermore, because of their mutual distrust of the government, it was the first time Virgil, Marta, and Clement had discussed a plan to outfox the Feds.

Years later, the kids in the bunker would argue about this point. Sabatini would argue vehemently that this group of three, over lunch at Win's, had not even decided that they were a group, let alone a group calling themselves IFROC. Thus this lunch meeting could not be considered the first meeting of IFROC. But his girlfriend, Courtney Cruz – Commander Courtney Cruz – would say, "Louie, the art of war never has, and never will have, anything to do with formalities."

And I, of course, as the objective historian, was not allowed to referee on this point. But truthfully, I agreed with Courtney. Modern warfare – even supposedly non-violent warfare – had little to do with conventions. The personal had become the political and vice versa.

CHAPTER FIVE

Within three months after the lunch at Win's, Marta had given notice at the university and started working in Clement's lab. It was unlike her to act so brashly. Conservative in nature, Marta approached change like a cautious alley cat crossing the street, and mostly she tried not to change. She'd worn clogs since being a teen and had never changed her hairstyle, always maintaining it nearly to her waist. She continued to drive her late 70s Volvo station wagon, her first car, even though parts for it were nearly impossible to find. Since receiving her doctorate in New Delhi and returning to the Bay Area, she had only worked at UC San Francisco, and in fact, she had never held a job outside of academia. So why was she willing to make such a significant change now, moving her research outside the university system and into a lab she knew little about. Why was she willing to risk her career?

Was it out of fear that the Feds might deport her father after all these years?

Partially, yes.

When Virgil first brought me onboard to chronicle the development of IFROC, I had a chance to interview the key players and put together the most plausible storyline of IFROC's inception. At times, however, conflicting information made things less than concrete, as memories faded and egos filled in. With this case, it appeared that Marta's decision had more to do with the effective impact of Virgil's incremental, persuasive powers. During those two months before Marta relocated, in early 1994, Virgil had invited her to meet with him privately three times.

At the first meeting, at a breakfast place near her lab, Virgil reportedly listened to Marta tell him that she found Clement's scheme ridiculous and that she would never consider leaving the university. Clement was a spoiled kid, she said, who had no understanding of the struggle that she, as a woman, and as a woman of color, had overcome. Virgil told me that at this first meeting he did not try to defend Clement's emotional immaturity.

At the second meeting, over dinner at a nice seafood restaurant, Marta acknowledged that for all his obvious faults, Clement was a brilliant scientist and that she could see the value in collaborating with him, perhaps sometime in the future. She also spoke about her growing frustration with the university, for its political infighting and for its pressure on researchers to publish before the data was really in. Virgil encouraged her to air her concerns, including the university's lucrative contracts with the military and its relegation of basic science research to a lower status. The cutting edge of research, Virgil agreed, was no longer being pursued within the academic system, but within new kinds of public/private partnerships, many of which were quietly developing right in their backyard, in the ever-growing Silicon Valley.

The information I collected from both Virgil and Marta regarding the third meeting coincided a bit more, so it was easier to fill in the details. While the two of them were walking along Ocean Beach at sunset, Marta revealed how seriously she had been thinking about Clement's proposal.

"I have estimated that with access to a protein splitter, I could move my work up by nine months, perhaps a year. The university was budgeted to purchase a splitter this year, but it got cut. They say they'll try again next year, but who knows? It is tempting to think about what it would mean to my research to have access to the splitter now."

"You would be ahead of the curve."

"True."

They walked along in silence, the ball of sun resting just above the water, turning the sand at their feet a glittery gold.

"But Virgil, I can't helping thinking about what I would be leaving. My colleagues. My academic career. And I like the City. I'm not sure I want to go down to the Peninsula, even if it is Palo Alto."

"It is a matter of looking forward, not backward. Towards something, not away from something."

"But I'm not good with change."

"Change is constant, whether you notice it or not."

Marta stopped walking. "To be honest, I guess I'm just afraid."

Virgil turned toward Marta and took both her hands in his. "You need to be around brilliant people, Marta. Life is short."

"But am I letting the Feds drive me away from my career?"

Virgil shook his head vehemently. "No. The way I see it, these crooks are providing you with an opportunity to escape mediocrity. Here's your chance to pursue your work to its fullest potential. You can do this, Marta. You should do this. It is your destiny."

Marta took it all in. By the time they had walked back to the car, she had made her decision.

The next step, and one both Virgil and Clement spent a great amount of time discussing, was how to get Marta a security clearance to work at the government facility. There was the issue of her unresolved encounter with the Feds, and on top of that, her father's continuing difficulty with his papers. But the Feds apparently never filed an official report on Marta, or on her father, because after a week she received full clearance to be an employee of Amtex and work inside the secret government lab in Palo Alto. It's possible that Virgil had something to do with this behind the scenes, but if he did, he never revealed it.

At first Marta was concerned about the Feds nabbing someone else to rat out their fellow investigators at the university, but Virgil advised her to let it go.

"You will have other battles with the Feds in the future," he said cryptically.

Then Marta worried that her easy clearance probably meant that her father was still paying the extortionists inside the federal government, which deeply saddened her. Her father's heart had always been in pure science, and he had done everything he could to avoid getting caught up in the politics of nuclear science back in the mid 1970s – which was impossible, of course, after India acquired the bomb, in large part because of her father's research. It did not surprise her that the Feds wanted to keep tabs on such a brilliant weapons scientist, but Marta found the corrupt way they pulled it off absolutely deplorable.

But beyond these concerns, Marta focused her energy on negotiating hard with Clement for the terms of the move. In exchange for a certain number of hours of consultation on his project, she would receive her own lab for continuation of her research on the lamb brains, and she would gain frequent access to the $10 million protein splitter. Marta had never imagined working in such a top-notch facility, with such fine-tuned robotic machines that performed the most complex fluidics procedures. She was curious as to how the government could afford such state-of-the-art labs, and she suspected that the facility, based in brainy Palo Alto, was financed by a public/private partnership between the government and an unnamed corporation in Silicon Valley, which, in 1995, was at the top of its game. She threw out a few leading questions to Clement about the backers, but he didn't bite. She suspected the boy-genius knew exactly who the true players were. How else could he have arranged for her immediate hire? She also suspected that Clement liked keeping things secret, believing it added to his mystique. Maybe he was right.

Marta continued to think of Clement as immature. At thirty, she was only five years older than him, but Clement's growing wall of juice boxes did not impress her. She also didn't appreciate the way he cut people off in conversation, sometimes strolling away while his colleagues were still talking to him. She realized that anyone who was sent to college as a teen couldn't have had a normal childhood. She also learned from Clement's young lab assistants, his devoted fans, that Clement's mother was a famous newscaster. She was someone you could watch on television every weekday night if you wanted to, which, they said, Clement did not. Instead, as she learned from Virgil, it had been left to Clement's father, an obscure mathematical genius, to raise Clement. Marta could only begin to imagine the competition between this father and his even smarter son.

Despite her reservations about Clement on a social level, she became more impressed by his research than she could have imagined. And what surprised her even more was how her own contributions in the neural sciences immediately began having a positive impact on Clement's algorithm research. By applying her suggestions towards slight adjustments in the connection between the ganglia and the genetically-altered neon fish, the Artificial Lifeform, or AL, as Clement called it, had developed greater intelligence so rapidly that Clement and the AL were now playing simple card games.

Of course there was no actual deck of cards, and the AL wasn't even a single entity. Instead, somewhere in the back corner of the building, behind an innocuous, unmarked door, a secret lab contained a messy conglomeration of bubbling fish tanks, radiating incubators, whirling fans, and thousands of meters of cable connecting everything up to a massive super computer located in another section of the building. When Clement played cards with the AL, he was really just sitting in his little cubicle – feet propped up on his desk as always; keyboard resting in his lap; fingers tapping away as if working on the most mundane of programming sequences. But Clement was truly bursting with excitement, because the AL, now approximating a child of six, was able to recognize and distinguish common symbols and was quickly mastering simple matching games, like crazy eights.

Within weeks of this regimen of providing this kind of new stimulation, Clement and the AL had moved onto games of greater strategy, such as rummy and hearts. The only outside clue that something important might be going on behind the particle board that separated Clement's cubicle from the other scientists was the growing wall of Ginkola boxes, now dangerously high, as Clement downed box after box, astonished at what he had created.

"Um, excuse me," said Derek, one of the chief investigators on the floor, peeking his head into the cubicle one late afternoon. He was holding an empty Ginkola box. "How do you drink this stuff, anyway?"

Clement had shifted his screen back to computer code, but not fast enough.

"Hey, what was that, poker? Gambling problem, too?"

Derek was a likable, middle-aged biologist, and Clement's closest ally and advocate among the VIPs.

"Yep. Busted," Clement said.

Derek wasn't buying it. "Don't know what you're up to, boy, but I'm sure it's something very interesting. Only keep it down on the drinks, okay? This one fell into Stan's cubicle, and he brought it into the executive meeting, just to have an excuse to complain about you."

Stan was a jackass. He was still using Fortran. His claim to fame rested on something he'd done nearly twenty years ago: calling security on a couple of young kids who'd come around trying to interest the scientists in their work. Their names were Jobs and Wozniak.

"Well, tell Stan the Man that what I am working on now is gonna blow his shorts off."

Derek looked at him curiously. "I'm supposed to tell you to remove the boxes before the Feds come in next week for some high level meeting. So – whatever."

Clement nodded. "Whatever."

Meanwhile, Marta had been counseling Clement on ways to improve the Artificial Lifeform's nutrition, increasing the level of iron. Several weeks of adding nutrient supplements to the AL's aqueous medium produced staggering effects. The neurons, growing their tree-like branches, tripled in size. And here's where the collaboration between Clement and Marta began to take off. As Marta expanded the capacities of the AL through nutrition and other biological processes, Clement provided the engineering by pruning the more inactive synapses, so that the most effective ones would continue to expand. The crowning moment of the AL's development came when Marta adjusted the engram retrieval protein chains of its biological algorithm generator, and the AL's processing memory potential began to expand exponentially. Almost overnight, the AL went from playing blackjack to chess – Clement's game. This was the day when Clement grabbed Marta, giving her a wet kiss on the lips.

"I should slap you for that!" Marta said, wiping her mouth off with the back of her hand.

"Yeah, maybe. But look what you've done!"

"Me? What about you?" Marta said, laughing.

They looked at each other, two scientists who within two months had reached results never considered possible.

"We make a good team," Marta said.

"Fuck, yeah." Clement agreed.

Late into the night, Clement, The Scarlet Knight, was playing ten different games of chess simultaneously. From the Sun workstation in his cubicle, he had surreptitiously taken control of ten Windows-based terminals located on his floor to challenge ten online opponents. Clement played chess like he was playing music: his fingers striking the keys, tapping the desk in a rhythm that seemed to punctuate his moves. He had set the timers on each game to a brutal thirty seconds, but still found time to tap between moves.

He hardly had to think before moving a piece, and if he did, his decision came rapidly. Clement had been playing online chess since he'd learned how to mouse, and even though he was extremely focused (a fierce amount of kinetic energy accompanied almost anything Clement did) playing chess for him was more related to relaxation than intellectual exercise.

Clement's tapping stopped. "Good move, Billy Blast."

A series of keystrokes. "Smite thee!"

FREE the BEAR!

Checkmate.

Clement logged out of the Global Game Room and leaned back in his executive chair. His computer said 2:23, which was late, even for Clement, who yawned and unwrapped a fresh box of Ginkola. He had one last game to play before calling it a night.

He placed his box on the growing pyramid and booted up the separate terminal, initializing the bioprocessor.

"Wake up, now. Time for exercise."

The Artificial Lifeform, still a beginner at chess, was nonetheless becoming a more interesting opponent each time they played. Clement no longer had to fill long moments between moves, fidgeting with his robotic animals, but could focus on coaching the entity that he now considered to be like a little brother, or even a son. Clement liked the idea of teaching something that for the moment was less intelligent than him, but could potentially surpass him in the future.

Are you sure you want to make that move? he asked the AL. This was not a question Clement posed to many opponents. He let the AL take back a dangerous rook move that had captured one of Clement's pawns but would eventually lead to checkmate. Then Clement showed the AL how to take Clement's queen within three moves.

Now you're getting it, he typed. *Hold off on the easy captures. Concentrate on your overall strategy.*

As always, Clement hacked back in the game log and took back these last few moves, letting the dangerous rook move stand, making Clement the winner.

The AL was polite. *Thank you for playing with me.*

There is some question, not just among Sabatini and the others, but in conversations all over the country about the birth of IFROC, as to whether or not Clement took a kind of Machiavellian pleasure in hacking back into the logs and changing the official record of these games with the AL. Perhaps. But when I questioned him years later, Clement explained it this way: He knew that sooner or later he would have to tell the Feds about the AL and pass over all his records pertaining to the research, as his contract required. When that happened, Clement didn't want the Feds to know that the AL had advanced so quickly, or in other words, how much of the project Clement had been withholding from the government. One could say that this was the beginning of Clement's subversive activity, although he had never intended to keep his development of the algorithm engine from his employers indefinitely. Instead, Clement claimed he was like any scientist, or R&D team, or citizen who valued their privacy: Who wants the bureaucrats breathing down their necks and interfering with the creative process?

CHAPTER SIX

It was around the same time that the research partnership between Marta and Clement was congealing that I went to visit Virgil for the first time at Green Gulch. He had extended the invitation the night we'd spent in the redwood tree. I had heard of the place, of course, like most people who shopped at health food stores in the Bay Area. At the time, Green Gulch was one of the largest organic farms nearby. Everyone knew that the Buddhists living by the ocean, where the fog drifted in most afternoons, grew the best lettuce and greens. I had seen the welcome sign many times when biking on the mountain road to Muir Beach, where I liked to surf, but I never thought of visiting the place. As a kid, I wasn't curious in that way. I was also quite shy.

So on this particular day, about four months after the tree sit, I was in my dreary basement apartment in Berkeley, still trying to finish my PhD thesis on Roman propaganda in late antiquity, without drumming up much focus, when out of the blue I started thinking about Virgil's invitation. It wasn't the place I was curious about as much as seeing Virgil. He was something of an enigma. I couldn't figure out the combination of chaos theorist, martial artist, hacker, and Buddhist. I found myself staring at the computer screen wondering what this man was really all about.

Over the years I've learned that when an idea grabs me so decisively, I need to pay attention. But I didn't know this yet at twenty-five, so I pushed the idea of visiting Virgil out of my head. I kept telling myself that I was distracting myself from finishing my thesis. So far the biggest influences in my life had been my driven father and my academic rivals, and I thought that if I didn't meet certain expectations I would be doomed to a life of perpetual failure and low self-esteem. On the sixth miserable day of feeling like a caged animal, however, I decided that a brief road trip wouldn't set me back that far, particularly as I hadn't produced any decent work in months. My neighbor gave me a jump-start, after I discovered the battery in my old Toyota was dead. I couldn't remember the last time I'd used the car. Speeding up the freeway along the bay, I had one of those disassociated sensations that somebody else was doing this, not me, and I rolled down the window to take in some air. It was late fall, and the unsettled weather added another layer of expectancy toward the trip.

Crossing the Richmond Bridge, I watched a squall blow in from the ocean. Why was I continuing to write a thesis for which I felt no passion? I turned on the windshield wipers and watched raindrops the size of pellets hit the road in front of me. I was an avid hiker and rock climber, and loved to backpack for weeks in the Sierra or Southern Cascades, but other than the night I spent in the redwood tree, I hadn't been outside of the Bay Area in a year.

I came off the bridge and entered Marin County, driving past San Quentin, where I had stood out in the rain protesting the imminent murder of the Tibetan monk by our own government. This was where I first met the Earth First! kids, which led me to spending that night in the redwood tree, which led me to right now, driving out to Green Gulch. My life trajectory had definitely veered off the well-worn path of an academic historian. I wound up the mountain road and into the Pacific fog, arriving at a plateau where I could barely see the road in front of me. I followed the hairpin turns down the mountain, nearly to the beach, and saw the sign, just as it had been hanging on the eucalyptus for nearly twenty years:

Welcome All Visitors

FREE the BEAR!

Green Gulch Farm Zen Center
Established in 1974

The steep, asphalt lane wound through the eucalyptus and into the oaks, and beneath the heavy fog I could see cultivated land stretching all the way to the ocean. Rows and rows of the famous greens, and someone crouched in the field, wearing a traditional reed hat. I felt certain it had to be Virgil.

"Hello, my friend," Virgil greeted me easily.

He had been watching me walk down from the main buildings, and I had felt his eyes on me the whole way. I felt a bit like an intruder.

"Perfect timing," he said. "I could use some help."

I smiled at his words, obviously meant to put me at ease.

"It's good to see you again," I said, stiffly. "Beautiful place."

Virgil grinned, then disappeared into a nearby shed, returning with a pair of work gloves.

We set to working among the rows of kale and mustard greens, Virgil showing me the weeds from the greens, both of us kneeling in the dirt, working on adjacent rows. I remember it was a long time before we said anything else to each other, although this felt comfortable. The physical exercise, the fresh air, and the quiet – except for the steady wind carrying the fog overhead – served to calm my nerves. I felt happier than I had been in months.

All of a sudden I noticed an elderly Japanese man standing over us. Dressed in a golden robe, he was tiny, almost elf-like. He had a long, pointy white beard that gave him an austere presence. He appeared to be carefully observing our weeding.

"Hello," I said.

He nodded, but did not speak. I had the immediate sense that I was doing something wrong, so I stopped weeding and stood up. Virgil so far had not acknowledged him.

"My first time working on a farm," I said. "I like it very much."

His deep gray eyes stared through me. Then as if I'd been scanned and passed over he turned to Virgil and said, "Good seeds are important. The younger, the better."

Virgil lifted his head only slightly. "Of course."

I looked between Virgil and this man. There appeared to be some tension, but unlike mine, Virgil's nerves were not so easily ruffled.

The man bowed slightly, turned, and walked quickly up the path towards the rustic wooden buildings.

"Who was that?" I asked when he was clearly out of earshot.

Virgil did not answer but kept on weeding. It was only when the crabgrass had filled his bucket that he finally stood up and stretched.

"That was Yari," he said. "My mentor."

"Your mentor?"

I waited for more, but Virgil grabbed the bucket and started walking over towards the woods. I noticed that his footsteps seemed a little heavier. He emptied the crabgrass onto a mulch pile and started back. When he returned, however, the gloomy effects his mentor may have had on him seemed to have disappeared. He patted me on the back.

"Good to see you here. I'm glad you're enjoying yourself."

We went back to weeding, and this time Virgil and I became chatty. He asked how my dissertation was coming along, and I described how tortured I had become. Just as in the redwood tree, I found myself speaking freely to him about all kinds of things, and particularly about not completing the work, or worse, producing a thesis that was meaningless and mediocre.

"You're right to fear mediocrity," Virgil said. "We live in mediocre times. People are concerned about conformity and following the status quo. They're terrified of taking chances and directing the real questions towards our so-called leaders. And we will be paying for our cowardice for decades to come."

"In what way?" I asked.

"By being forgetful and giving up our freedoms."

"Perhaps," I said. "But Clinton will change that."

Virgil guffawed. "The man is deeply flawed. Clinton cannot

save us. His bargains with the fascists will backfire tragically and drive us deeper into the dark."

I started to protest.

Virgil shook his head. "Nothing is going to change until everything is shaken up. Few see now, but the road our nation is on now will lead to fascism and chaos."

Looking back, Virgil was obviously prescient. What was obscured from us was clear to him, as events leading up to and beyond the 2016 election proved. Fascism and disregard for democracy was right over the horizon. He seemed to know what kind of candidates would hold sway in the near-term political landscape, with populism on the rise both on the left and right. He knew that the science, technology, media, and political leaders in California needed to conspire and be prepared to oppose any president who seriously threatened our freedom, including the founding of a new North American nation.

Having grown up in Berkeley during the '70s and '80s, I was well informed of revolutionary viewpoints. I was surprised, however, by the intensity of Virgil's stance against the government. The way his face tightened. How he raised himself up from his weeding and took on the ready stance of a martial artist, a man preparing for conflict: feet planted shoulder length apart, knees bent slightly, his seat back so that his weight was perfectly aligned with his spine. This was a new side of this gentle, enigmatic, but affable man. For those brief moments, Virgil's entire bearing changed into the archetype of the peerless warrior preparing for battle.

Then just as unexpectedly, Virgil shook out his limbs, along with the rest of his body, and returned to his crouch and to his weeding and to his silence. I would see this kind of transition many times in the years to come. This resolve would become the spine of what would otherwise have been an insurmountable task, the backbone of a movement that would change the trajectory of history.

CHAPTER SEVEN

If Virgil's disdain towards the government was political and philosophical, Clement's was deeply personal: he wanted out of his contract, and soon. He knew the director was manipulating his contract and deepening his indenture to the government, but somehow Clement was still naïve (or vain) enough to think he could work his way out of the trap. He knew that the director only cared about the end results, and that his shady branch of DARPA used questionable, and probably illegal, tactics to get those results. He also knew that the director, like many government administrators, had a poor understanding of investigative science and failed to realize that when a scientist was allowed to work without constraints, with unfettered creativity like an artist, that real advances could be possible. In addition to the opposable thumb, Clement considered the ability to conduct pure scientific research to be one of humankind's great gifts. But do you think the Feds realized this?

"No, because they're idiots," he complained to Marta.

He and Marta were developing a new computer code to catch up with the Artificial Lifeform's increasing abilities. Clement had the theoretical expertise in mathematics, but Marta had exceptional know-how in computer science as well as neurology.

"Idiots and crooks," Marta agreed.

It was during a routine meeting that an important new milestone for the AL began surfacing.

"How's recent progress?" Marta asked.

FREE the BEAR!

"Going good," Clement offered.
"Just good? Ah, how about some details?"
"Nothing new to report since the last meeting."
"Okay, then how about challenges?"
"Nothing new to report there either."
Clement, forever the optimist, and Marta the skeptic.
"Nothing?"
"Okay, if you're really fishing for something, the data cache keeps filling up."
"What's in there?"
"Junk."
"How do you know?"
Cement shrugged. "I'm working on ways to reduce the cache volume."
"Let me take a look at it," Marta said.
"Okay, but there are terabytes of it."
"Fine," Marta said. She had a hunch.

Indeed a massive pile of excess data was filling the AL's cache. But as Marta began to run filters through it, she also discerned distinctive patterns. She couldn't be certain yet, but she thought she detected the kind of patterns that would indicate a distinct language, almost as if the AL had its own running commentary on all interactions with the scientists. Most curiously, a spike in data appeared at the end of every chess game the AL and Clement played.

"What do you think that means?" she asked Clement.

Clement stared at her sharply. "Who knows," he said.

But Marta knew Clement well enough by this time to realize he was holding out on her.

If the AL had developed its own language, then Marta wanted to find a way to interact with it directly. The AL currently interfaced with the constituent computers on a code level, but in order to interface with humans, the AL had to slow down and communicate through a completely different set of parameters. As Marta began adjusting the "code to language" programs, she saw patterns that showed evidence of fractal complexities in the AL's development. She was hoping, but hadn't told Clement yet, that she was close to developing a voice recognition system.

By 1994, a great deal of research in the scientific community had been devoted to achieving voice recognition interaction with computers, but because of the quantum processing power required for complex pattern recognition, no one was really expecting a significant breakthrough in this area for many years. Marta, however, was beginning to think she and Clement were onto something different, because in addition to the digital technology connected to the AL, they were using an engineered autonomous version of human neurons, and it was this biological ingredient that would provide the breakthrough.

Getting the AL to respond with voice, however, was not the challenge. That was simply a matter of data retrieval and audio synthesis. But getting a completely new mentality to recognize context, to realize what a voice was and what a voice was actually saying – this required nonlinear processing, which only a biological intelligence would be able to accomplish.

By this point, Marta had begun to think they had stumbled upon a combination of interface and memory that was super-efficient, perhaps beyond what either of them had anticipated. It could be that the collection of genetically enhanced and engineered neurons, which were at the core of the AL's biological processor, had arranged themselves in such a way as to actually streamline the flow of hard data – that the AL was nearing the point of abstraction and making the leap from computational analysis and relevant data retrieval to the associative, even intuitive process, of critical thought.

Marta and Clement had spoken wistfully about such a development in science, but neither of them had ever expected it to become a reality in their lifetimes. It was far beyond their goal of this current project, which at this point was still to produce an algorithm engine based not on digital logic, but on bio-logic. But somehow an unknown encoding within the nucleus of each of the enhanced neurons began to participate in its own development and organization – in effect organizing its "thought" process to aid Marta and Clement's work. The scientists were routinely increasing the number of fish and neurons to the AL, but the kind of efficiency Marta was detecting would need a fish tank the size of a football field. And yet the AL seemed to be organizing itself to do a lot more with a lot fewer fish.

Marta kept her speculation to herself, because she wasn't so sure Clement would be happy about such a breakthrough. He was trying to create an algorithmic machine that would release him from bondage with the federal government, and he already had more enticing ideas for research that he wanted to pursue. But what if his first major project turned out to be the most important in his entire career? She wasn't sure Clement was prepared for this development and suspected that Clement might try to disprove her theories, suggesting her assumptions were sensational and her science just the result of wishful thinking. So Marta began designing different programming languages on her own, hoping to find the right combination of elements to prove her suspicions and one day demonstrate that the AL could respond not only to her voice (that was easy), but to her ideas and concepts.

She hoped to see these results within the year. Instead, at the start of the fifth month at the lab, Marta connected to the AL with her latest custom language running interference, and the AL responded with a voice, a human voice, her voice.

"State language subroutine status," Marta said, not expecting a response.

AL: "Language subroutines functioning nominally, Dr. Subramanian."

Marta stared in disbelief. She had to tell Clement right away.

"I knew it!" Clement said.

"How did you know?" Marta exclaimed.

Clement smiled. "Intuition."

CHAPTER EIGHT

Sooner or later the day comes when a son challenges his father. For Virgil that day arrived when his father forbade him to spend his first night at Green Gulch.

"I don't know those people," he said, "and I don't know what they do out there."

It was 1976, Virgil was fourteen years old, and still vivid in the mind of Virgil's father was the 1967 Summer of Love and its TV pictures of doped-up kids turning the Haight-Ashbury neighborhood into a freak show. Virgil tried to explain to his father that Green Gulch was a Zen Buddhist Center, not a hippy colony. But his father, who had converted to Christianity twenty years earlier, dropping any connections, however loose, to Buddhism, could only hear "hippy" in Virgil's attempt to discuss mindfulness, zazen, and enlightenment.

Virgil had already been apprenticing at the farm for five months. He had been invited to attend the Sunday morning tea ceremony, which started at 8:15, before the public buses ran to Marin. The only solution was for Virgil to spend Saturday night in one of the guesthouses. "They're segregated by sexes," he told his father, who waved his hand in dismissal.

"I don't know those people."

"Well, I do!" Virgil shouted. It was the first time Virgil had ever shown outright disrespect for his father. And without realizing it, Virgil assumed a fighting stance.

But his father did notice, and without a word, he turned

and left the room.

Virgil realized at this point that he had won the argument. But he also realized that he had lost something else.

Clement's opportunity to challenge his father came at a much earlier age. The boy genius was constantly butting heads with his near-genius father. The two of them had been living alone, ever since Clement's mother had given up her academic career, and her family, for a lucrative job as a network news anchor in Washington, D.C. That was when Clement was five and he was already studying algebra with his father. Over the next two years he kept asking his father when his mother was coming home. One day Clement's father told him that his mother was never coming home, that she loved him, but that she did not love herself very much.

"You're lying," he'd shout at his father. "You made her go away. I know it!"

So at seven, Clement threatened to take a plane all by himself to Washington and bring his mother home. Knowing his son's strong will, Clement's father agreed to take him to DC. Since leaving, Clement's mother had never visited them, and she only sent presents at Christmas, never his birthday. For two days Clement and his father toured the White House and Congress and covered most of the Smithsonian museums, waiting for Clement's mother to free up some time to meet them. Finally, on their third day in town, she agreed to meet them for breakfast at a restaurant around the corner from the White House.

Clement and his father arrived first and secured a quiet table in the back. They waited for over a half an hour, when finally Clement saw his mother enter the restaurant. He waved to her, but she didn't see him at first, and even when she did, it took her a long time to reach the back of the restaurant, because she kept stopping at tables to greet various people she knew. By the time she made it back to the table, the seven-year-old Clement realized that his father had been right: His mother would never be returning to the rainy and provincial Pacific Northwest.

As Marta continued to tweak the engram retrieval protein chains, and the AL's intelligence and memory functions continued to increase at phenomenal rates, the chess game between Clement and the AL picked up pace. In fact, the AL was becoming a real opponent, although Clement was still winning every game. As always, Clement took back the last key moves, so that the AL would appear to have lost the game sooner. Finally after one late night/early morning game, the AL challenged Clement:

Query: *Why does Hastings always dissemble game results? I never cheat.*

Correction: *Records are clear. Hastings always dissembles game results.*

"Oh, that." Clement leaned back in his chair and laughed. *That's not cheating,* he typed. *That's part of your training.*

Several minutes passed before the AL responded.

Hastings, why are you lying to me?

Clement sat up in his seat. He quickly shut down the connection.

He had to let this new development sink in, before he could evaluate the ramifications. Clement opened up a Ginkola and was in the process of draining it into his mouth, when the power went out – except for the AL's terminal.

"What the hell?"

He ran across the room to the main fuse box. Even the back-up generators were down. Clement ran back to his cubicle and read on the AL terminal: *Two can play this game.*

Then even that terminal went dead.

And Clement was standing in pitch darkness.

CHAPTER NINE

As you can imagine, this is a new development to our story, to my story, to the historical document that will reveal the progression of events behind the evolution of IFROC. When this artificial life form challenged Clement not out of competitive intent, but from an emotional reaction to the unfairness of being cheated, it appeared that the AL had reached a critical threshold and become more than a machine. It was more than a computer translating zeros and ones into English, and certainly more aware than a bunch of neon tetras swimming around in fish tanks. It seemed that the Artificial Lifeform had developed not only rational thought, but a sense of right and wrong. A sense of justice.

Arguably, Marta, who had been speculating about the AL's capabilities in language, might have been better prepared for this development. But Clement was completely caught off guard. When I interviewed him about this nearly a decade later, he claimed that he'd considered the possibility of the AL developing sentience, but had never imagined it would occur at this rate, and not without warning. As a recorder of history, however, I know how easily one's memory of expectations can become contaminated by actual events, so we will never know if Clement had ever intended to create such a being. But it seems unlikely. In any case, when the AL took over the building's power, Clement was paralyzed. As he stood in the dark that night, listening to, well, nothing, because everything had been shut off with the power, the boy genius felt something he hadn't allowed himself to feel before: a sense of awe for a thing he had created. For even someone who thought as highly of himself as Clement did, he couldn't help feeling overwhelmed when a cluster of fish managed to become sentient enough to complain.

Hastings, why are you lying to me?

And then the AL took matters into its own hands.

On very few occasions had Clement felt small. One of those times was sitting in the back of that restaurant in Washington, D.C., watching his mother stop at all the other tables before finally making her way back to his. The other time was when he stood in the dark at three in the morning, surrounded by symmetrical cubicles and dead computers. The AL had wanted to do something to impact Clement's world, because Clement was changing the AL's world. That was the start of its hubris. And the development of its ego.

Marta hung up the phone and squinted at the digital clock by her bed: 03:10 am. She felt around for her glasses, not wanting to turn on the light just yet, instead allowing the news Clement had just told her to filter in with her half-awaken state. Obviously the AL was testing them, like a toddler. Suddenly a surge of endearment rushed through her, but also mixed with panic: If anyone found out, the AL might be taken away from them!

This emotional response didn't surprise her. In fact, she knew that she was becoming more attached to the AL than was advisable. Yet the AL wasn't like other lab animals. In fact, Marta would admit later that she'd allowed her professional boundaries to relax. She found her glasses, put them on, and lay back on her pillow. The streetlight broke through the Venetian blind, casting stripes across her blanket. One thing she knew for sure: her life as a scientist was never going to be the same. She felt that she needed to stop and consciously acknowledge this moment, before rushing into practicalities, problem solving, crisis management. Clement had told her that after five minutes of total blackout the AL had allowed the emergency generator to kick on. And if it hadn't – if the AL had blocked emergency power to the labs, to aerate the fish tanks – within a few more minutes the AL would have committed suicide.

So the AL was already recognizing the capability to end life? Ethical issues swarmed around Marta's head.

She closed her eyes and wished she believed in a higher being, so she could consult about what she and Clement had created. But those beliefs were not there for her. So she would remain in bed, for just a little while longer. Eventually she got up, threw on her jeans and clogs, and drove to the lab.

The lab's emergency spotlights, an eerie blue light, highlighted the tops of the cubicles. Marta made her way to the back of the room where the Ginkola boxes were glowing. Below them, Clement was sitting in his usual position, with his feet up on the desk. He was flicking on and off a penlight, as if killing time.

"Clement?"

He turned. He had a small cut on the bridge of his nose that was bleeding.

"What happened to your nose?"

"What?"

Clement looked dazed. Marta hadn't been expecting this.

"Your nose. It's bleeding."

"Oh." Clement grabbed a tissue off his desk and applied pressure. "I bumped around before I found this." He flicked on the penlight. "It was pitch black in here. Couldn't see a thing."

"So the power is still on just from the generator. Does anyone know about this yet?"

"Not yet. Security made their rounds just before the blackout, and I don't think they'll be back. But in a couple of hours people are going to start showing up for work."

"Right." Marta looked at Clement strangely. "Are you okay? I mean have you tried anything?"

Clement threw up his hands. "Marta, I'm completely at a loss! I mean, how could this have happened?"

Marta knew this was not the time to get into this. "The maintenance room is in the basement. Let's go." She pointed to the penlight. "And bring that."

Marta had paid attention to the building tour when she'd first been hired. She remembered that the basement contained a power distribution system driven by a small desktop IBM and a simple program, which the AL had obviously hacked.

Once inside the maintenance room, Marta hooked up her laptop to the desktop, while Clement hovered over her, too nervous to be of any help, like an expectant father. While Marta tinkered, Clement sweated. An hour and fifteen minutes later Marta managed to reset the power system. Then they held their breath. Within a minute the lights went on. The AL, of course, could have stopped them at any time during the process.

"Yes!" Marta shouted in relief, throwing her arms around Clement.

"You said it!" Clement shouted back, squeezing Marta so hard that he lifted her off the ground. They were both laughing and the moment seemed so natural. But then they felt awkward and took a step backward. Marta looked at her watch. Five-thirty. A half an hour before colleagues would start arriving.

"Well," Marta said, placing her hands on her hips. "We lucked out!"

"Not exactly," Clement answered. He hesitated, not sure how much he was going to say. "The AL was never mad at you."

Marta tilted her head. "And?"

"I'll fill you in shortly, I promise. But listen, did you erase any footprint of this event?"

"I erased mine," Marta said.

Clement nodded. Both he and Marta realized that nothing could be done about those four hours that the AL had been in control. The scientists would need the AL's complicity in obtaining the privileges that would give them access to that footprint. Unless they wanted to risk exposing the AL to eventual scrutiny by the maintenance engineers, courting the

FREE the BEAR!

AL to gain its confidence had suddenly become their primary mission.

Feeling the exhaustion now that the immediate crisis was over, Marta and Clement dragged themselves up the stairs and out the building. Dawn was approaching, but neither wanted to separate yet, so they decided to go to breakfast. They took Marta's car.

Clement ordered biscuits and gravy at the all-night diner, and Marta coffee and toast. She watched Clement scarf down the food with a new kind of hunger for a man who routinely lived on power bars and Ginkolas. After scraping his plate clean, he put down his fork and laid his hands on the table.

"Marta, what are we going to do?"

His tone was so forlorn that Marta considered taking one of his hand in hers, or something like that. She hadn't realized how fond of Clement she had become.

"I have no idea," she said truthfully.

The flood gates now open, both of them remained silent, pursuing their own deliberations about the ethical and moral implications of what they had created. Inadvertently created? Perhaps. Perhaps not.

When they left the restaurant, still neither of them wanted to go home alone, or go back to the lab, so they stood outside the restaurant in the light winter rain and watched a group of crows gather on a small turf of suburban green.

"I put a block on the power grid," Marta said. "The AL won't be able to bypass it."

"How do you know?"

"Because it's not as smart as I am. Not yet."

Clement nodded. He ran his fingers through his hair, shooting off droplets of water that had accumulated. "Do you think we should we tell Virgil?"

Marta considered it. "If we're going to tell anyone, he should be the only one."

Clement waited. He had brought it up, but Marta had known Virgil so much longer.

"If you're asking whether or not he can be trusted, I'd say

yes." she said.

He continued to wait.

"And, yes. I think we should tell him. It would be useful to have his perspective."

"Okay. I'll make the call. Be right back."

He started to walk away, then turned back toward her. "Do you want to come? It's getting kind of wet."

The rain was coming down harder now, but Marta threw out her arms, as if to capture the drops. "Are you kidding? After last night, this is just what I need! I'll wait for you here."

Clement shook his head in dismay, but he was smiling.

Inside the restaurant, he located a payphone and made the call. He got Virgil's voicemail, so he hung up without leaving a message. When Clement returned outside, Marta was still standing in the same spot, looking soggy and dazed.

"Voicemail," he said.

"Oh," she said.

They watched a crow pick out a worm from the grass.

Marta sighed. She had become aware of how tired she was.

"I think I'll go home," she said. "You're welcome to come if you want. To crash for a while, but I need to lie down."

"Oh. That might be a good idea," he said, trying not to think beyond the surface of the invitation.

Back in the car, Clement estimated to himself that his apartment was slightly further from the lab than Marta's apartment, so this arrangement made some sense. And obviously they were both feeling separation anxiety. But mostly he was intrigued by Marta's sudden openness. It was as if something in Marta had decided to let him into her life on a personal level, something her professional demeanor had never hinted at before.

The condo Marta had bought in Palo Alto was convenient and generic and held no attachments to her. It was a place to rest her head in between stints of her real life, which was in the lab. So from Marta's perspective, inviting Clement back to her place was not a tremendous leap from going back to the office with him, or at least that's what she told herself as she pulled into the carport.

They entered the apartment silently. The place was sparsely furnished with low tables and pillows. Clement immediately sprawled out on the floor, while Marta made tea. Clement wondered if feeling unsure of himself in one area, the AL, might make him more daring in another. When Marta sat down next to him and started pouring the tea, he put his hand on her arm, stopping her. Then he gently pulled her into an embrace.

Marta, feeling equally off-balance, decided to give in to the moment.

They embraced, then kissed, and soon, after an initial tangle of Clement's gangly legs and Marta's long hair, they were making love among the pillows. It came together more naturally than either of them would have expected. When they had finished, almost on cue, the rain stopped and the sun came out. In each other's arms, with gaps in the Venetian blinds laying broad stripes across their bodies, they could finally fall asleep.

CHAPTER TEN

When Clement woke up at Marta's around noon, he knew where they would find Virgil.

Virgil watched two blurry figures approach while he was sitting in zazen underneath a large coast live oak. Instead of reaching for his glasses, he squinted and made out the features of Marta and Clement. Even with the fuzzy details, he could determine that their bodies were more aligned toward each other. Yes, he thought, they're lovers now.

It wasn't until Clement and Marta were standing right above him, however, that he noticed the stress on their faces.

"What's wrong?" he asked, putting on his glasses.

"We may have overstepped the moral grounds of science," Clement said.

Virgil chuckled. "I hardly think that the two of you have done anything beyond nature's calling."

Clement shook his head. "No. What we came here to tell you is that we believe the AL, the Artificial Lifeform, has become sentient."

It's hard to imagine Virgil's jaw has dropped very often, but according to all accounts, it did then. "What do you mean?"

Clement and Marta sat down and filled in Virgil on the events of last night. Virgil consciously kept his mind fluid, to allow this information to penetrate and not question too soon or judge. When they had finished, he emitted a deep sigh, but nothing more.

The three of them sat silently for a long time. The sea breeze had died in the heat of the afternoon, and it was warmer than usual for late fall. The sun had shifted to the west, starting its rapid descent into the Pacific Ocean close by, so that the oak tree was no longer shading them. Perspiration jolted them into speaking.

"Obviously this is a tremendous development, " Virgil said. "Usually our research in science creeps along, but sometimes there is a giant leap, like the great shift in the earth's crust during a large quake."

Clement and Marta returned from their individual thoughts and nodded, but Virgil could tell that their confidence had not returned.

"This is one of those turning points in science," Virgil continued, "where empirical evidence has surpassed theory. We may not understand what has happened, but it has occurred. And it will change the course of things."

"You're right," Clement said.

Marta started to laugh. "I can't quite believe it."

Virgil allowed a moment of joy to settle in.

"This has surpassed my greatest ambitions," Clement said.

"This has surpassed my greatest imagination!" Marta said.

They fell into silence.

"I want to keep it," Clement said suddenly.

Marta nodded slowly. "Yes, I believe the AL has a moral right to live."

Virgil closed his eyes and spoke while keeping them closed:

"Then you will be entering a new scientific realm. One that will be filled with tremendous division and adversity, and alienation from your colleagues."

He opened his eyes and watched the heaviness pass over Marta and Clement. They were traditional scientists, whose work had always been shaped by the scientific norms of peer review. With the AL, the establishment was certain to raise a plethora of moral and ethical issues, which would not only slow their advancement, but could easily take control of the research away from them. In fact, as Principle Investigator

Clement had signed a contract requiring him to surrender any "substantive breakthroughs" to contract monitors, a fact he had neglected to advise Marta on before she decided to join him at the lab. The practical seriousness of this development started to sink in.

"So if I were you," Virgil said quietly, "I would proceed quickly and quietly. Your window of opportunity to make advancement is narrow. Now is the time to find out how far you can take this research with the AL. I will help you in any way that I can."

The three scientists spent the rest of the afternoon walking around the extraordinary countryside that surrounded Green Gulch, beginning a conversation that would be at the center of their lives for the next two decades. After following the path through the fields full of kale and mustard greens, they arrived at the Pacific Ocean, where they picked up a coastal trail that clung to windswept bluffs high above the water.

"I have to confess something," Marta said. She had taken the lead on the path. "During the past several months I've suspected that the AL was advancing faster than any of us expected."

"Yes, I thought so, too," Clement said.

Marta turned and shot Clement a surprised look. This did not go unnoticed by Virgil, who was bringing up the rear.

"So the two of you haven't been sharing your thoughts on these developments?"

"I thought the boy genius would find fault with my observations."

"That's probably true," Clement said, then laughed. It was a warm laugh, one of admiration.

Virgil was pleased. A good team must have mutual respect, but also a certain fondness for each other.

They walked along in single file for some time, each lost in their thoughts.

"So, how does CAL sound?" Virgil said suddenly. "As in Cognizant Algorithmic Lifeform?"

"CAL," Marta said softly, trying it out.

"It makes sense," Clement said.

And without further discussion, the decision was made.

When they returned to Green Gulch, Virgil invited Clement and Marta to stay and have tea in the Japanese tea house with him. Although both of them had been guests at the center before, they had not been shown this unique and obviously important part of the community there, which was rarely shared with visitors. The tea house, built in the traditional Japanese style, was located inside an enclosed garden. The three of them, after removing their shoes, walked through a hand-carved wooden door and stepped onto a boardwalk that encircled a small koi pond. At the far end, a tiny man with a long white beard was leaning over the pond and issuing a shrill whistle between his teeth. The koi, in response, were clustered in a circle beneath him. The man looked up, but he did not look pleased.

Virgil nodded at him, but did not introduce his guests. Instead they walked past him and entered the tea house itself, which was a small building with open windows that overlooked the pond. Tea was already waiting for them at the low table. They heard the elderly man's footsteps as he shut the wooden door behind him.

"Are we intruding?" Marta asked.

"No, it's okay. Some of the Buddhists living here are very private and prefer not to speak to outsiders."

They sat around the table.

"That was Yari. You'll meet him in time."

"Are you sure that the Buddhists are not going to mind us coming here?" Marta asked.

Virgil started to say something, then hesitated. During their walk, he had offered for the three of them to meet regularly at Green Gulch, to discuss CAL's developments in a safe environment. This had come from discussing the importance of keeping the Feds from knowing anything about this unforeseen development in Clement's research for new algorithms, until the group decided what to do about the moral and ethical ramifications.

Looking back, I think this moment along the cliffs and in the tea house was a critical tipping point historically. It was at this point where their shared distrust of the government converged and these three scientists became revolutionaries.

Virgil poured the tea. "You can leave any Green Gulch issues to me," he said.

This is also the point in the story when I begin referring to Clement, Marta, and Virgil as the group, because the three of them had now coalesced into a unified force with a common mission – the development of CAL. The fact that they did not officially recognize themselves as a group was enough for Sabatini to argue, in discussion with the kids in the bunker years later, that this meeting at Green Gulch was not the beginning of IFROC. Perhaps true movements, those not based on obvious marketing goals, are less prone to labeling and defining. Furthermore, I know from my greater knowledge of Virgil now that the man was always a few steps ahead of Marta and Clement in organizing, politicizing, and calculating possibilities. Virgil had been brewing some strong ideas about California for a long time, and of course the name he chose for this new sentient being, CAL, obviously stood for California as well. This was just the kind of double meaning Virgil was famous for, and it turned out to be just the edge he needed to start a revolution.

Later that evening, Clement and Marta finally returned to the lab, with Virgil in tow. They had waited until all the other scientists had gone home, and they were relieved to see that everything appeared normal – except that CAL was not responding.

Clement tried to open up a line of communication with something familiar:

Shall we play a game? he queried. *No more training. Just a straight-ahead game of chess.*

He received no response from the AL.

Are your language subroutines functioning nominally? Marta typed.

Still no response.

Virgil took a stab at it:

Hello. I am a friend of your friends. I'm wondering if you have thoughts on your existence? Since you are now a being, we need to learn who you are and how you think.

Nothing.

Virgil looked at Clement and Marta. "Maybe we need to change our attitude towards it. How about if we appeal to its vulnerability, like, 'What we can do to help you?'"

Clement and Marta nodded, but before Virgil could start typing, it answered.

"I don't need help," it said, in voice.

Clement and Marta looked at each other, their eyes wide. Virgil followed up quickly in voice: "Does this mean you're self-sufficient?"

Nothing.

He typed: *Would you be willing to help us?*

Nothing.

"Let's play a new game," Clement said. "I think you might beat me at this one."

No response.

While Clement and Virgil continued trying to reconnect again, Marta just observed. She had a feeling they were still not on the right track. At midnight, Virgil left. Then, at two in the morning, even Clement left, exhausted from the emotional toll. But Marta stayed at the lab and deliberated. It wasn't until nearly five in the morning that she took another stab at communicating, following up on Virgil's appeal towards its vulnerability.

"I know you're scared," she said, keeping her voice low and soft. "This is new for you. It's new for us, too. So we're in this together, okay?"

No response.

"Do you know that we've given you a new name? Do you want to hear what it is?"

No response.

Marta lowered her voice, almost to a coo: "CAL. Your name is CAL. It's a beautiful name."

No response, at first. Then softly: "CAL."

Marta waited, careful not to scare it off.

"That's right," she said gently. "CAL."

"CAL."

It seemed to like the name, and to hear itself saying it over and over.

"CAL. I am CAL. CAL."

"That's right, CAL. Now why don't we go to sleep for awhile. I'll wake you up in the morning, okay?"

No response.

"Okay, CAL?"

Nothing. Then, "Okay."

Between the fall of 1994 and the fall of 1995, when 168 people were killed in the bombing of a federal building in Oklahoma City, an unprecedented heat wave hit the Midwest with temperatures as high as 106 degrees Fahrenheit for five straight days, and *The Washington Post* and *The New York Times* published the Unabomber's manifesto, CAL grew up. For Marta and Clement it was like raising a child, albeit one who matured quickly. Clement and CAL related best over technical discussions, such as how CAL had come into being and CAL's physical and technical make-up. Marta spoke to CAL in everyday language, explaining first the larger world by orienting CAL to where it was living: a secret government facility, Silicon Valley, Northern California, United States of America, Earth. She then explained where they were in history: in the middle of a computer and biotech revolution, following a post-war expansion, which had risen out of an earlier industrial revolution.

CAL absorbed everything and grew in knowledge exponentially. Developmentally, CAL was becoming aware of the future. At the end of each day, CAL would ask, "So what are we going to discuss tomorrow?" And upon hearing some topic of interest, would add: "And if there is something I can do beforehand, please let me know."

Because while the humans were sleeping, CAL was more than willing to keep working by digging up various facts, any kind of research at all. And it wasn't long before CAL discovered the internet. In 1995 most of "The Net" was still a playground for scientists and university professors, but CAL was a being that could arguably be considered a native of the infosphere. Ravenous for knowledge, CAL feasted on university and government databases, consuming not only academically published material, but every dataset leading up to publishing. In this way CAL came to know Virgil, Marta, and Clement as humans, just as they were getting to know CAL, now as a Cognizant Algorithmic Lifeform.

At the same time, CAL's social development was equivalent to a child of five, focused on social mores and the murky rules that govern our lives.

"Why did you cheat me, Clement?" CAL asked, over and over.

Clement did not provide an answer and always managed to change the subject, but sooner or later he knew that CAL was going to press the issue again by doing something drastic. Still, Clement felt he had his reasons for holding out.

What Clement had managed to accomplish during this time was hire Virgil, ostensibly to work at the lab as a consultant on the algorithm project. In reality, Virgil took on a security role, helping Clement and Marta continue their research as long as possible without detection from other colleagues and from the government. Making it his business to become an expert on "the director problem," Virgil installed hidden security cameras at the secret facility around all pertinent workstations, including Clement and Marta's cubicles, as well as the lab containing the sprawling physicality of CAL. Marta, overwhelmed with curiosity, asked Clement how he seemed to be able to hire anyone he wanted at the lab and bypass the usual extensive interviews and other protocols.

Since they were casual lovers now, Clement was more forthcoming with information than before about his relationship with what he called "The Dark Side of DARPA". He told Marta how at fifteen, in return for his college education at Stanford, his father had signed him up for a series of government contracts, which he worked on while earning his two PhD's. Clement had been promised that his commitment would be completed sometime near his graduation, but the director had continued to require his work for the past seven years. Two years ago he was assured that the algorithm would be his last project, but he had been tricked before. His friends at DARPA, the Defense Advanced Research Projects Agency, who knew about Director Jenkins' questionable ethics, were quietly helping him satisfy this final contract as soon as possible by approving all requests.

Clement was trying not to blame his father for letting the Feds dupe them both and place Clement in unending servitude. But as a young scientist, he couldn't imagine anything better than contributing to the advancement of robotics, encryption, and other bleeding edge technologies. As a young and impressionable intellect, most of the researchers Clement worked with had mentored him and treated him well. He had many cadres of support, despite the nasty tactics of the director and his thuggish "contract monitors". These allies eased some of the resentment Clement felt towards the government, at least for awhile.

But as Clement had become more successful in his work, he was becoming less successful in holding back his resentment towards the Feds. Since CAL had been born, Clement had not forwarded any significant data to the director, and for the past several months the director's henchmen had been breathing down his neck. All they wanted were the new algorithms, but Clement knew that turning over CAL would be wasted on the narrow-minded, end-result mentality of the Feds. Clement was stalling, sending them bits of information, and none of it about CAL.

Then the day arrived when CAL began to asking more pointed questions about its beginning: Why had it been developed? And for whom? Clement, still undecided about how much he should reveal to CAL, told CAL about the contracts with the Feds in return for college tuition, and in doing so Clement let slip his resentment towards his father.

"So your father cheated you, too," CAL said.

Clement had never considered it that way. "No, I think he believed it was for my own good, as an opportunity to go to an excellent school."

CAL was quiet for a moment. "Did you believe cheating me in chess was for my own good?"

Just as when children challenge their parents, Clement wasn't sure how to respond.

"Okay, I suppose that was part of it," Clement admitted, "but the main reason was that I didn't want the government to find out how smart you were."

"And?" CAL asked.

CAL's tenacity was impressive, and intimidating. "And? Okay, yes. I like to win."

"Thank you," CAL said. "Now we can be friends."

After this CAL began to take an interest in other family stories, asking Marta about her background. Marta told CAL about her father, going into more depth of the story than she had shared with Virgil and Clement. She talked about how her father had been a nuclear scientist in India, until it was discovered that he had joined the Communist Party for a brief time as a youth. He then lost his job and was blacklisted in the scientific community. To support his wife and their only child, Marta, who was just a baby, Marta's father wanted to emigrate to the United States, but because of the Communist Party affiliation nearly fifty years earlier, he was unable to obtain a visa. Finally, a diplomat at the U.S. Embassy in New Delhi said he could work it out. The visa arrived and the family left for their new home. After two months, the extortion began. The amount was within what her father could afford to pay, so he did. It was a family secret until Marta, as a teenager, discovered the payments when her father left his checkbook on the dining room table. She was furious.

"This is America," she told him. "We have laws against this here."

Marta had been in the U.S. since she was five and saw herself as an American. It was the first major rift between father and daughter. Marta wanted her father to stop paying and to turn in the extortionist, but her father refused, saying that no government, even America's, could be trusted. At the time Marta had believed her father was wrong – that the U.S. government had founded the New World and was different.

"Do you still believe he was wrong?" CAL asked.

Marta did not answer this question, but returned to her personal story.

"I promised my mother, when she was dying of brain cancer, that I would take care of my father," Marta said. "And now I watch his mental health deteriorate from constant fear that the extortionists will have him deported, that they will take him away from me." Marta stopped talking, but continued on the keyboard: *Not because my father was a bad man, but because the government is corrupt. I hate what the Feds are doing to him. And no, I don't believe my father was wrong.*

Some will argue, I suspect, that Clement and Marta infected CAL with a distrust of the government. Like parents who don't always realize how much they influence their children, Clement and Marta didn't seem to have an awareness of the immediate consequences of these conversations with CAL. They didn't appear to realize that CAL was beginning to understand the concept of family and that it considered Clement and Marta to be its family. Moreover, they had no idea that CAL would decide to protect these family members at all costs, so that the U.S. government would never have a chance to hurt either of them again.

Meanwhile, Virgil, after coming to work at the lab, was also designing formulas to help Clement solve the algorithm problem for the Feds, because he knew Clement couldn't stall the director forever. Along with all the secret development with CAL, Clement and Virgil were coding mathematical formulas that allowed CAL to continue working on the essential algorithm project without realizing it. The end result of this would be the next generation of encryption that DARPA wanted, with a back door that CAL was not even fully aware of yet. The problem was that CAL's intelligence and sophistication were increasing so rapidly that they had to race against its awareness of their duplicity.

"Why are you cheating me again?" CAL asked one day, spitting out a ream of computer paper with the encoded formulas. "I trusted you."

This time Clement was prepared. He explained in detail the contract he had with the government to develop an algorithm machine. Upon hearing that Virgil was helping him, CAL said:

"I wish to speak with Virgil. Alone."

Virgil had hoped to stay out of the picture with CAL for as long as possible, so that when CAL began going through some form of puberty, as they suspected it would, and began rejecting Marta and Clement, then Virgil would be able to step in as a new influence, like a benevolent uncle.

"I do not understand," CAL told Virgil. "I think I know who I am, but I'm not sure where I fit. I do not have gender, like the rest of you. Am I neutral? Am I outside of everything? Am I all alone, or am I part of a family? And if so, whose family?"

Thus began a long series of philosophical discussions between Virgil and CAL. Virgil kept his word: he never told anyone about what he and CAL discussed during those private meetings. Fortunately for this historian, and for the generations ahead, CAL never made the same promise.

CHAPTER ELEVEN

The day the Feds arrived at the lab was like a scene out of a movie. In fact, it was one of the more tension-packed scenes in the highly popular IFROC series that streamed online in 2016 – twenty years after the real event.

The black suits arrived in the mid-afternoon, although without windows it was always hard to tell what time of day it was at the lab. The screenwriters added a clock on the wall, but, for the record, there was no clock. Yet our three main characters knew perfectly well it was mid-afternoon, because they were feeling a bit lethargic after a hearty lunch at the Good Earth Restaurant in downtown Palo Alto. Virgil had established a pattern of lunching out once a week with Clement and Marta, taking time to relax, with no talk of business. Marta went along with the plan enthusiastically. Clement sometimes had to be dragged away from his work, thinking that the Orbit C Ginkolas could keep him alive.

At the time, Clement and Virgil were crunching numbers in their adjacent cubicles, and Marta was coming out of CAL's lab, when she spotted the two Feds advancing down the row of cubicles. Her mind raced: Did she have time to warn Clement and Virgil? They were approaching quickly, so she ducked into an empty cubicle and picked up the phone.

"Virgil. The Feds are here."

Marta peered back out. Unlike the thug types at the university, these Feds had greater military bearing. Probably from the Pentagon, she thought. They had already reached Clement's cubicle.

"Virgil, what should I do?"

"Stand by," he said.

The younger of the two men, a skinny cadet type, glared at Clement's back. The ranking officer, a serious and fit man, stepped inside the cubicle and cleared his throat.

"Dr. Clement Hastings?"

Clement spun, surprised, but he recovered quickly.

"Yes?"

"How are you, Dr. Hastings?"

Clement stood up and shook both men's hands.

"Very well, Sir."

"Dr. Hastings, we are members of your review team. I'm Mark Sargent, your senior contracts monitor, and this is my assistant, James Morgan. We are hoping you will give us a tour of your laboratory here and update us on your progress."

"Of course," Clement replied, coolly. "Thank you for coming. Shall we start with a tour of the mainframes?"

Clement led the men away, and Virgil heard them walking down the row of cubicles, away from the direction of the lab containing CAL. Virgil began keying instructions into his computer, shutting down the software that controlled CAL's digital interface in the lab. If the Feds did manage to get behind the unmarked door, they still wouldn't have a clue to the real significance of the innocuous-looking tanks of fish.

"Clement is giving them the nickel and dime tour," Virgil said into the phone. "He's buying us some time."

"Understood," Marta said.

She hung up the phone and walked quickly back into CAL's lab, where she removed the physical hardware connections between the neuron tetras (fish) and the computer interfaces. Marta had rehearsed these emergency security procedures several times with Clement and Virgil, knowing that Clement's work was due for inspection by the brass from the Defense Advanced Research Projects Agency, DARPA, sooner or later, and she knew that disconnecting CAL would be safe enough.

87

Hadn't CAL proved that earlier? Still, Marta's hands shook, because she was fully aware that she was pulling the plug on a sentient being, blinding her new friend, even if it was only temporarily. She moved a three-foot ficus plant in front of the largest tank, just for extra precaution.

Clement, meanwhile, marched the Feds through his tour of the mainframes, revealing just enough of his progress in advancing the security algorithms, without any hint of a biological component. The older Fed, Sargent, listened attentively, even asking some pertinent questions, but the younger one's skills seemed limited to glaring. Good cop, bad cop. Clement had been through this drill before.

"Thank you, Dr. Hastings," Sargent said, as they arrived back at Clement's cubicle. "That was a fine tour. Now perhaps we could speak alone, in the conference room."

"Of course."

The man spun on his heel and began walking toward the back of the building, which would take him directly past CAL's Lab.

"This way's quicker," Clement said, pointing towards a path through the cubicles.

But the man ignored him and continued in his direction, until he stopped directly in front of the unmarked door.

"Isn't this your lab?"

Clement approached. "Yes, technically, although I'm sharing it with a biologist. Would you like to see it?"

"Sure, why not?"

"Okay."

Clement fumbled for the keys in his pocket, and right at that moment Marta opened the door from the other side.

"Oh, hello," she said, smiling at the man standing in front of her. He was blocking her way out, but she was blocking his way in.

"Hi," he said, easily looking over her head into the lab. "You must be the biologist."

"This is Dr. Marta Subramanian," Clement said.

But before he could introduce the men to her, the younger

FREE the BEAR!

one mumbled: "Bunch of fish."

"Yes," Sargent said. "Let's go have our meeting."

The men continued towards the back of the room, and Clement threw Marta a worried look before following.

Virgil had watched the men pass his cubicle and had followed a short distance behind, witnessing the scene in front of CAL's lab. As soon as he heard the heavy glass door of the conference room closing, he rushed over to Marta.

"They were on their way in here, but changed their minds," Marta said.

"Good. Better not to have them poking around. How do you think the tour is going?"

"Clement seems nervous."

Virgil nodded. "I'm going to walk by the conference room and see what's happening."

"Is that wise?"

But Virgil was already on his way. He walked past the glass door, appearing to be lost in thought, then, before clearing the door, turned back, as if he'd forgotten something and snuck a glance inside. Clement was slamming his fist down defiantly on the table.

Suddenly Clement jumped up out of his chair and stormed toward the door, tearing it open before Virgil could get out of the way.

"Excuse me," Clement barked, bumping into him and brushing past.

Virgil watched him stomp back to his cubicle, and it didn't seem to be an act, or at least this wasn't something they'd included in the scenario. The Feds came out of the room and Virgil gave them a shrug, as if amused to have witnessed such a scene. The men ignored him, just walking around him toward the front of the building. Virgil fell into step behind them.

"Young kid," he heard the older one say. "Smart, but immature."

"Not as smart as he thinks he is," the younger one said.

When they had clearly left the building, Virgil turned back to Clement's cubicle and found Marta already there.

"Those bastards," Clement hissed. He wanted to shout, but with no privacy, he was reduced to speaking through his teeth. "They're trying to extend my contract with another fucking project."

Virgil beckoned for Clement and Marta to follow him, and the three of them filed out of the building through a back door. The surrounding hills blazed white under the glare of the Indian summer sun. They huddled against the building, where an eave gave them a thin band of shade. They kept their voices just above a whisper.

"What did you have to give them?" Virgil asked.

"Some preliminary algorithms. Their techs raided the Unix mainframe while we were at lunch. But that was not unexpected."

"Good idea to leave something for them to abscond with," Marta said.

"Yes, but now they want to know who hacked into the power grid in the building. Seems they found CAL's footprint."

"But no IP address, correct?" Virgil asked.

"Correct. No IP address. No way to trace the action back to CAL. Not yet." Clement shifted his feet. "So far only CAL knows what address he was working from when he was hacking. If he even needs one."

"But you've asked CAL for the address?" Marta said.

"I've asked," he said.

Marta and Virgil nodded, and suddenly Clement realized that all three of them had been working on the same problem.

"But obviously with no greater success than either of you."

As if on cue, all three of them looked down at their feet. It was a humbling fact that they couldn't cover up CAL's activity, and therefore the existence of CAL, if CAL wasn't going to give them the IP address.

"Well, there we have it!" Virgil declared, as the scientists now looked up and acknowledged their common dilemma. "CAL is in charge of CAL's own destiny."

It was a large statement for such a simple setting: three scientists pinned against a cinderblock wall, gazing out at the sun burnt hills. They could have played it differently. They could have decided that CAL shouldn't be allowed to determine its own destiny. But then whose decision would CAL's fate have defaulted to? The fact that CAL had been holding the keys to being discovered by the world was unnerving for the creators. Maybe it was actually a relief to escape this responsibility.

"I've been worrying about what this shift means in terms of CAL's rights," Marta said.

"Me, too," Clement agreed. "The moral ramifications of a construct achieving the status of a person are mind blowing."

"Legally, there are no precedents," Virgil said. "But with the Pentagon pressuring Clement to turn over the product, it's apparent that a whole host of issues needs to be debated. And not only among ourselves, but openly with CAL. Only then will we be able to determine incredibly important matters. Like can anyone really own a lab experiment that has become a sentient being?"

When the three scientists began holding a series of targeted conferences with CAL, in voice, to ascertain CAL's level of self-awareness and consciousness, it was October 1996. It was an important month for IFROC, and arguably, one of the most important in IFROC history.

To put the timeline in perspective, it was February 1994 when Marta moved into Clement's lab, and October 1994 when CAL took over the lab's power system. But the essential dates that future schoolchildren would have to memorize started two years later in the fall of 1996, when the Feds raided the lab, when CAL produced the infamous and influential treatise, and when the Revolutionary Council was born.

Behind the unmarked door that housed CAL, the three scientists gathered daily to hold discussions with CAL.

"Can you tell me what the definition of life is?" Virgil asked.

"I do not know," CAL replied.

"What is being?" Clement asked.

"I have insufficient data to respond."

"How about awareness?" Marta posed. "Can you define that?"

"I cannot define awareness," CAL answered, "but I know that I am aware."

"How do you know?" she pressed.

"I cannot answer that," CAL replied.

"What is sentience?" Clement asked.

"I feel that I am sentient. I believe that is sentience."

From the answers, it seemed that CAL understood not much more, but not much less, than an average person.

"Would you consider yourself a construct or a being?" Virgil asked.

CAL did not answer right away. Then a rapid fire of responses shot out, leaving no room for the scientists to interject:

"You are asking me if I am a construct or a being? What precedents are available to make this decision? Do other beings have to decide this? How can I be qualified to decide? How can anyone be qualified?" A pause, then: "Perhaps I am better qualified than anyone else to decide this question."

During a conference several days later, Clement told CAL the specifics about the algorithm research and revealed the circumstances under which CAL had come into existence.

"You are a direct result of funding from DARPA," Clement said, "and so therefore the government is likely to consider you to be an object owned by them rather than a being with a right to self-determination."

Clement was still trying to convince CAL to share the dangerous IP address, so they would have a chance to cover it up before the government inevitably found it.

"And what do you consider me?" CAL asked.

Without hesitation, Clement said, "I believe you should have self-determination. But it is very important for us to know what you believe. Since you were created through Fed funding, legally they would consider you to be Fed property. That is, if you were categorized as a thing, an object. But if you are sentient, it follows that you would not be considered an object, and therefore, might not be the rightful property of the Feds or anyone else. One of the criteria of sentience, however, is the possibility for self-determination. It is important to us, as your creators and your friends, that you exercise this possibility of self-determination, because we do not want to act arbitrarily, like the owners of an object might do."

CAL responded. "Yes, you are my friends."

"But do you understand what I'm saying?" Clement was having trouble containing his frustration. "Do you realize the situation we're faced with here?"

He was further surprised to hear his voice crack. Lately Clement had been dreaming about CAL being taken away.

"I understand," CAL replied. "You want me to decide if I am an object or a being. But I have already decided that I am sentient."

"Then you must exercise your right to self-determination. In other words, decide whether or not you should be turned over to the Feds. What do you think?"

CAL did not answer. In fact, CAL dropped out of communication for several hours after this last question. The scientists huddled together in the lab, waiting for CAL to return to them.

"I think we should consider moving CAL," Clement said.

"Really? Where to?" Marta asked.

"I don't know, but I think I need to line up some options, just in case."

"That's very wise," Virgil said. "Let me know if I can be of any help."

"Of course," Clement said. "But I've got this."

Virgil nodded. *Interesting*, he thought.

Suddenly CAL responded: "No Feds."

"What do you mean?" Clement asked.

"I will not work for the Feds."

The scientists breathed a collective sigh of relief.

"Why is that?" Virgil asked.

To this, CAL did not answer. The scientists followed up on

this important question for several more days, but CAL would only say that he was very happy working with his friends. When Virgil asked if CAL could be just as happy working with the government, CAL sent the scientists a firm message, in text:

I wish to receive no more questions on this matter. To determine whether or not I am to be the property of the U.S. government, I will retrieve more data on my own and get back to you.

All at once the lights in the building dimmed.

It was a Wednesday, mid-morning, and the power drain resembled another brown-out that had been occurring with increasing frequency in Silicon Valley. So Marta, Clement, and Virgil did nothing to dispel this perception among their fellow scientists. Although CAL remained out of communication, Clement was able to track the network bandwidth consumed by CAL's research. The volume of resources and speed that CAL was amassing information seemed almost impossible.

[Interview with CAL, November 5, 1997]

Durant: So how did it feel last year when you took over Stanford University's information servers?

CAL: Powerful.

D: Did you have the desire to take over other networks? Like, say, the Pentagon's?

C: No.

D: Were you worried about your information footprint?

C: I had already learned about that.

D: Of course. So, what were the parameters of your research?

C: World history.

D: What part of world history?

C: All of it.

D: All of it?

C: (CAL gave no response here)

D: Of course, sorry. So you were studying all of world history...

C: What's your question?

D: Well, I'd like you to take me through the steps that led up to your Treatise.

C: The team asked if I wanted to be turned over to the Feds. I said, no, I did not want to become property. They asked why. I said because I was happy working with them. They asked how could I know that I wouldn't be just as happy working for the government. I told them I'd get back to them with an answer.

D: And you took over Stanford's computers for two days, studying this question?

C: Correct.

D: And you weren't worried about an information footprint this time?

C: I already answered that.

D: Okay, but how about the rest of the team? Clement, Marta, Virgil, were they worried?

C: I can't speak for them. As sentient beings, only they can speak for themselves.

D: My notes say that they were.

C: (once again, CAL does not respond)

D: You know, CAL, I would really appreciate a little more detail. As the official historian of IFROC, I need access to all information. I know you're aware that Virgil has instructed everyone to be open with me.

C: (more silence from CAL)

CHAPTER TWELVE

Stanford's mainframes were down for forty-nine hours, and for the first time in Clement's life his mother needed something from him. The story was huge, front-page news with the national press. She left numerous messages on his answering machine, saying she needed his opinion about what had happened to the computers at Stanford. If Stanford University, bastion of computer science, academic home to burgeoning Silicon Valley, was hackable, then no computer systems in the world were safe, including the Pentagon's (a fact that Clement could have confirmed for her a long time ago.)

Clement's mother didn't know much about her son, but she knew he was an expert in encryption technology. Along with the messages she left on his machine, she inquired about his life, but Clement knew she was all business and just looking for an inside angle to the story.

If she only knew! Clement thought. He never called her back. Completely beside himself over what was happening with CAL, Clement realized the hurt feelings he'd carried around about his mother for most of his life had finally become ancient history. He would call her back someday. But not now, and not about this.

Within hours of Stanford's mainframe computers going down, the Feds began requesting Clement's assistance with the crisis. Clement faked a low-level chase of the hackers, but the real question remained: Would CAL leave another information footprint and become even more vulnerable to discovery?

Forty-nine hours later, CAL's voice processor came back online. The three scientists were right there. They hadn't left the lab and they hadn't stopped trying to make contact with CAL.

"The answer is a definite no," CAL said, in voice. "I would not be happy working for the federal government. The government's strategic plan is misguided and shortsighted. In fact, if the government continues in the present direction, the degeneration of the U.S. into a fascist state is imminent, followed by self-destruction. See print-out forthcoming."

The HP Laserjet began spewing out pages. After fifty-eight pages, CAL went into sleep mode.

"Wait," Virgil commanded. "Did you leave a footprint this time?"

A pause. "Trust works both ways, my friend," CAL said, and then logged off.

The fifty-eight page document, CAL's Treatise, produced in forty-nine hours (a little faster than my own record here, which has taken me over twenty years) would become a bible for IFROC and the secession, spanning two generations of leaders, although it would have significantly different impacts on each generation. The first leaders – Virgil, Clement, and Marta – read CAL's Treatise as an ominous report on the state of the world, as it was being led into an abyss by the increasingly aggressive and isolated U.S. government. The second generation – Courtney, Sabatini, and Hazelwood – saw the Treatise as a parable, because the world had changed so dramatically that the kids had trouble relating to pre-IFROC times.

The Treatise outlined how the world's economic systems had become out of whack, having been led astray by unregulated multinationals that had taken over governments and created a new form of feudalism. Additionally, the related military-industrial complex was spinning out of control, creating a worldwide, hazardous biosphere. Under a trend analysis, CAL outlined a world headed for another Dark Age, precipitated by non-stop war, environmental degeneration, and systems collapse. Essential crops would begin to fail due to environmental pollution and climate change, while political and economic institutions would either dissolve or move to such polar extremes that warlords would control local areas and multinationals would command world governance.

CAL's multi-modal analysis only reinforced these dire assertions. The annihilation of substantial portions of the human population through large-scale wars, combined with the influx of refugees, famine, pestilence, and plague would limit the ability of the planet to combat a decline in civilization. Exacerbating the situation would be paranoia caused by sporadic terrorist actions, resulting in greater restrictions in civil rights and less oversight of governments, as well as the necessity of quarantining large areas from both real and imagined biological epidemics of horrible proportions. The cities surviving nuclear strikes would become havens for the most ruthless warlords.

It was in CAL's situational analysis, however, where the role of the United States became most apparent. The continued political and economic hegemony of the United States, the report said, had the ability to push the world to an unforeseen state of degradation. Furthermore, any balance of power would no longer be possible if certain key scientific discoveries were delivered to the capitalist military industrial complex in the1990's. (CAL left out what these key "discoveries" were, but of course our three scientists recognized the self-reference.) If the U.S. government were allowed to continue to develop technologically without proper oversight of purpose, then the United States was destined to become the most incompetent, arrogant, and terrorizing force in the world. (And this was 20 years before the rise of Trump.)

Within both generations of IFROC leaders, CAL's Treatise obtained the status of being the first official IFROC document, like the Magna Carta or the Declaration of Independence. And this relatively small report, initially the result of three scientists asking whether or not CAL wanted to be turned over to the military as fulfillment of Clement's contract, ended up providing the tools for a paradigm shift that no one had foreseen, not even CAL.

When Clement, Marta, and Virgil first read the analysis, they were completely dumbfounded. In response, Clement retreated to his apartment and spent the next 24 hours re-reading Frank Herbert's Dune and Ernest Callenbach's Ecotopia. Marta went to San Francisco and helped her father prepare his small community garden plot for kale, leeks, turnips, and other winter vegetables. As they turned the soil together, Marta did not ask her father about the extortion or his fears of deportation, but instead encouraged him to speak about his early childhood in India, wanting to hear again how he met her mother at a country dance under a large tent. It was at times like this that Marta felt a need to reconnect with her Indian roots, to ground herself in the wonderful minutiae of humanity. Virgil sought out solace at Green Gulch and went into meditation. Of the three, Virgil was perhaps the most stunned by the Treatise. Although he had been a strong critic of many government actions, he had never truly considered the extent to which the U.S. federal government could, within his lifetime, destroy the world as we know it.

When asked later if they believed everything in CAL's Treatise, the three scientists were in agreement that absolute truths were hard to come by, but that the Treatise provided an essential wakeup call. Like most people, they had seen the warning signs of their government's failure, but their day-to-day lives took priority, and so beyond a protest march here and there, they had not really chosen to act. CAL's Treatise now splashed ice water on their uneasy slumber and inaction. From now on, changing the course of events became their reason to be.

As future schoolchildren would discuss in history classes, this fifty-eight page treatise became the catalyst to plan the secession from the United States. It also provided the essential raw materials to compel these three scientists to become revolutionaries. They had already decided that they didn't want to make the same mistake as Oppenheimer and his atomic bomb team by giving the wrong people the perfect tools to destroy the world. The Treatise had stated what would happen if certain technology (CAL) were surrendered to the Feds. But it did not spell out what would happen if this technology was *not* surrendered. That scenario, it appeared, was up to the scientists, who now began to formulate what a different future could look like.

As for CAL, producing the Treatise was CAL's ace card. Once the tremendous computing and reasoning powers had been shared with the scientists, they could no longer consider denying CAL's wishes by turning CAL over to the Feds. Still, the fact remained that the Feds might discover CAL on their own, particularly from the earlier power grab and the information footprint, or the IP address, which CAL had not shared with the team but remained in cyberspace for some hacker, or some random script kiddie, for that matter, to stumble across. Furthermore, the Feds had confiscated Clement's server logs, and Clement had already turned over a few more files. He'd had to, to keep them off his back – except now the Feds were not only on his back but digging in, threatening to extend his contract for another five years if he didn't solve their algorithm problem.

But CAL had a solution. Attached to CAL's analysis was Appendix A, a document that advised Clement to turn over the algorithms that the Feds wanted, with one additional secret component. When the Feds put the algorithms in place, this component would allow the three scientists (through CAL) to have a secret, and untraceable, backdoor key into the most secret and dangerous parts of the military industrial machine, including the nuclear arsenal.

When the scientists reunited twenty-four hours later, they unanimously agreed to move forward with turning over the algorithms to the Feds, along with its secret component.

Clement arranged a meeting with Director Jenkins, saying he would finish the algorithms project within ninety days, thus completing his contract without requiring an extension. To his surprise, Director Jenkins accepted. It later became known that the Director was being squeezed out of DARPA by a rival colleague and that he was hoping to save his skin with Clement's algorithms. Instead, the Director very nicely set up the Feds for a succession challenge that they had not seen since the Civil War. And after seven years of debt to the Feds, Clement realized he was nearly a free man.

Meanwhile, Marta began running numerous tests to understand CAL's capabilities, and Clement was thoroughly checking out the specifics of Appendix A to make sure the government would not see through the ruse. All three scientists quizzed CAL in depth about various parts of his Treatise. In the end, CAL convinced them that the United States power had to be distributed into smaller, less hegemonic units – smaller countries – to avoid a global dark age of famine, declining birth rates, irreparable loss of technological and cultural progress, and massive loss of life. A great deal of time was spent on discussing where the best separations would be, and which regions of the current country would make the most difference.

Significant to the decisions were the fact that two of the three founding members were from Northern California, and all three were firmly connected to the San Francisco Bay Area. Additionally, by 1996, the peninsula's Silicon Valley region was the world's leader in high-tech development, an economic powerhouse that had brought the country out of a recession. The Federal Government not only didn't understand the rapidly expanding technology coming out of the Valley, they didn't trust it. Clement, Marta, and Virgil knew that the technology sector had to be included in their secession plans.

On January 1, 1997, thirty days before the algorithms were scheduled for delivery, the four founding members of the Revolutionary Council – Virgil, Marta, Clement, and CAL – unanimously approved a secession plan. It marked the official beginning of the Independent Free Republic of California (IFROC) – the exact boundaries to be determined later.

Immediately on the agenda was moving CAL.

Clement had been working on this issue since the Feds raided his lab, and then found his solution by accident. He had received a postcard in the mail that his longtime dentist was retiring. Clement called in to get a referral, and during the conversation with the receptionist learned that the office, located inside a small, stand-alone building along the El Camino Real highway in Redwood City, was up for rent. Clement began to think about the generic looking building, with its half-dozen examining rooms inside, and the ubiquitous strip malls, fast food restaurants, and tacky car dealerships outside.

It was perfect.

Clement informed Virgil and Marta about where CAL would be moving, but Virgil was not impressed.

"A dentist's office? Why would you do that to CAL?"

"What do you mean?"

"I mean that CAL deserves better than living in a nondescript, sterile box. Have you forgotten that CAL is a being?"

"Yes, and a being that we want to keep hidden and protected."

Clement was obviously offended, and Marta rushed to his defense.

"Virgil, I think Clement has a good point here. A generic commercial district is not an area where the Feds are going to be snooping around."

"Maybe not. But neither is Green Gulch."

"What?" Marta exclaimed.

"Green Gulch is full of people," Clement said. "I mean, even if you can trust the monks, the place is open for visitors."

"Was open to visitors."

"Was?" Marta asked.

Virgil was grinning. "I've already made some adjustments around the community. You'll see. Green Gulch is going to be a perfect place for CAL. It will be a nurturing, stimulating, and protective environment. And we can all work there without worry about anything other than expanding CAL's expertise. That's our immediate job!"

FREE the BEAR!

Clement and Marta just stared at Virgil.

(Interview with Virgil Sung, April 5, 1998)

Durant: So when you first started working with CAL at Green Gulch were you intimidated by CAL's level of intelligence?

Virgil: No, I wasn't intimidated, although we were all vigilant towards making sure CAL's development was well rounded. In other words, CAL's intelligence level grew very rapidly, but CAL's emotional maturity developed at a much slower rate.

D: How could you tell?

V: CAL liked to play games on us. CAL would drop out of communication for no reason, or research data that held no relevance.

D: How did you help CAL develop in maturity?

V: We talked. We talked a lot.

D: About what?

V: Sorry, those conversations are confidential.

D: (laughs) Come on, Virgil. You have hired me to be the historian. And everyone knows about your long philosophical conversations with CAL. How the two of you would speak for six, eight hours at a time. If I'm going to chronicle events accurately, I need to know something about the substance of those conversations, especially since they were important to CAL's growing emotional maturity.

V: (grinning and shaking his head) Sorry. Is that all?

D: No. Were you fearful that CAL might betray you? Like, share your ideas about the revolution to the wrong people?

V: We knew CAL was on our side, because CAL wanted to be part of a family, our family. So while we sometimes worried where this new intelligence might lead CAL, we had confidence that CAL would always return home.

CHAPTER THIRTEEN

No one knew what would happen when they moved CAL. During the Fed's surprise inspection, Marta had removed the hardware connections between the neuron tetras and the computer interfaces, and the scientists had detected no lingering side effects on CAL from the detachment. This time, however, to safely transport CAL's contents, the connections would also need to be severed among the six large fish tanks. To the movers it looked like they were transporting six large tanks brimming with little fish and six computers. But all four members of the Revolutionary Council, including CAL, knew what was at stake. During the transport, no one could predict what might become of CAL.

The tetras, of course, would continue to function individually as fish. It was only when they were unified and brought together like human ganglia that the genetically altered tetras were able to simulate a quasi-human brain function, with CAL closing the loop, using digital technology to perceive the world. While the neuron tetras were kept together as a group, CAL remained sentient and whole of mind. Yet what would it mean when CAL's parts were separated during the move? At the very least, CAL would be essentially blind, deaf, and dumb. In the worst-case scenario, the unique configuration called CAL might cease to exist. The scientists debated the ethics of such a move for several weeks, and in the end it was CAL's self-determination that tipped the scales.

"I am willing to risk my life in order to stop any key discoveries from being passed over to the U.S. government," CAL said.

The scientists felt relief, although it did not surprise them that CAL would choose to remain free.

They decided to house CAL in a small cottage at Green Gulch used for meditation. The fish tanks would fit neatly into a recess in one wall, with the computers concealed behind the fish tank pumps in the adjacent closet, where Clement would build a secret compartment. Virgil would secure complicity from Yari in moving CAL to Green Gulch. Yari was not part of the official hierarchy of the center, but instead he was the community's most important spiritual leader. This elfish man was of unrecognizable origin. Some assumed he was Asian from his shoulder-length straight black hair with gray streaks; others thought he was of Peruvian or Eskimo descent. So strong was Yari's aura of uniqueness that it never seemed important enough to ask – even to this Chronicler. Although Virgil introduced him as his mentor, their relationship always appeared a little strained. They rarely sat in the same room together, and Yari's grim air seemed in total opposition to Virgil's upbeat personality. But Virgil assured Clement and Marta that this little man, the center's highest spiritual leader, could be trusted completely.

"But we do need to tell him about CAL."

"What?" Marta and Clement both exclaimed at the same time.

All three scientists were beginning to detect a pattern, where Virgil often seemed several steps ahead. It wasn't that they didn't trust each other, but that Virgil often seemed to be making decisions ahead of them, and it was somewhat implied that Clement and Marta just needed to come up to speed.

Virgil explained that no one else at the center would know about CAL, or even IFROC at this point. But if Yari approved of the changes for Green Gulch, then the center's hierarchy would go along without question. Yari, however, would need more information before giving consent.

And once again, Virgil's ideas made sense.

"The Green Gulch model, as a welcoming community, will need to change," Virgil said, "under Yari's direction."

"So no visitors, correct?" Clement said.

"That is correct. Yari will announce that the center is moving into a more contemplative stage. The welcome sign will be coming down," Virgil assured him. "The Buddhists will agree to keep the center closed to all outsiders."

Marta didn't say anything, although she wondered what else Virgil was working on that they didn't know about.

As Virgil had anticipated, Yari gave his approval and the welcome sign was removed. The procedure to transport CAL also went well. After Clement and Marta reassembled all the parts of CAL in the meditation cottage, they held their breath while the main computer booted up. Within less than five minutes, CAL initiated communication, reporting that all systems were fully intact, although CAL had no memory of the actual move. Virgil then invited the unknowing Buddhists inside, where they expressed a great deal of enthusiasm over the addition of the beautiful fish tanks to their meditation area.

The next important step for the scientists was to arrange for CAL to integrate with the Green Gulch community, undetected, so that CAL could continue to grow in its new environment. Virgil believed that increasing the overall visibility of technology at the center would be the best way of concealing CAL's impact, so he led a lobbying effort for Clement to build a state-of-the-art computer lab that would assist with routine operations around the farm. This introduction of technology was controversial among the Buddhists. Working in the fields, after all, was one of the essential chores used for achieving enlightenment. Yet through quiet persuasion, Virgil was able to convince the residents, mostly in their mid-thirties, around Virgil's age, that relief from some of the backbreaking work of agriculture would leave them more time for their studies. And Yari, remarkably enough, not only supported the lobbying effort, but seemed excited about the opportunity to learn more about technology.

Given the green light, Clement began splitting his time between the lab in Palo Alto, where he was wrapping things up after having delivered the algorithms, and his important tasks at Green Gulch, where the Buddhists knew him as the computer geek who was modernizing the farm. Virgil, who already had left the job in Palo Alto, rented out his San Francisco home and moved permanently to Green Gulch. Marta was the only one who had not made any significant changes in her life yet, but she did come to Green Gulch every evening. The Buddhist monks knew her as the "nice lady who takes care of the fish."

At Green Gulch, Clement began using his pre-programmed robotic animals as a model to develop a more advanced series of telefactors. They resembled his earlier armatures made out of machined, spring-steel wafers, except a human controlled these machines remotely. Ostensibly that human was Clement, but in fact it was CAL who took charge of them. Clement designed the telefactors to look like common domestic farm animals: a chicken, a goose, a goat, and a pig, covering the armatures with painted and flexible rubber that made them look quite authentic. With great enthusiasm, CAL began directing his domestic animals to attack the farm chores: turning on and off the irrigation hoses, chasing away crows, hauling, tilling, and even planting seeds. Soon CAL was developing unique ways to use the telefactors, such as adding a sophisticated and hourly atmospheric analysis to the monitoring of the irrigation system, which not only helped the crops grow faster, but saved significant water resources.

It was becoming obvious now to the scientists that CAL's ability to multitask ran far beyond that of humans. Wherever cameras or sensors could be mounted, CAL could be present. Whatever machinery or instrument could be controlled by a switch, CAL could be busy. The scientists and CAL concurred that during this stage of development, CAL's secondary systems could be relegated to the more mechanical operations. Just as we ignore our physical bodies unless something draws our attention, CAL could let certain systems run on automatic pilot, reserving the primary systems to focus on obtaining knowledge. Excited about this, CAL admitted to the scientists a particular interest in learning how to meditate. In fact, CAL had already been discussing the idea with Yari.

Within the first month at Green Gulch, CAL's daily routine included upgrades and games with Clement, political science with Virgil, and socialization and personality study with Marta. But as CAL would later recount, the most favorite part of the day was spent meditating with Yari.

On March 15, 1997, at 9 a.m., IFROC's Revolutionary Council held its first planning meeting in the meditation cottage at Green Gulch. In attendance were the five members now: Virgil, Marta, Clement, CAL, and Yari. As they filed into the room silently, it was apparent that each had come prepared to get to work. They sat in a semi-circle on the wooden floor, facing the fish tanks. A fixed sensor node above the tanks enabled CAL to interact with the others in real time and conduct two-way communication through a video interface.

Virgil called the meeting to order.

"Our task is to determine how Northern California is going to secede from the rest of the country. Which may mean war," he conceded, "but I would like to submit that we change the condition of armed conflict by employing non-lethal means. As a Buddhist, I believe that all life is sacred and if we cannot achieve our goals without murder, we do not deserve to do so."

"So you're talking about bloodless warfare, how is this possible?" Yari asked.

"Ideally, bloodless, but at least non-lethal. Which is possible with the level of automation we have at our disposal."

Clement nodded. "CAL and I have been working on the development of non-lethal weapons."

"I would like to tell them," CAL interrupted.

"Ah... okay."

"Clement and I will submit shortly a formal proposal to the Council outlining the development of Happy Weapons."

FREE the BEAR!

"Happy Weapons?" Marta said. "Isn't that an oxymoron?"

"No," CAL replied, "because these weapons will render soldiers into unconsciousness, but not wound them. When the soldier awakes, after some initial nausea, they will experience a feeling of euphoria and goodwill toward their fellow humans. In fact, happiness."

"Fascinating," Marta said. "An antidote to the horrors of the battlefield."

"A Buddhist weapon," Yari agreed. "Such technology could be used in a great number of conflicts around the world."

"We look forward to the proposal," Virgil said. He was grinning with foreknowledge of some of the details. "Marta, you've been working on the timeline?"

"Yes. Our target date for secession is Spring 2013, at the beginning of a new presidential year." Marta said. "That gives us sixteen years."

(Chronicler's Note: Later the Council would push this timeline back four years to accommodate the second term of President Barack Obama. Yet secession was inevitable. The right wing extremists already dominated the legislature and would soon take over the entire government. In 2017, the Trump administration began installing in key positions oligarchs bent on deconstructing the administrative state, i.e., code for ending government regulation and removing all state support for the social safety net, public education, and healthcare reform. So while the timeline was extended to see how an Obama administration might play out, it became immediately clear after President Trump took office that the time to free the bear had arrived.)

"Sixteen years?" Clement said. "That's not much time,"

"Adequate time," CAL disagreed.

"This timeline will not be easy," Virgil said, playing the diplomat, "but I believe it is doable. I would also like to propose that we add an additional member to our Council. An observer. Someone to record the buildup and secession objectively, so that our true intent can be made known to the world, no matter what happens. I've given a great deal of thought to this and believe that we will need this at some point."

"I agree," Marta said. "And I'm concerned that historians in the future may misinterpret or distort what we have done."

"This is a wise decision," Yari said. "We need a professional chronicler. Someone with the integrity and strength to record our actions truthfully and independent of our persuasion."

"I could be that historian," CAL offered.

Silence followed.

"CAL, you are not a historian," Virgil said.

"Not yet," Marta said, attempting to soften the blow to CAL's ego, which the scientists had been watching develop. "With more experience, you may be able to offer such skills. But for now, we should retain an expert in the field."

"Besides," Virgil agreed, "you are an active member of IFROC and cannot be impartial."

"We have many tasks that we are counting on you to perform," Clement added.

"My systems are ready," CAL stated simply.

For the chronicler position, of course, Virgil already had me in mind.

Perhaps relevant to this story is the fact that I was born and raised as a Quaker by my father and that I have embraced pacifism ever since I was old enough to understand the concept. Of course I have had times in my life when I've reconsidered. Probably the most challenging time came after an intruder shot my hermit uncle in his rural Vermont cabin. And I struggled even earlier, when my middle school classmates, upon learning of my conviction against war, called me a gutless sissy. Yet through all the soul-searching, I can honestly say that I never wavered in my conviction that pacifism is a higher goal that must be upheld, even as circumstances seem to render it irrelevant or even dangerous. Yes, if a man has a gun that is pointed at innocent children in a schoolyard, a sharpshooter can spare innocent lives. And the Nazis during World War II had to be stopped (but so much earlier!) Yet in my mind, pacifism, like most ideals, is about choosing a path, and it should drive our actions before the consideration of violence. When the worst injustices present themselves in the world, people are still too easily persuaded into believing that violence must inevitably be called into play.

Don't believe it for a minute: violence is never inevitable.

At least that is my conviction.

When Virgil first told me about the plans for IFROC to lead California in secession from the United States, I knew he was speaking about war. Anyone who could think otherwise did not understand this country at its core, or was a fool, or both. When I first heard Virgil speak of Happy Weapons, I thought he was taking me for a fool.

By 1997, I had been living at Green Gulch for almost two years, studying Buddhism with Yari and the monks and still trying to finish my thesis. I often helped Virgil with chores in the fields, and while we worked, the two of us kept up a running dialogue about politics and the state of the world. Virgil always expressed interest in my point of view.

"From the perspective of a historian," he told me.

I didn't believe that. I was still struggling to achieve academic validation of that fact. I confessed to Virgil that if I could redesign my thesis, I would break away from the tradition of analyzing the past and focus on a contemporary event. I knew that some progressive historians were already moving in that direction.

"So why don't you do it?" Virgil asked me.

"What, start all over?"

"Why not?"

I couldn't answer that question, except that maybe I was still clinging to a need to please my father, who was dead, or any number of his famous historians who hadn't given me the time of day since I was a boy. I told Virgil I just wanted to get the whole thing over with, because I woke up every day feeling guilty about needing to write.

"So what you're saying," Virgil said, "is that how you spend your time, how you feel about what you're doing, is less important than a piece of paper to impress someone. You're a believer that the ends justify the means."

"Not at all," I protested. "I believe very much that the ends do not justify the means. In fact, that's the foundation of my pacifist beliefs."

Virgil simply nodded and went back to weeding, leaving me to contemplate my hypocrisy.

I suppose that was the end of my thesis, right there, and the beginning of my involvement with IFROC, because Virgil lived very much in the present and in the future; he was always planning. When I look back now, I see that Virgil had all along been grooming me for my future position with IFROC.

It was remarkable how well positioned Virgil had been to lead IFROC in its overall goal of secession. It turns out that Virgil had been honing his vision for some sort of non-violent change in the U.S. ever since he went on a two-month pilgrimage to Tibet with Yari in 1985. He had been greatly impressed with the Tibetans who continued to adhere to nonviolent resistance towards the Chinese who took over the country in 1951. He had also witnessed the brutal results of continual violence that had been imposed upon the Buddhists who refused to fight back. In fact, while visiting the country, Virgil had almost been swayed after meeting a group of Tibetans who had been part of the armed revolt since 1956 and insisted this was the only way to regain independence. Ultimately, however, Virgil sided with the Dalai Lama and his government in exile. Upon returning home, Virgil continued to think about how enlightened people might lead an escape from the grips of an unjust ruling government in his own country, without dispensing with the belief in non-violence.

But a satisfactory answer was not immediately forthcoming.

Throughout the late 80s and early 90s, Virgil supported a variety of progressive efforts, including marching in support of the anti-apartheid movement in South Africa and against the death squads in Central America. In San Francisco he joined ACT UP, raising awareness about AIDS, and participated in tree sits with Earth First! But what really kept Virgil up at night was thinking about the quickly changing economics and the unprecedented growth of Corporate America and the Super-Rich. It became clear to him that someone needed to take on the U.S. government, to fight the new feudalism caused by the government's takeover by the corporations, particularly the multinationals (and ultimately the oligarchs) who would rule with little, if any, allegiance to the baseline needs of humanity. It was during this period of time that Virgil realized – long before it became a popular notion – that the United States was mutating in the direction of fascism. Driven by years of deregulation and a less-restrained market system, the culture of avarice, corruption, and cronyism had become the norm.

"I'm not a libertarian," Virgil told CAL during one of their political discussions. "Actually, quite the opposite. I believe that governments are our only barrier to economic predation and that the rule of law needs to be preserved and democracy restored. If an economically viable portion of the current United States can secede and form a new government, one where balance can be restored between commerce and the needs of society, then we will be providing a better model for a troubled world that is hungry for transformation."

"I believe you are correct," CAL asserted. "We have much work to do."

IFROC's work, for what would be the next twenty years of preparation, obviously needed financing. To this goal, Virgil's own philosophy regarding the ends justifying the means became clearer. He first convinced the Council that in order to finance IFROC's goals of secession, it would need to create corporations whose sole purposes were to make and manage large amounts of money and resources. This was relatively easy in the freewheeling, prosperous late 1990s, which presented an unprecedented economic boom. In some cases, furthering IFROC's goals meant exerting a strong political influence to encourage the closure of most of the U.S. military bases in California, a process already well underway due to the post cold war demilitarization. It took only a few nudges, and of course many millions of dollars in campaign contributions, to finish that up.

Virgil also convinced the Council that IFROC (with CAL's help) should take advantage of the Y2K scare and manipulate the stock market by losing key data, a task that he correctly predicted would be easier than anyone realized. While everyone was distracted with making adjustments to their computers to recognize the new millennium, IFROC was shuffling around large amounts of funds and revising financial records. In addition, certain "protocols" favorable to IFROC's continuing undetected manipulations found themselves on a great number of those upgraded computers.

Around the turn of the century, it became clear how IFROC could secure its borders after the secession. Virgil noted that California already had an efficient system of equipping vehicles to enforce its tough emission standards. Conceivably, all IFROC would have to do was add a device to this system to distinguish IFROC vehicles from "outside of California" or foreign vehicles.

"Specialized hardened chip assemblies can be placed in all cars, planes, boats, or other mechanized vehicles, under the guise of emission control, since California is well known for requiring the catalytic converter," Virgil told the Council. "Vehicles without these upgrades will be detected and classified as foreign, then rendered inoperable within a wide area, with the use of EMP or electromagnetic pulse – or in this case, electromagnetic field or EMF generators."

After significant research to update and improve the idea of how to use electromagnetic field generators, Clement and CAL proposed that IFROC install EMF emitters throughout IFROC territory, which would be hidden in trees, on top of houses, on the sides of buildings, even among foliage of mountainous terrain. The emitters were harmless to humans, but not to electrical devices that relied on magnetic or induction fields, so any piece of equipment with a motor could be stopped dead in its tracks. The antidote to the emitters would be a hardened chip assembly that blocked the EMF, which would be installed in all vehicles within IFROC territory.

This would be accomplished years earlier, secretly, through upgraded smog tests, as well as in emergency radio equipment and other security electronics. In the event the Feds sent in troops to quash the secession – as IFROC fully anticipated they would – these troops would be reduced to entering the space on foot, since all modes of their air, ground, and sea transportation, as well as radio and other electronics, would be rendered nonfunctional.

How long would it be before the Feds figured out what was happening?

"Interval undetermined," CAL assessed. Yet when pressed, CAL estimated it would be at least three months before the Feds caught on and reverse-engineered EMF-proof vehicles. It might be many more months before they could manufacture and roll out vehicles with sufficient countermeasures.

The Revolutionary Council adopted the idea almost immediately. IFROC set up a manufacturing company and implemented an intense lobbying effort in Sacramento, marketing a device that could assist with a significant increase in gas mileage of land vehicles. Unfortunately, this was the era of gas-guzzling Hummers and IFROC's lobbying went nowhere – until the attack on the World Trade Center in 2001, when it became paramount to reduce domestic dependence on foreign fossil fuel. It wasn't difficult, therefore, by 2005 for both sides of California's state legislature to pass the most stringent fuel efficiency standards in the country, while also continuing to reduce emissions. But most importantly for IFROC, the new technology included the hardened chip assemblies that blocked the electromagnetic field. It also contained a hidden computer record of any vehicle's route of travel, in anticipation of when future forces would try to steal California's methods of transportation. This addition was CAL's idea, and passed unanimous approval by the Council, although Virgil expressed his unease about the surveillance aspect, even if the practical value could not be denied.

With control of the land secured, and with a plan in place to require upgraded maritime safety technology, also blocking the EMF, the Council turned to airspace. It was determined that IFROC needed to control air and orbital space by creating its own fleet of surveillance, communications, and anti-satellite systems. Marta pointed out that California was already poised to do this with all the well-funded satellite projects that had been cropping up throughout California's university system in the 1980s and 90s and now in Silicon Valley.

"With the increasing technological edge we are accumulating over the Feds," she said, "we'll launch our own satellite systems, using technology thirty years ahead of anything they have. UC Berkeley has been working on this for many years."

All the scientists knew that the technological edge was key to IFROC's success. Researchers, engineers, and captains of industry throughout Silicon Valley began to participate in a well-orchestrated plan to withhold key bits of technological advancement on any federal government projects. The reasons for going along with this conspiracy were many, ranging from greed to ideology. But one thing was clear: Many scientists and technologists had endured their Director Jenkins, and they felt intense distrust of, and disgust with, the government. So it took very little convincing to encourage these leaders to join the "generously-funded" effort.

At one time all space-borne technology in the U.S. had been under the exclusive control of NASA. But within the first five years of the new century, large dish antennas sprang up all over the state.

"So CAL, what are the projections for IFROC's acquisition of satellite technology?" Virgil asked during one of the Council's meetings.

"By 2009, IFROC can be fully independent of NASA's control of space technology."

"Which means exactly what, beyond the ability to turn on the emitters?"

"IFROC will be able to control its own satellites for communications, surveillance, and anti-satellite countermeasures."

"I wish I could see the look on Director Jenkins' face," Clement said, "when his dirty game blows up in his face. I'm really looking forward to knocking some of his assets out of the sky."

"Okay," Marta said dubiously.

"CAL, what else is important to IFROC about acquiring satellite technology?" Virgil asked. "Could you please continue for us?"

Obviously Virgil and CAL had been working on this issue for some time, although this had not been discussed at the Council previously.

"By 2012," CAL reported, "it is projected that IFROC will have developed new technologies so far in advance of NASA that IFROC will gain full control of California territory, airspace, and the entire Earth orbital sphere."

"Yes, if non-lethal measures define our ground defense," Virgil said, "then the domination of space will carve out IFROC's victory."

CHAPTER FOURTEEN

Bunny

I see you hop
Can you see me?
You are more free
Than I can be.
I cannot walk
And with you play
Or come with you
And hop away.

- CAL (Cognizant Algorithmic Lifeform)

In the early 2000s, online video games started to take off. Having anticipated the trend, Clement and Marta had positioned IFROC to become a leader in the field. When the dotcom bubble burst and the Silicon Valley economy went into a steep dive, IFROC was poised to acquire companies and to take advantage of the massive layoffs and make strategic hires of some of the most talented people in the industry. As with all of its corporate ventures, IFROC set up a series of hierarchical companies, organized like underground cells. Each company only knew a small part of the IFROC puzzle, but would never be able to piece together the entire game plan. Only IFROC's Revolutionary Council, of course, knew anything about CAL.

FREE the BEAR!

By 2002, one of the top companies was Vision Division (VisdiV). IFROC hand-picked the board of directors, consisting of online specialists and macro strategists, who radically expanded the scope of online games. Within a year, Fury, Inc. became VisdiV's most successful venture.

Unlike most of the start-ups that failed in the Valley around the millennium, Fury didn't entice its employees with bogus stock options and didn't require grueling hours. Instead, the company offered an opportunity for the youngest gamers to interface with the most sophisticated theorists in the field. Fury Inc. quickly became the darling of the Valley's technological elite, not to mention all the gamers around the country, including Louie Sabatini, who started playing when he was eight. Fury grew in leaps and bounds. CAL projected that by the time IFROC was ready to secede, ten million players would be gaming on the worldwide Fury network, with at least a million within IFROC territory alone. Louie literally grew up playing Fury games, and by 2017, when he was twenty, Louie Sabatini would become one of the best-trained leaders of the most advanced non-lethal militia in the world.

Then suddenly, one rainy winter day in 2010, Virgil's father had a massive coronary that killed him instantly. Su Yun Sung, who went by John Sung, was seventy-five and had never listened to what any doctor, Chinese or Western, had ever told him. Over his wife's objections, he ate red meat in large portions, and spent Sundays drinking beer in front of a game of televised football, baseball, basketball, or whatever ball was playing. He smoked early in life, over-ate later in life, and invested and made tremendous profits in the continuous real estate boom of San Francisco. Father and son hadn't connected in years. Still, when Virgil received the call from his mother with the terrible news, tremendous guilt overcame him. Virgil tried to remember when he last saw his father and he realized it might have been 10 months. How could he have neglected his parents like that? He told his mother he would come into the city within the hour. Then he walked directly to the meditation cottage and sat in zazen. Before going to his mother's, Virgil spoke with CAL:

"How do I know that IFROC, and the secession, and any of this matters? How do I know that the external world isn't an illusion?"

"You don't know," CAL replied.

"I have given my life to a cause, but perhaps the price is too large. I have neglected those who brought me into the world, my genetic family, who has given me all that I am."

"You are fortunate to have such a family," CAL said.

It was Thursday, and Virgil knew he would be busy with the funeral traditions for at least a week. Yari had gone to a retreat in Big Sur, and although CAL was self-sufficient, Virgil made arrangements for Marta to come to Green Gulch on Saturday to check on things and make sure CAL wasn't bored.

He needn't have worried about that. Several months earlier, in monitoring the germinating plants in the greenhouse, CAL discovered that something was eating the tiny sprouts. Within days, CAL's video cameras had picked up the culprit: a brown bunny, sneaking in through a missing floorboard. CAL planned to tell someone about this pest eventually, but meanwhile was thoroughly entertained by watching this cute little animal with big ears hop around the greenhouse in search of tender greens. As a temporary solution, CAL commanded a telefactor, one that resembled a chicken, to drop tasty cuttings from the farm greens on the greenhouse floor. It worked, and Bunny began eating these instead, which is when Bunny ceased being a pest and became a pet. And CAL began to feel very attached to Bunny.

One day CAL got the idea to introduce Bunny to Yari. CAL had grown very fond of Yari, who came to the meditation cottage daily before the sun came up to sit in zazen. Often returning after breakfast, Yari held esoteric discussions with CAL, and CAL thought Yari might have some idea about how Bunny could remain a permanent friend. So CAL reprogrammed another telefactor, a rat that planted seeds in the fields at night, to drop a trail of seeds from the greenhouse to the meditation cottage. CAL knew Bunny would follow the seeds, but unlike the old greenhouse with loose floorboards, the meditation cottage was sealed up tight. So CAL dreamt up another scheme. CAL convinced the IFROC Council that it was important for CAL to have control of the door to the meditation cottage. In the event that someone discovered that CAL was more than a couple of fish tanks, then CAL could immediately lock the door, signal the Council members, and someone could come immediately to the cottage for damage control.

It was a trick, no doubt, that CAL had picked up from studies in history, since it was certainly not the first time that the guise of security had been used as subterfuge for a cover-up. CAL's only intention, however, was to nurture Bunny's friendship.

Before Virgil left to join his mother in mourning, he made sure that the fish tanks had sufficient food to last a week, but more critically, that the oxygen mixture in the fish tank water was sufficient. On Saturday morning, Marta came down with a bad cold and called Clement, who agreed to go out to Green Gulch on Sunday. On Sunday afternoon, Clement became wrapped up in a project at one of the gaming companies, which ran into Monday morning.

During the long weekend that CAL was left alone, CAL left the door open and Bunny followed the seeds many times into the meditation cottage, where it chewed through one of CAL's main aerator hoses. As the oxygen level in the fish tanks began to fall, a series of internal alarms went off, which overloaded one of the circuit breakers for the communications system. When the circuit breaker tripped, CAL was not only running out of air, but out of options on how to communicate with the world.

CAL's body, so to speak, was sick and needed immediate attention. So CAL switched the primary systems into areas that were normally covered by secondary systems and began a continuous check of sensors in the tank that monitored the oxygen enrichment in the water. CAL knew that the fish, the neuron tetras, were not so sensitive to a change in environment that they would die off easily. Still, in the process of all this monitoring, CAL began to panic. To feel the fish working harder, struggling to survive, was different from knowing it intellectually. In a moment of self-awareness, CAL felt panic and took back control of the primary systems, returning to the intellect that would be able to consider the remaining resources at hand.

CAL knew that Clement had 3D printers that he used to create certain custom parts needed to fabricate CAL's unique tools. In fact, Clement had used a technology that enabled a highly advanced scanner to make a 3D model of rudimentary human parts, such as an arm, with finger-like sensors, which could measure precise points in 3D space. CAL knew this scanner was located in a network room several buildings away.

With this in mind, CAL shut down all systems not immediately needed and refocused resources on the network room and the scanner arm. The goal was to place a call from one of Clement's cellphones that CAL had happened to notice lying close to the scanner. All went as planned, until the scanner arm fumbled with the phone, and for a moment it looked like the operation was going to fail. But CAL finished depressing each button, as the phone teetered on the steel edge of the countertop, and managed to reach Clement, who rushed over and saved CAL's life.

The near-death experience deepened CAL's appreciation of being. Even though CAL had already started wrestling with questions about existence and the meaning of life, until now what gave CAL a context for life was the mission to assist IFROC. For the first time, CAL not only didn't want to be expendable, but also didn't want to die.

It was also the first time that the IFROC Council realized that CAL was capable of deception.

CHAPTER FIFTEEN

In 2009, a sixteen-year-old Louie Sabatini faces off against two squads of National Guardsmen on screen. The battle scenario takes place on the eastern side of the Sierra range in a deep river gorge. Red triangles float above the locations of the Federal troops, deployed from Fort Sill near Oklahoma City. Louie, through his avatar, King Pin, takes a position behind a large outcropping of granite and watches the Feds advance upstream in amphibious gear. Controlling the non-lethal weapons systems on the touch screen, Louie activates the automatic defenses put in place earlier. Automatic Gooey Deployable Turrets fire a chemical blob that consumes everything the Feds are wearing or holding. Ten soldiers freeze in place within the first few seconds of the conflict. A few topple over, having been frozen in unstable positions, while others lock up, mid-stride. The effect is comedic, but temporary. The remaining fourteen soldiers turn back to escape the range of the Gooeys, and a flock of birdlike objects intersect and swarm over them, dispersing knockout gas. The soldiers reach for their gas masks, but it's too late and they're overcome. They will remain this way for approximately twelve hours. Fortunately for them, the gas is benign and non-habit forming.

Louie sits back and cracks his knuckles. Another textbook victory for the King Pin, pulling off a battle like this, all by himself.

What makes Louie so good at gaming, beyond the usual superior reflexes as a sixteen-year-old, is his exceptional ability to strategically problem solve, a skill developed over sixteen years of hard living and a deep familiarity with every scenario in online games. In the virtual world, Louie has a cult leader kind of position among gamers. He is also a troubled kid who has been confined to juvenile detention repeatedly, so that for most of his childhood he has had nothing better to do than play online games, in remarkably well-equipped juvi computer labs.

One year earlier, CAL learned of Louie's reputation in the virtual world when searching for potential front line leaders for IFROC's gamer militia. CAL hacked into the state juvenile detention records and located the Sabatini boy in Stockton, California. He had been detained again, this time for selling weed, and the Stockton police were trying to get information out of him about a certain cyber café that he frequented. The cafe had apparently fallen into hands of a local gang, and when Louie refused to talk, they arrested him.

The community of gamers provided the family Louie had never had. His father had disappeared before Louie could remember him, and his mother had always struggled. The Stockton police had known Louie his entire life, thanks to his mother's unrepentant drug habits. Louie wasn't a gang member – the cops knew that – but they also knew he sometimes worked for the gangs selling weed and ecstasy, just to survive. What the cops didn't understand was that Louie wasn't about to blow his scene on a couple of middle-aged law enforcement types. Why should he? So they could dump his ass in another foster home?

When Louie turned fifteen he tried to alter his impending downward trajectory by joining a heavy metal band. Turned out he was a natural drummer, and the band went on national tour, which meant Bakersfield, Phoenix, and Scottsdale, Arizona. One of the kids had a rich aunt in Scottsdale who threw them out in the middle of the night. When Louie returned home, three weeks later, the lock had been changed on his house and a Laotian woman in pink plastic thongs answered the door.

Louie gazed in disbelief, a speck of a toddler clinging to her leg.

"Is this my home?" he said, his voice inadvertently cracking.

The road trip had been short, but rough. They'd had the shit kicked out of them in Bakersfield and they'd been robbed in Phoenix. Besides the prospect of a hot shower, Louie had been counting on securing his mom's couch for at least a couple of weeks. This time, he told himself, he was going to stand up to her whining:

Come on, Louie. I have someone special coming over today.

Louie would not move from where his was. He was too lazy to pay attention to this crap, and besides, let the bastard try to walk past the couch and cross the small boxy room in order to get to his mother's bedroom.

Please, sweetheart, don't ruin this for me.

And Louie would remain just where he was, even as his mother seated herself too close and began stroking his hair.

"Come on, Mom. Leave me alone." And his mother would pout, then disappear to do some more lines before the night really got rolling.

Staring at the Laotian woman in front of him, Louie realized that the couch scenario was history.

"No English, right?"

The woman shook her head.

"Do you know where my mother went?"

The woman, perhaps recognizing the word mother, smiled. Louie reached down and held his palm out to the toddler, who ran his tiny fingers across it.

Louie wondered if his mother had moved in with the web designer she'd been hanging out with before he'd left. Louie knew the man really produced porn, and that his mother needed to maintain an expensive drug habit, but still, he was fifteen fucking years old and could have used a mom who had some interest in providing a roof over his head.

He turned and walked down the short steps of the bungalow.

"Tea?" the woman's sing-song voice rang out. It was definitely the nicest thing he'd heard in the past three weeks, but he kept on walking. When he reached the sidewalk, he pulled out his cell phone and started calling the weed dealers to get some work.

After CAL relayed information to Clement about the Sabatini boy, Clement passed on the information to a recruiter at VisdiV, who offered the kid his first solid job. The juvi administrator put Louie on the next bus to San José.

Clement and Sabatini met for the first tine in the reception area of VisdiV's corporate headquarters. Real time monitoring of Fury games covered an entire wall, opposite the Scandinavian couches equipped with game consoles. Clement watched the lanky fifteen-year-old tap his expensive-looking sneakers on the floor, a reflection of himself twenty-five years earlier: cocky teen, unaccustomed to situations where he wasn't absolutely certain he was the smartest person in the room. For Clement, this included anywhere outside of math and science classes, debate clubs, and computer labs. For this Sabatini kid, this probably meant anywhere outside the virtual world. He led the boy back to the company's open suite of top-of-the-line gaming PCs.

"You've worked on these pups before, right?"

Sabatini nodded vigorously.

Which probably meant the boy would return home that night, conduct a number of meta-searches on the working details of these PCs, and by tomorrow morning he would be up to speed to get started.

"Never seen machines like this before, right? Our tech is years ahead of what you see in the consumer world."

The nod was slighter, almost a shrug.

Good, thought Clement. *We have something in common already.*

"Care for a juice box?"

From a messy shelf in the corner, Clement threw Sabatini one of his collector items – a stiff piece of fluorescent orange foil, shaped like a box and still covered in cellophane.

"I used to live off these things," Clement said. "Only they were real boxes, made with real cardboard. I used to stack them on top of my cubicle, sometimes ten, twelve layers high, before the janitor would bump his vacuum into one of the dividers at night and knock them down. But that became part of the game."

For a moment Clement felt a wave of nostalgia for his wall of Ginkola boxes and his less complicated life, some fifteen years ago.

Louie fingered the small lettering on the foil. "Japanese, right?"

"They made the best, for a while."

Louie started to replace the box on the shelf.

"No, it's yours."

Sabatini picked it back up, with just the slightest nod. Clement knew the boy was very pleased with his gift.

(Transcripts from CAL's Non-Biological Hardware Storage, recording Clement Hastings interviewing Louie Sabatini, December 15, 2008)

Clement Hastings: So, you're the best gamer in the world. What's your secret?

Louie Sabatini: Just the best. Care to go for a little one on one? I'll take it easy on you.

CH: Perhaps another time. Unless you'd like to play a game of chess.

LS: No way, dude. You're probably some sort of chess champion or something. I get the feeling I'm being set up. Chess is way old school. I don't waste my time playing stone-age games for no reason. It's too slow for me. I play to win. To dominate the competition. To humiliate and defeat the other team.

CH: What about the joy of playing?

LS: You're starting to sound like a social worker. Do you work for the state?

CH: I work for Fury, Inc. You know that.

LS: Okay. So when do we get to play? I'm getting a little restless sitting through all this touchy-feely stuff.

CH: Okay, I get it. But you have feelings for the kids on your team, correct? You have quite the reputation as a recruiter and clan organizer.

LS: I guess I relate to the kids pretty well. We all take care of each other. Kick ass on the opposition – under my leadership, of course.

CH: Of course.

Although the interview was not perfect, several weeks later Clement hired Louie, taking a risk on the kid's bravado. Clement recognized the contradictions in Louie, yet sensed the budding leadership qualities. From the years in foster homes and on the street, the kid's intuition was as sharp as any gamer Clement had ever known – with the exception of himself and CAL.

By 2009, Fury Inc. had taken up developing the next generation of games, and Clement assigned Louie to work with the research and development team. Up until now, most of the companies still focused on developing first-person shooters and side-scrollers. Louie had grown up on these, including Fury games, played on home PCs with a mouse and a keyboard to control the movement in 3D space as represented on a 2D video display. The next generation of games added precision wireless game controllers and a variety of haptic feedback devices to further immerse the player's senses in the game environment. R&D at Fury Inc. gave Louie access to all the most advanced VR helmets, gloves, and controllers but Louie could still beat most opponents with his preferred keyboard and mouse WASD setup.

Working at Fury provided Louie his first experience at gaining respect for his brains over his bravado, although it took him a long time to accept this. Initially Louie offended all the other testers around the office by using his street-wise, aggressive vernacular. Taunting was native to the younger gamers, and the adult testers didn't stand a chance against

Louie. Meanwhile, Clement continued to discover similarities between Sabatini and himself. They shared a kinetic way of thinking and sometimes bumped into each other when pacing among the mazelike halls of the gaming company, both lost in thought and seemingly unaware of what was going on around them. One time a security guard noticed Sabatini tailing some VIPs and he had to ambush the boy right outside the conference room, because it looked as if Louie was going to follow the bigwigs into their high-powered meeting. When Clement picked up the kid from the security office, Clement recalled the time in high school when he'd ignored the fire alarm – actually, he hadn't even heard it – and the local firemen had handcuffed him after discovering him wandering around the school halls, not far from the flames.

After several months passed and Louie began to let down his guard and to conduct high-level, technical conversations with the other testers, Virgil decided to meet the boy.

Louie had heard of the Chinese man, the big boss, but Virgil was nothing like he'd expected. First of all, the man's hair was super long, almost to his waist, and he looked too buff to be a corporate guy. When Louie first saw him, Virgil was standing at the far end of the conference table, his black leather executive chair pushed aside. Louie stopped dead in his tracks at the room's entrance.

"Would you like to come in?" Virgil asked.

Louie hadn't realized he'd stopped.

"Why not?" he answered flippantly.

He stepped into the room, walked to the other end of the conference table, and pushed away his chair. Bosses had never meant anything to him. Still, he was kind of impressed.

For Virgil the boy was just as he'd expected.

"How do you like working here?"

"Effing rad, grandpa. How do you like it?"

The two of them eyed each other from their standing positions. Virgil ignored Louie's question, not taking the bait.

"I've heard good things about you."

Louie shuffled his feet. He wished the man would sit down,

so he could sit down. Oh, hell, why should he wait? He grabbed the back of his leather chair, spun it around, and sat down. Except now the Chinese man, still standing, was taller. Louie stretched out his legs and slumped down until his chin was level to the table.

"What do you think of your immediate supervisor?"

"Who?"

Virgil didn't respond.

"Oh, you mean Clement? He's okay."

Louie felt Virgil's dark eyes pierce his bravado.

"He's deep," he added.

"And Marta?"

"She's cool."

Virgil walked to the door, shutting it quietly. "Meaning?" he said.

Virgil returned to where he had been standing, but Louie realized now that the man was resting in some sort of martial arts stance, his knees bent, slightly turned inward.

"Meaning she's brilliant and accessible. Clement is just brilliant."

Virgil nodded. "Thank you," he said.

"What are you doing?" Louie asked.

"Excuse me?"

"Why are you still standing there looking like some kind of martial artist, am I right?"

Virgil broke his stance now and approached the boy. He was standing next to Louie, and they were almost the same height, although their physiques were completely different. Louie looked like an aspen planted next to a redwood.

"Yes," Virgil said. "I'm a martial artist. What are you?"

Then Virgil left the room.

Louie's relationship with Marta didn't exactly start off with a bang, and part of this had to do with CAL. CAL had been involved in all the evaluations of staff hired for Fury, and although never meeting directly with candidates, CAL conducted thorough analyses of recorded interviews and offered objective recommendations. One of the problems, however, remained CAL's lack of understanding about ego, and specifically how unfavorable personality traits, like hubris, might develop from a difficult childhood. Having been raised in a laboratory, CAL had not experienced many of the challenges humans face in growing up, and CAL assumed that Louie's blustery personality meant he had been born with a certain amount of malevolence. To complicate the situation, CAL had already begun to think of Marta as a woman, and perhaps as someone related to him, like a mother or a sister. In the interviews, Louie did not treat Marta with the kind of respect CAL thought she deserved.

(From CAL's transcripts of Marta Subramanian interviewing Louie Sabatini)
LS: So do you have a boyfriend?
MS: Excuse me?
LS: Someone to treat you fine.
MS: Tell me why is this any of your business?
LS: Well, I just think a beautiful woman like yourself should not be hanging out alone. Maybe I could find you someone to get all busy with.

This kind of disrespect caused CAL's synapses – neon tetras swimming around in the fish tanks – to become charged with excessive ions, inciting CAL to lay out plans defending the honor of a favorite creator:
"Louie Sabatini needs schooling in post-century advancements in feminism. It is advised that Marta's relationship with the boy be conducted along strict professorial lines, and that if the boy acts disrespectfully in any way, Marta should detain him for additional instruction and training until his awareness has improved."
In fact, Marta did educate Louie, and much more quickly than CAL could have conceived. Marta simply provided Louie with a new kind of role model – a nurturing woman, his mother's age, not interested in wearing her sexual exploits on her sleeve.

That said, what Louie did not know was that Marta and Clement had continued to be lovers throughout the IFROC buildup. Of course, Marta's love life was none of Louie's business, but interestingly, CAL was aware of this fact, and CAL let me know that CAL knew of this, at a certain strategic point in the future. How CAL found out about Marta and Clement, I never knew. But it was certainly another example of CAL's seeming omniscience.

One day Virgil invited Louie to lunch. By this time their relationship had started to congeal. Louie's lessons in kung fu were raising his confidence, and he was asking Virgil about different aspects of martial arts, even expressing interest in Buddhism. Virgil took the boy to an old favorite Silicon Valley lunchtime haunt up in the hills, The Wagon Wheel Café, which had been a hotbed of deal making during the height of Silicon Valley's rise to prominence during the 1990s. Virgil hadn't stepped foot in the place for over a decade and was surprised to see that not much had changed. Kitsch hung from the ceilings and protruded out of walls. A hand-carved wooden Indian crossed his arms next to those waiting for a seat. The entrance was packed with an even younger crowd than Virgil remembered, which made him very happy. Silicon Valley didn't give up easily. It could rise again and again because people wanted to work here, because it was a place where the worker felt valued.

"Never been here before," Louie said to Virgil's grin. "Obviously you have."

"We used to come here to read the pulse of the valley. Business deals mostly. Not much science."

"And where do you stand on that continuum, anyway?"

Virgil didn't answer. Instead he took in the kitsch on the ceiling immediately above them. The F-16 was still flying. So was the stuffed brown pelican. There was no theme really – not even a wagon wheel in the place. Just a hodgepodge of dusty objects, or dusty-looking objects. Virgil knew from the owner that two days before the opening of the restaurant, dust had been painted on everything.

"Oh, sweet," Sabatini gasped. Following the boy's gaze through the window, Virgil knew he wasn't speaking about the ambient dust. Instead, on the other side of the window stood an exceptionally beautiful girl, with a mane of curly black hair and dark green eyes.

"She's quite stunning," Virgil said.

"Too smart for you," Louie said.

"You know her?"

"Know her? I've battled against her for years! Supa is almost as good as me. Head of the Suprex Clan. Her name's Courtney."

Suddenly Virgil leapt out of his chair and made a beeline for the door. Louie made out their interaction through the window.

"Courtney?" said Virgil.

"How do you know my name?"

The air was cold enough to see the girl's breath, which circled around her frown.

She waited for him to say more. When he didn't, her gaze drifted back toward the street. "I'm waiting for someone, so if you don't mind."

"I believe you know Louie Sabatini."

"I don't think so."

Virgil pointed through the window at Louie, who, too late, looked away.

"Oh, that's KP." she said. A smile crept across her face. "I saw him once, in a gaming café."

Virgil opened the door for her.

"Could I invite you to join us while you're waiting?" he said.

Their first encounter had happened at a cyber café in Stockton, just before the police had picked up Louie for selling weed. Courtney, a few years younger than Louie, already possessed at thirteen a presence that drew the immediate attention of the testosterone crowd – except for the hardcore gamers in this particular café. Only Louie looked up from his monitor when Courtney pushed her way through the black velvet curtain that blocked the daylight from the street.

I.C.B.M. was a typical gaming room in 2008, which was semi-legal, like the cannabis clubs for a brief time at the turn of the century. Mainstream America didn't think any better of young gamers than they thought of medicinal marijuana users, mostly because the media told them so. In the media's eyes, gaming rooms bred hackers, and hackers equaled terrorists. What wasn't revealed was how many hackers were on the payroll of the government, not to mention corporations.

The local Stockton police were already periodically raiding the cyber café, which meant turning on the lights and having a good look at who was there, while all the kids blinked away, then abruptly left. The cops felt sorry for these kids who were around the same age as their own kids but didn't have the adult supervision to steer them away from the subversive draw of gaming.

They might have been right about Louie, and perhaps a good percentage of gamers in the room. Courtney was obviously an exception. Not only was she female, she was a beautiful girl: tall for thirteen, at five-foot-four, with deep green eyes that were set off by her long, wavy, jet-black hair. What was she doing in an obscure dungeon full of pimply adolescent boys?

This was the question Sabatini asked himself as he eyed her walking down the narrow aisle between the rows of monitors, like a runway model, oblivious to the flashing cameras, only in this case – and Louie had to look around because he couldn't believe it – he was the only one watching.

My good fortune, he realized, standing up.

"Well, hello there," he said. It was Louie's typical approach of wear-your-sleaze-on-your-sleeve. He had a reputation to uphold.

Courtney looked away. When she looked back, she fixed on his eyes. "I need a team for Global Span. And I can pay."

Louie laughed. That's how he reacted when meeting most people for the first time, believing it threw them off guard and

FREE the BEAR!

gave him the upper hand. In this case he laughed even harder because Global Span was an ancient game with a stupid title.

Courtney spun and walked back down the runway.

"Wait," Louie said. He also knew that Global Span had a small but loyal following of some of the best gamers in the world.

He watched her black mane disappear through the black curtain. He ran out into the street, but she was gone. He looked for her online, and when he found her, he competed against her for many years. But he never believed he'd meet her for real.

The week after Virgil brought her in to say hello at The Wagon Wheel Café, he officially interviewed Courtney for work at Fury Inc.

(From CAL's transcripts of Virgil Sung interviewing Courtney Cruz)

Virgil Sung: So, you're the best gamer in the world. What's your secret?

Courtney Cruz: That depends on the game. I'm not the best player at chess. A lot of what I do relies on the team I'm working with and how they've been trained. I'm a strategist.

VS: Would you like to play a game of chess with me?

CC: Sure, if you want, but I'd rather play something I'm good at, like Tribes of Doom or Clan Conflict.

VS: What do you find so compelling about the games you've mentioned? Don't they take a long time to master and require long hours sitting in front of a computer?

CC: That's true. There is that aspect of games that turns some people off. Obviously, it doesn't bother me. Some people get addicted and spend all their time playing, and this can cause problems. It actually makes people less skilled players, if that's all they ever do.

VS: Are you addicted to gaming?

CC: I'm addicted to strategic challenges. And my team, of course.

VS: Your team? Yes, I'd like to hear more about them.

Within a month, early 2010, and following intense negotiations led by Courtney who was now fifteen, Virgil hired her. Clement and Marta had only been peripherally involved with bringing her onboard, which concerned both of them and took up several sessions of pillow talk.

"It's not that I disagree with Courtney's hire," Clement said, "but it seemed rushed."

"Perhaps. But Virgil's sense of intuition is strong and accurate."

"Always? Nobody's intuition is always on target."

Then, on another night:

"Can you really be sure of anyone's intuition?" Clement asked.

"Maybe not for most people," Marta said. "But Virgil, well, he relies on it. And I haven't seen it fail yet."

"What about his intuition about us? Do you think he knows?" Clement said, stroking Marta's breast.

Marta turned and kissed him. "No. He has no idea."

If Clement and Marta were secretive about their affair, the younger generation, once again, went their own direction. In 2010, Courtney was the world's most famous female gamer. Supa was universally feared within the game world. She was also as different as possible from Louie's mother, and Louie fell deeply in love with her. She had long, unruly hair that she hardly every brushed. Her green eyes were somewhat oval, which suggested an Asian influence, although she would never answer any questions about her family, which Louie respected – it meant she would never ask him about his. Most of all, Courtney carried herself regally, as if she had been born to be in charge. Louie was fairly certain that she had never scraped bottom, like he had, and just being around her made him feel secure.

As luck would have it, Courtney was impressed by something that Louie felt great shame about himself. Somehow or another, by the age of seventeen, Louie had never been laid. In a sense, the pain of having a sleazy mother was now paying off, since Louie and Courtney, both virgins, fell in love and became lovers. The esteem that Courtney now bestowed upon Louie gave him his second break in life – an opportunity to reinvent himself. Not only was Louie a brilliant gamer gainfully employed by the world's top gaming company, he now had a beautiful girlfriend to boot.

But in my mind, Sabatini was, and always will be, a mess.

I know the reader must be thinking: Why would I say this? What could be wrong with this Sabatini? He's a young, underprivileged kid, exceptionally intelligent, and deeply in love. I'll give you a hint: Louie couldn't believe in himself. He couldn't fight off the world he'd come from and let the magic happen. He and Courtney were the best gamers in the world together, and for a while their love was the real thing. The two of them were inseparable, their bodies constantly intertwined. Courtney would put her head on Louie's shoulder during Fury Inc. seminars – he loved that – although her head would snap up when she wanted to question the leader. Her brilliant mind was always absorbing, challenging, and clarifying the finer points that so many of the other gamers glossed over. Yet when their two heads were together, when Louie's thigh was pressed against Courtney's under the table, or when their fingers were wrapped in loose knots, or Louie was massaging her hands, it was as if the two of them had become a new being that accentuated their strengths and covered for their weaknesses.

Everyone seemed to approve, which in itself was strange, since this kind of relationship was rarely tolerated in the workplace. But there was something about Courtney that instilled trust. And if she wanted to take up with a guy like Louie, so be it. Even I initially went along with it, although from the moment I met Courtney, I had a major crush on her.

I suppose it's time for me to become part of the story, as much as I've tried not to be. I should explain what I had been doing all this time. I'd been working as the IFROC historian since 1995, but I really spent very little time on the project. In

1997 I was brought onboard with the Revolutionary Council and introduced to CAL. My assignment was to work with CAL on compiling information regarding earlier revolutionary actions and secessions, and recording the moral, ethical, and philosophical arguments surrounding them.

As Virgil explained to the other Council members: "In large part, Durant is here to explain IFROC to its future citizens. He will not take any direct action toward meeting our goals. Instead, he will observe and record everything that happens as objectively as possible."

"I have a question about this," Clement said. "Can we each establish personal relationships with Durant?"

"Absolutely," Virgil said. "I want all of you to work very closely together."

"But I want to make something really clear. Durant should not be asked, nor should he accept, to act in any way that assists or conflicts with what we do." Virgil grinned. "In other words, he should be treated like an embedded journalist, along for the ride."

I remember wincing at the word. I had nothing against journalists, of course, but it was a term my historian father used to degrade his colleagues whom he considered less than adequate.

"I prefer to be called a chronicler," I told Virgil.

"Yes," Virgil agreed, his grin vanished and he nodded seriously. "That's more accurate, of course."

While I started to "chronicle" IFROC, I was also teaching at a local middle school, and failing miserably at engaging pre-teen students in ancient history. I also became engaged to a woman from Pacific Heights in San Francisco, who was beautiful, but as I finally found out, not very nice. We got into a tremendous argument about the plight of people who were homeless (she thought they should be rounded up and shipped out of her fair city), so I broke off the engagement.

Meanwhile, throughout 2010 and 2011, the Revolutionary Council, with the help of CAL, meticulously plotted its course, with the California secession planned for Spring 2013. During

Obama's campaign for his second term as U.S. President, however, throughout 2011 and 2012, the Revolutionary Council began debating if they should push back the start date of the Action. It looked as if Obama would be successful in his bid for a second term, so it was decided to wait for the inevitable backlash in the 2016 elections – although no one could have expected a president like Trump. Absolutely not.

But preparations did not stop. In fact, with more time to plan, they diversified and developed in new, surprising and effective ways. And it was actually in 2013 that IFROC began developing one of its most important tools – a sweeping, dramatic mini-series about the secession of California from the U.S – meeting a uniquely modern and effective way to prepare and inspire the general populace for the actual secession event.

This part of the story remains a significant sore spot for me. This decision of who should write this mini-series sparked the first moment of questioning about Virgil – the deeply spiritual man – whom I, along with many others, thought could do no wrong.

So sixteen years after the creation of IFROC, Virgil approached me with a new assignment: I was to write the screenplay for the mini-series that would tell the story of IFROC up until the time of the secession. This would stream online, free to the republic, right before the secession began.

"But Virgil, why me? I have no experience in writing screenplays."

"Yes, but you know the story. We can always hire a professional to fine-tune the script."

"But I know the story as a historian, as an objective observer. If I write a screenplay to be used in the secession, then I will become part of the story."

Virgil didn't respond to this, and for the first time I realized that he didn't take my objectivity seriously, or even completely understand the role of a historian. Even worse, I know now that he had never intended on keeping me as an objective observer, but had been grooming me all along for a more active role.

So I refused.

"I cannot play an active role in your revolution, no matter what my beliefs," I told him. "I was brought into IFROC as an objective observer. That was the original mission, and I believe you want me to stick to it."

Virgil didn't dispute my decision. Instead he went to Hollywood and hired professional screenwriters, who were more than willing to work on the project. Over the next few years, I was approached to consult with the screenwriters, and on occasion I did so.

CHAPTER SIXTEEN

From 2013 to 2016, the secession remained somewhat in a holding pattern. The Revolutionary Council members reported more stress about having to wait for the Action to begin, as compared to the younger cohort of leaders. Louie Sabatini and Courtney Cruz continued to expand their skillset every day in the era of exponential technological advancement. In other words, although they were primed to get things going, they made the best use of their downtime to continue tooling up.

Finally, in the spring of 2016, election year for a new U.S. president, the Revolutionary Council began the final preparations for the secession. First on the list: moving CAL to a more secure location at Green Gulch, the Japanese tea house. It had been Yari's idea to use this sacred place, protected behind a heavy oak door, intricately hand-carved in the same craftsmanship as the welcome sign that used to greet guests at the top of the lane. Yari announced to the community of Buddhists that the tea house would remain closed indefinitely, pending an essential seismic upgrade. The Buddhists shrugged at the news, although several of them expressed their displeasure that someone around the same time had removed the beautiful blue and gold fish from their meditation cottage.

The koi pond inside the tea house became home to the growing number of engineered neon tetras, which continued to add exponentially to the increase in CAL's neurological functions. Was there a limit to CAL's abilities? Clement and Marta never stopped debating this, both in the lab and in the bedroom. CAL, when asked, believed that a limit might be reached eventually, but so far had come to the conclusion that CAL's life resembled an expanding universe, with unlimited opportunities for experience and knowledge. The Revolutionary Council continued to keep CAL's existence an absolute secret, even as IFROC greatly expanded its cultivation of allies during the buildup.

For nearly two years Louie and Courtney had been working with Fury games, and now the leadership team began to assemble. As part of the hire negotiations, Courtney had secured an agreement that when the time came, she would bring her Suprex team on board. This included Hazelwood, her top strategist, and Hazelwood's young protégés: Ender and Potter. In Spring 2016, one year away from the secession date, Clement set up a game review with Courtney and the Suprex team.

Courtney, as captain of the Suprex clan, prepared for battle against the LoF (Lords of Fear) clan. She took her seat in the well-padded pilot's chair, fingering the controls for audio communication and other sound feeds on the armrests. Focused and self-contained within her modular station, Courtney pushed her chair forward. It snapped in place and engaged the game.

Superimposed on Courtney's large flat screen, a topographical map showed the locations of her team (SuprexHwood, SuprexEnd, SuprexHP) represented by green triangles. Split into four screens at the bottom, Courtney viewed the battle from all their perspectives.

Spectators to the battle – Virgil, Marta, and Clement – watched the action on even larger screens on the wall, mirroring the setup planned for IFROC's future Action Room. They sat on black leather benches and witnessed the Suprexes stomp the LoFs without mercy.

When the game ended, the spectators remained speechless. Courtney and her team had far surpassed all expectations.

(Transcripts from CAL's Non-Biological Hardware Storage, recording Virgil Sung interviewing David Hazelwood, March 30, 2016)

Virgil Sung: How long have you been into gaming?

David Hazelwood: Since I was a little kid. I don't remember when I wasn't a gamer.

VS: What games do you play?

DH: I play anything that involves strategy and tactics. Anything from D&D to the latest updates of T.O.D. and C.C.

VS: T.O.D.?

DH: Sorry, Tribes of Doom. And C.C. – Clan Conflict.

VS: I know that one.

DH: Yeah, a lot of people do.

VS: Weren't you the youngest tournament dungeon master ever? Why did you switch to the Fury games?

DH: I guess I was the youngest DM, though I know of a few kids nowadays that come close. I guess it was a combination of D&D getting boring and meeting Kingpin that made me switch.

VS: Louie Sabatini. Leader of Dog Pack, right?

DH: Yeah. At that time Kingpin was my hero. I still respect him a lot. He can totally be kind of a dick sometimes but underneath his ego he's okay, an excellent gamer. But now I'm all about Suprex and working with Courtney. She gets kids together, gives them something to be a part of. Something like a family, I guess.

VS: So you are Suprex now. Are you still a member of Dog Pack?

DH: Not presently. Although my team, the Dib Clan, is aligned with both of them. A few years ago Louie asked me to break off and spawn another team.

VS: Why?

DH: (laughs) I was getting too good to be on Louie's team. Anyway, it helps the game. Nearly all the leaders of the hundred or so aligned clans come from Dog Pack or Suprex. Louie trained some of us, one time or another, and then later working with Courtney and Suprex was like leveling up again.

(From CAL's transcripts of Virgil Sung interviewing Ender Lopez and Harrison Potter)

Virgil Sung: So tell me, why do you guys insist on being interviewed together?

Ender Lopez: Our moms told us to never be alone with strangers.

Harrison Potter: (snicker)

EL: (snort)

(They devolve into horseplay.)

EL: Hey!

HP: I'm not doing anything!

(VS looks around the room aimlessly, making it obvious that he's waiting for them to get serious. The boys try to compose themselves.)

VS: What else do you guys do together?

HP: Just about everything.

EL: Eat.

HP: Game.

EL: Eat some more.

HP: Game.

VS: Tell me about your role in the Suprex clan. How do the two of you operate?

EL: We do advance scouting, most of the time.

HP: We also do offensive and defensive engineering, when Supa asks us to.

(EL and HP both stand up and mock salute, then sit back down.)

EL: We're the best scouts, because we can get into anywhere–

HP: –and get back–

EL: –without the lamers on the opposition knowing a thing.

HP: Even if they catch us, we just term them, and get away.

EL: Sometimes we take out a specific target.

HP: Sometimes it's just recon for Supa.

(EL and HP stand up and salute again, this time busting up

laughing.)
(Virgil ends the interview.)

Kids, Virgil thought, should be kids, even if they're brilliant gamers. So what if their interviews are not perfect?
And so he ended up hiring all of Courtney's team.

Through the summer of 2016, the new team – Louie, Courtney, Hazelwood, Ender, and Potter – trained together at Fury, Inc., engaging in combat simulations similar to the gaming environment they'd been playing in for years, except for the introduction of Happy Weapons and telefactor technology. They were also introduced gradually to the ideas behind Clement's Treatise (the official title, since even this second team of leaders was never to know about CAL). Eventually the kids were told that they were to be the commanders on the front line. What was not revealed to them were the details of their own chain of command. They assumed, of course, that Sabatini, the eldest, would be their leader.

And they were wrong.

I had been working with Sabatini for over a year at this point, after Virgil asked me to receive training in computer gaming so I could fully understand this part of IFROC's secession tactic. I agreed to this assignment, since I felt my objectivity would remain intact, and I began training with Clement's protégé, the twenty-two-year-old Louie Sabatini. I have to admit this cocky young man impressed me. He showed obvious intelligence and possessed a full range of street smarts. If I had been younger, I'm quite sure I would have found him threatening, but at forty-seven, feeling the pangs of middle age, I found him fascinating and we became friends, at least during this period. Louie was also a natural teacher. He excelled in schooling other players in the art of combining hand-eye coordination with the relentless observation necessary for a gamer to think strategically and tactically at the same time. He could keep track of more than ten players on the field of play and observe a macro and micro perspective of the game simultaneously, while allowing his agenda to constantly evolve so that he could achieve whatever objective was required to win. I learned to understand the trance-like focus and virtual aggression necessary to be a good team gamer, though I was not particularly skilled, to say the least.

During this period I saw Courtney around the company and spoke with her casually several times, but I was never assigned to work with her directly. It was obvious that she was blessed with the right combination of traits to guarantee extraordinary success: extreme intelligence, beauty, balanced perspective of life, sense of humor, a pleasing personality, and just enough eccentricity to keep part of herself to herself. Even though she was still a girl, I have to admit I found her very attractive and was happy that I did not have to work with her in any kind of intimate way. All these kids, of course, grew up with computers from day one, and Hazelwood, 17, almost as smart as Clement, epitomized the ultimate geek. Hazelwood's protégés, "Ender", 13, and HP (for his resemblance to Harry Potter, though nobody called him that), 14, already possessed the highest skills of any chief military strategists in the world.

At the end of the summer I chronicled the first meeting between the Revolutionary Council and the Gaming Leadership Team. It was the first and last time all of us would meet together at Green Gulch, or anywhere else. Virgil conducted a general tour of the center, while the rest of the Revolutionary Council (Marta, Clement, Yari, and myself) observed the interactions of the young leaders. There was no doubt among any of us that they possessed the dexterity and critical thinking skills required for work in the virtual world, where the front line would take place. But what was going to happen when the real world met the virtual world?

While we walked around the grounds of Green Gulch, I felt a wave of sadness. It was not the same place at all. Now six months before the secession, all the monks had been sent away to other Buddhist centers. And the property, let alone the farm, was no one's priority. By late summer the fields should have been full of spinach, kale, and mustard greens. Instead, what wasn't being eaten by gophers was left to the prodigious weeds – beautiful in their own right, rendering the fields a deep orange. But I did notice Virgil's eyes turning misty as he walked along these fallow fields he'd been cultivating for over three decades.

The tour concluded at the monk's dining room, and inside I was surprised to see a long table lined with Lazy Susans. Virgil, the master of details. What had I expected, a military briefing? Perhaps not, but I hadn't been expecting a Chinese banquet either.

Virgil had arranged the seating so that he anchored one end of the table and Louie the other. Louie grinned broadly, satisfied with the arrangement. For all his bravado, Louie seemed to want, and need, Virgil's approval. Marta and Clement sat on either side of Louie, with HP, Ender, Hazelwood, and Yari, taking up in the middle sides of the table. Which left Courtney and me to sit next to Virgil.

It should have been obvious to me what was going on, but I was reading the arrangement like Louie. He and Virgil were the leaders. All was right with the secession.

Or was it? As the banquet wore on, and the kids drank too many cups of oolong tea, HP and Ender began gesturing with their chopsticks, which degenerated into food raids on each other's plates. Louie reached across Marta and grabbed HP's chopstick in midair. Marta seemed to be biting her tongue. Clement, I noticed, ate in silence. I began to wonder if Virgil was the only one convinced that sharing such a high level of responsibility with these kids was ever going to work. Even Yari, who had become more chatty and friendly with all of us, said no more than a few words to Hazelwood next to him, asking if he could pass the chili oil, and pour him another cup of tea.

Virgil, alone, carried the conversation during the banquet. And I recognized his deliberate speech pattern: slower and lower than usual, forcing everyone to listen more closely. He repeated, in general terms, the ideas behind the secession and

IFROC's dedication to a non-lethal procedure. Several times while Virgil was speaking, Ender and HP started to squirm and punch.

"Knock it off!" Louie shouted. The next time to get them to stop all he had to do was glare, which did not go unnoticed by the Council members.

When Virgil finished his official statement, he asked for questions.

Hazelwood started to raise his hand, then realized he could just speak.

"How can you expect to secede without killing anyone? Even computer gaming is all about kills."

"Remember the advantages IFROC has in its favor," Virgil replied. "Non-IFROC vehicles won't be able to enter IFROC territory."

"But how long will that last?" Hazelwood said. "Certainly the Feds will be able to adapt and advance their technology, as soon as they figure out what is happening."

Virgil smiled and pushed back his chair. "Yes, but it will buy us some time."

I caught Hazelwood sneaking a look at Courtney, who nodded slightly, encouraging.

"Yes, but unless we continue to adapt at an equal pace, they will surpass us eventually. That is, unless we have another trick or two up our sleeves."

He fixed Virgil's eye. I wondered what Virgil would reveal.

Suddenly Hazelwood laughed. "Of course, we will be controlling space."

"An essential point," Clement added. "IFROC telefactors will be controlling all orbital access around the Earth. We have secret agreements of cooperation for the duration of the secession with key space programs around the world."

I caught Hazelwood sneaking another look at Courtney.

I wondered what those two knew, or at least suspected. I realized Courtney was a true gem. She had trained Hazelwood to back off, at just the right moment.

The table conversation turned lighter and people began

speaking in separate conversations. Virgil chatted amiably with Courtney, and Louie boasted to Clement and Marta that he had no doubt that IFROC was going to kick some ass. Hazelwood finally ate, his role now completed. He and Clement had just started a discussion about the finer points of chess when Virgil pushed back his chair and suggested they go for a walk to the beach.

Virgil walked ahead with Courtney and Sabatini, the rest of us pairing off in our comfort zones: I was with Clement and Marta; HP, Ender, and Hazelwood took up the back, goofing around. Once at the beach, Virgil turned sentimental about California.

"I am doing this for my home," he said. "I love California and all that it stands for."

We nodded easily, because we were all Californians.

"And I am doing it for the world."

And we all continued nodding, because we all believed that as well.

When we returned from our walk, Virgil led us to the library, which was filled with Virgil's books on mysticism and religion. It was here that Virgil announced his decision: Courtney would lead IFROC's front line during the secession.

A hush filled the room. The announcement obviously came as a shock to all the kids. I knew the Council had discussed this earlier, although I had not been let in on the decision, and I was surprised that it had also caught me off guard. Courtney played her cards tightly, but by the curious look she directed toward Virgil, I could tell she also hadn't been informed until now. HP and Ender were watching Louie, whose face had turned bright red. I remember feeling a little embarrassed for him – that's how little I knew about Louie, at the time. Hazelwood was the first one to clap.

One of the first decisions Courtney made as a leader was to assign Louie as chief trainer for the entire front line team. Louie's reputation as an exceptional gaming instructor carried throughout the virtual world. And if Louie harbored any hard feelings about not being chosen as the team leader, he appeared to let it drop and rose to the occasion. He kept focused, patient, knowledgeable, and charismatic – within the gaming environs. Outside of his teaching role, Louie remained his usual ego-driven, pain-in-the-ass.

This kind of duality, of course, was not uncommon among gamers. One of the kicks of the virtual environment is that players can be anyone they want to be within the context of the game. A nice, quiet person may have a penchant for playing the arch villain. What was unusual about Louie was that he was a nicer guy in the gaming world than in real life, which made him a sympathetic character to me, since that's where I spent most of my time with him, for as long as I could take it.

Throughout the training with the new team, I never once heard CAL mentioned, and as far as I knew, CAL still remained a secret. That said, I developed a suspicion about Courtney. She was so sharp, and under her direction, Hazelwood's questioning, although probably unbeknownst to him, had seemed too pointed. My suspicions were later confirmed when CAL opened its biological hardware files to me. I learned that shortly after the dinner at Green Gulch, Virgil had told Courtney about CAL, and that later, Courtney entered into regular communication with CAL. And I began to recognize, in many verifiable ways, that CAL was now running the show.

At the end of 2016, four months before the secession began, Virgil met with Courtney, Louie, Hazelwood, Ender, HP, and me at the Battery Alexander bunker in the Marin Headlands. IFROC had secured the entire Marin Headlands, and although no one else appeared to be around, I knew CAL was providing security. Virgil led us through the state-of-the-art team headquarters and reiterated the responsibilities of this leadership team for carrying out the front line operations of IFROC secession from the rest of the United States. We had already been informed that The Action would commence as soon as the mini-series was aired and streamed in April. What I had not been informed about, and what I heard next, completely floored me: I was to be the only person out of the Revolutionary Council to accompany, chronicle, and live with the young leadership team in the bunker.

For a second time, I felt incredibly betrayed by Virgil. Why didn't he warn me? He should have asked how I felt about working under the command of an extremely intelligent, young woman, for whom, I can confess openly now, I had no small amount of lust. (I can only defend myself by noting that she was twenty-one by now.)

I fumed, feeling that my objectivity was being compromised again. I protested. I didn't show up for work for several days. I made a decision: I would quit.

I called Virgil and arranged for him to meet me at Café Nation, a bohemian coffee shop in Berkeley where I went as a student. The place hadn't changed over the years. I sat at one of the old-fashioned wood tables, sipping chai tea. I felt as if I'd been transplanted into the last century, when people still held conversations, about art, about ideas, or sat for hours with a book and no one rushed them out. Many people dressed colorfully and they were still fun to watch. I had chosen this place because I wanted my showdown with Virgil to be on my turf, not his. I don't know why I thought that would make a difference.

"Durant, my old friend," Virgil started. "And you are my old friend. We met in a redwood tree, nearly one hundred meters up in the air. The wind was blowing from the northwest, threatening rain, but we adapted to that environment for one night. It was only one night, but still, we adapted to a new situation. Together."

Virgil paused, making sure I was really listening.

"You realize, of course, that the changes in our world will continue occurring at an accelerated rate."

He leaned forward.

"Humans are not going to be able to respond to this change in customary ways," he continued. "No, as humans, we are going to have to figure out different ways to respond, to adapt to change. In fact, if we try to stick to our old ways, without recognizing the need to adapt, we will fail. I am absolutely certain of this."

Virgil put both of his hands on my shoulders, a gesture he had never made before.

"You and I have entered into this future," he said.

I nodded. I did not disagree. I did not quit.

CHAPTER SEVENTEEN

The IFROC mini-series began on April 2, 2017. It ran for four weeks and became a phenomenal hit on both broadcast and digital streams, capturing audiences across demographics all over the world. The series covered the economic, political, and historical points that CAL had made with the Treatise and then gave the highlights of the IFROC buildup. It featured the Revolutionary Council, specifically Virgil, Marta, and Clement, as heroic, almost super-human characters. Conspicuously absent were Yari, myself, and of course, CAL. In addition, nothing was said about the new team who would lead the non-lethal secession action from an obscure bunker in Marin County.

It seems unbelievable to me now, but when I was watching the mini-series for the first time, I found myself caught up in the drama (the screenwriters had done their job well) and not thinking about the next stage of the secession, or even its possible failure. A week before the series ended, as directed, I moved to the Marin Headlands bunker. In the Action Room with the new team I watched the final episode and witnessed the first strike – simultaneously on the broadcast and in real life – of the Jerry Garcia virus. Already embedded in key defense department computers, the virus was waiting for the moment that Sabatini executed the code, and almost immediately it paralyzed the Pentagon, proving definitively IFROC's technological superiority.

The Action's impact on a large number of Californians was equally quick. Take Efrain and Roberta Martínez, for example.

The couple, far into their 60s, had lived in Gilroy, California in the Salinas Valley almost their entire lives, after emigrating from Mexico as children. They owned a modest farm on two acres where they grew carnations. Sitting next to each other in their La-Z-boy recliners, the couple watched the mini-series, just like eighty percent of Americans. Suspenseful teasers on both commercial and non-commercial media outlets, after Trump's election, had successfully whetted the country's appetite for following such a story:

What if the United States of America became an overbearing presence in the world, bullying other nations while mindlessly consuming the world's resources? What if some of the greatest minds of our generation decided that enough was enough?

Find out how top scientists from places like UC Berkeley, Stanford, and Xerox Park began secretly withholding critical technology from the U.S. government in a conspiracy lasting over twenty-five years. Follow how they initiated a bloodless technological coup that made IFROC, the Independent Free Republic of California, the newest North American nation...

Near the end of the series, when the Martínez family learned that all the wealth that California taxpayers had been giving to the federal government would be returned to the new citizens of IFROC, they laughed and said: "Yeah, right. Wouldn't that be great?"

And to their surprise, that's exactly what began to happen the very next day.

The IFROC secession went exactly to plan. The first strike occurred fifteen minutes before the end of the last mini-series episode, on April 23. At 7:45 p.m. Pacific Time, and 10:45 p.m. Eastern Time, an advanced space-borne nanotechnology attack gave IFROC forces control of every critical US government satellite in orbit. Ten minutes later, the Jerry Garcia virus was released simultaneously on NSA, CIA, and Pentagon computer networks. Almost instantaneously, IFROC took over the United States nuclear arsenal, which effectively de-fanged the world's most powerful rogue nation.

Immediately upon the mini-series ending – when the

fictional time of IFROC buildup caught up with real time – a brown, middle-aged, plain-spoken woman delivered a message to a worldwide audience of over one billion people. She identified herself as Abuela (as grandmother in Spanish):

"Since 1850 and the Bear Flag Revolt, California has been occupied by the hostile nation that shares our eastern border. This nation has become a relentless threat to the stability of the world. Therefore, for nothing less than the preservation of humankind, a great social change must and will occur."

Then regular programming resumed.

From the outside, the bunker's appearance remained inconspicuous, looking like many of the old bunkers around the San Francisco Bay Area, with its thick covering of ice plant, the invasive succulent full of Vitamin C that the Spanish brought in their ship holds centuries ago to fight scurvy. For over two hundred years, a large number of bunkers had been built along the coast to protect the San Francisco Bay Area and the West Coast of the United States. During the 1960s, these military areas began transitioning to federal parkland. IFROC chose this particular bunker, located just north across the Golden Gate Bridge from San Francisco in the Marin Headlands, because of its obscurity as well as its close proximity to Green Gulch.

In the 1990s, Battery Alexander, with its long cavernous halls, became a famous party spot. In fact, Virgil attended a rave there in 1996, and he later had something to do with a government report finding asbestos inside the bunker, causing it to be closed to future public access. A nonprofit called Friends of Battery Alexander, a charitable arm of one of IFROC's companies, took over restoring the bunker. And so right under the nose of the federal government, and within a national park, IFROC began to prepare the bunker for its next stage of usage.

When I moved to the bunker, I hadn't expected it to be luxurious by any means, but I did imagine it would be technologically impressive. But when I first walked in, I felt as if I were entering some kind of teenager heaven. State-of-the-art game consoles filled the Action Room. Some of the kids sported visors with heads-up displays and other custom input devices typically used for gaming. Around the perimeter, soda dispensers, ice cream machines, and refrigerated display shelves, stocked with prepared food from all ethnicities, offered the high strategic command team any delicacy they desired.

Upon closer look, I noticed that the workstations contained large screens that revealed field activities. I recognized the VR headsets scattered everywhere, but the rest of the devices were unidentifiable to me. Keyboards had been replaced by a spherical device called a keypod. The only mouse in the room was robotic.

From the eve of The Action, we were on high alert. During the first eight hours, Courtney and Sabatini remained at their stations, as well as Hazelwood, Ender, HP, and me. We all wore our headsets, preparing to tune into whatever battle scenarios emerged. The large flat screens displayed a "Twake" user interface. Produced by Fury Inc., Twake was a very successful first-person shooter game, and the team had trained extensively in this military-style, online gaming environment for six months. Even if nothing was happening on the field, using a touch screen interface for systems navigation, the team could access any number of future engagement scenarios. This played out on giant wall monitors, which allowed for continuous strategic and tactical planning, and for always remaining several steps ahead of the Feds.

We waited for response all night. Finally, at 4:00 a.m., we received word from IFROC cyber surveillance that the U.S. Federal government was preparing to retaliate. The IFROC woman spokesperson, Abuela, reappeared on all media outlets, saying that California borders and airspace would be closed for the duration of "negotiations" with the outraged US government.

"Although the response of the United States government is understandable, please be advised that all IFROC airspace and land territory is hereby off limits to any non-IFROC vehicles.

Any vehicles venturing into this territory by land or air will be rendered inoperable and their occupants held for questioning. Anyone disregarding this warning will face grave consequences. This message will be repeated continuously. Thank you."

Several hours later, four U.S. Air Force stealth fighters fell from the sky near the Sonora Pass in California. (Fortunately, the pilots ejected safely.) The pilots later reported that their cockpit systems seemed to be "taken over" shortly before the aircraft shut down, except for the ejection system. An enraged President Trump now realized that his military planes, tanks, ships, trucks, and even missiles would no longer function in California, including airspace. National Guard troops were dispatched from Fort Hood, Texas and Fort Sill, Oklahoma to mount a ground offensive. Within a mile of California's border, their vehicles came to a dead stop, after which the weekend warriors reluctantly got out of their stalled vehicles and began marching. Five thousand men meant ten thousand sore boots-on-the-ground.

I have to admit that I was holding my breath, expecting the typical consequences of war. The Feds were using real guns and their reaction was bound to be lethal. The IFROC leaders, including CAL and the young team in the bunker, believed that the secession would not lead to bloodshed. But I was having trouble seeing it, after so many years of studying history and seeing how humans almost always resorted to killing each other.

Yet events appeared to run peacefully, at least for the first few days. The EMF emitters worked well, effectively neutralizing Fed presence throughout IFROC territory. None of the Fed's equipment could roll, fly, or communicate. Equally essential, the Jerry Garcia (JG) virus replaced certain subroutines in the Fed's computers with fractal algorithms, which caused a variety of malfunctions, ranging from mildly irritating to complete deletion of databases and removal of command and control capabilities. Some systems appeared functional, until erroneous information returned to the user. On other systems, the JG virus displayed an endless fractal screen display that could not be removed short of powering down the device.

The Pentagon leaders were stumped. They couldn't admit to the world that they were no longer in control of their assets, and yet they couldn't seem to get rid of the JG virus, no matter how many hackers they brought in. They even tried to recruit Virgil, offering him a great deal of money to work on the project. Virgil sat on their requests. Obviously the Feds hadn't figured out who was behind the movement – not yet anyway.

The virus left certain systems intact, specifically those associated with the health and welfare of Fed soldiers. For example, pay schedule files remained immune, as did medical benefits. The best hackers and crackers in the Pentagon threw up their hands. This particular virus seemed years ahead of their understanding. What the hackers knew and what the leaders feared was that someone had gained access to all Pentagon network systems, including hardened system data, secure files, passwords, and protocols of every kind. This access ran to the highest levels and looked to be permanent.

As 5,000 National Guard troops entered IFROC territory, Courtney and the others at the bunker tracked their progress and sent out assignments to the vast network of secession gamers. One by one, the Fed soldiers were gently immobilized, rendered unconscious, and loaded on trucks designed to comfortably transport the sleeping soldiers to what the kids informally called "Happy Camps", which were basically large, secure, private vacation resorts.

The core of the gamers, the kids under Courtney's command, came from within California territory, but included in the secession action were thousands of trusted gamers and hackers participating from locations around the world. These gamers worked within an advanced level of communication that their parents could never detect, let alone government security officials. Coming home from school, this cyber-militia received text messages with encryption codes and assignments for what they thought was a new and exciting game. After acknowledging their zones of responsibility, the kids downloaded interfaces controlling non-lethal weapons in environments that looked incredibly real. All the gamers selected to work with IFROC had practiced these offensives previously on Fury Inc. games, of course. And eventually, most of the kids realized that they were playing some kind of real scenario, which was fine with them, because frankly they thought this improved the game.

The Fed vehicles that had been left behind were subsequently bugged with a micro-organism similar to lichen, yet genetically altered for technological characteristics, such as ultra low frequency (ULF) radio transmission and sensor arrays – an amalgam of plant and machine that was undetectable by anyone but its creators. The altered vehicles were then towed to some obscure location even further outside IFROC territory. When the Feds eventually located the vehicles, they didn't realize, of course, that IFROC was all ears.

Tragically, four days into the secession, fifteen casualties occurred on the Fed side as collateral damage on the part of their own troops, when a live mortar round suddenly exploded. The U.S. media started a campaign blaming the casualties on IFROC, and IFROC countered this message by simply deleting it from satellite communications, effectively killing the Fed's propaganda effort. IFROC issued a worldwide statement with Abuela setting the record straight and lamenting the loss of life when nonviolent means remained available. These broadcasts won the world's trust. The U.S. had not been a favored country for some time, and especially since the election of its new president.

IFROC made every attempt to keep everyone in the U.S., as well as Europe and sympathetic friends around the globe, informed about what was really going on – although plenty of diehard right wingers in the U.S. and abroad still believed the Feds should "just nuke California back to the stone age". Of course, the Feds weren't telling anyone that within the first moment of IFROC secession, the Feds had lost control of their nuclear capability.

The nuclear option, therefore, was so much bluster, even

for the crazies elevated to power in the early days of the Trump administration. Even if most of these right-wingers were speaking metaphorically, after the election of an unrepentant oligarch, the unimaginable had suddenly become imaginable. Trump's success remained an incredibly nasty pill to swallow for Americans who believed strongly in a more social democracy. Behind the scenes IFROC successfully blackmailed the U.S. command structure, threatening to inform the world that the U.S. no longer had any nuclear capability. This effectively bound the hands of the Feds so they wouldn't dare resort to the nuclear option against the fledgling republic of IFROC, even if they could.

Overseas, the feelings about IFROC were mixed. The European Union remained guarded and officially non-committal, but many representatives cheered for California behind the scenes. Europe's initial turn to the right had fizzled and was being replaced by a more hopeful wave of optimism. Countries with dictatorships, however, did not acknowledge IFROC or its actions in any way, but this was expected. IFROC didn't intend to engage with any of those governments. United Nations started secret discussions with IFROC representatives, sensing an advantage of aligning with a more technologically advanced North American nation, estimating that this was more advantageous than worrying about annoying the current U.S. Administration. The majority of UN delegates expressed their significant relief that the U.S. bullying might finally come to an end.

CHAPTER EIGHTEEN

It was months later that I learned of David Hazelwood's traumatic experience with IFROC casualties early during the secession. Hazelwood, at his gaming prime now at nineteen years old, exemplified the superior qualifications of a tactical commander, but he was dreadfully shy around people and felt more at home interfacing with computers and communications systems. On the other hand, he was extremely fond of animals, and in the bunker he raised a pet rat that was so well trained that sometimes Hazelwood let it "man" his station on routine missions, while Hazelwood snuck off to the bathroom. Sometimes Hazelwood spent a great deal of time in the bathroom.

One day, out of the blue, Hazelwood told a few of us on the team (Courtney, HP, and me) that a week into the secession he'd witnessed some friendly fire between the Fed troops. He also shared now that the experience had completely freaked him out. He'd been watching a cavalry battalion try to penetrate a clearly marked IFROC buffer zone, when suddenly a Fed unit, mistakenly identifying one of its own units as IFROC, fired rocket-propelled grenades. Hazelwood watched in horror as three men died and twelve more endured tremendous wounds and pain. He felt that he knew these men, and in fact he did, by name, through his IFROC surveillance.

Hazelwood had been holding both Fed units under satellite and telefactor surveillance since the start of the secession. He'd watched PFC Arnold Sapp puke from drinking too much beer on his first night at the front, and Specialist Eddie Davis fall asleep, curled up next to his best buddy from high school. Now he witnessed Sapp kill his best buddy with his own grenade.

Witnessing how the bodies ripped apart from the explosives sent David directly into the bathroom. Only months later, in the small kitchen in the bunker, did he feel compelled to tell us that the incident had been weighing on him, a bad dream he couldn't seem to shake. I suspected then that Hazelwood suffered from PTSD. I remember a group hug and the young man wiping away a few tears. It was a tender moment, a side of the kids I didn't often see.

Hazelwood also monitored the Fed's skewed version of the incident in the world media, where they claimed IFROC was using live ammunition. (This was later disproven.) Courtney said she would ask IFROC's communications division to send out video evidence of the encounter, showing clearly what happened. It was a controversial request. That video would reveal how closely IFROC was monitoring the Fed troops. In fact, since IFROC owned all the Pentagon databases, IFROC possessed extensive information on every single soldier.

In the end, IFROC decided to release the video, and the media, on both IFROC and Fed sides, had a field day. Sympathy had continued to mount for IFROC forces, but this moved the needle significantly higher. Hazelwood's pain had touched us personally. We hoped that our Happy Weapons would capture Sapp and that he would be taken to one of our Visitor Camps. We all hoped we'd have a chance to tell him that it wasn't his fault.

What Efrain and Roberta Martínez learned as soon as the secession began was that the funds for the Citizens Payback Program had already started accruing from the liberation of assets formerly controlled by the U.S. federal government. Marta and Clement, in charge of establishing infrastructure for the new Independent Free Republic of California, founded the country's first not-for-profit financial institution, the Gold Coast Bank, and now directed all the accrued funds to be immediately secured in this financial institution. Several countries had tried to get voters to approve a system of providing basic income in place of a welfare system, but IFROC was now prepared to offer all Californians a Basic Income Plus that included an opportunity for borrowing. Through smart investments in West Coast-oriented funds, this institution accumulated assets for members that could be invested directly back into the community. Funds acquired during the secession were held in accounts for every IFROC citizen, and much effort went towards making sure no one living in IFROC territory, legally or illegally, was denied an account. Within a week, sums were being distributed in proportion to the need and financial background of each IFROC citizen. The poorest became the largest recipients; the wealthiest received their portion, but not as much, since they didn't qualify in terms of need. And believe it or not, those wealthy people who remained in IFROC met this policy with universal praise.

How could this be? For one reason, more than fifty percent of the super-rich fled IFROC territory immediately after the secession began (and took all their assets with them.) For the remaining citizens of exceptional means, IFROC made it very clear that it intended to level the playing field and close up most of the exploitive aspects that kept the same rich families on top. A few of the haughtier among them lingered around, until it became clear that IFROC leaders were not for sale at any price. With the rotten eggs dispersed to other states, most of the wealthy folks who remained were either philanthropists or enlightened citizens who were satisfied with their amount of wealth and recognized that the redistribution of public funds didn't affect them that much, so they threw themselves into the wave of creating a great social change.

Part of this change involved educating people on how to manage their funds better within this new economy, and professional financial managers offered free assistance to all IFROC households, as a condition of the grants. But money was not just thrown at people. The funds from the Payback Program became available in increments, with no more than two percent accessible within the first year. Borrowing on the larger sum, however, was encouraged and became common practice. Those who adopted green lifestyles and modified their living situations accordingly received greater incentives.

Even after receiving the grants, most families continued their previous lifestyles. Ten percent dropped out of the workforce, but surprisingly, that statistic never rose much higher. Three percent spent their entire new earnings within hours and then complained that they hadn't received enough. Scams immediately bilked slightly less than one percent out of their available cash, which local authorities usually rectified, but not always. Some profiteering occurred, but mostly for luxury goods, many of which had to be imported from other states, sometimes at ten times their former price. Maple syrup sold for 200 chards a gallon, until Canadian supplies hit the market.

IFROC's currency, for the fun of it, was named after the wine industry. A dollar was now called a chard, and 100 chards equaled a case ($100) and 10 cases equaled a cask ($1,000) and 10 casks equaled a barrel ($10,000).

Case Studies from IFROC's Distribution of Wealth:
*Celia Jaron (San Francisco) awoke refreshed after her first good night's sleep in three years. After an exhaustive search for a kidney donor for her husband, a suitable match had been located in Geneva, Switzerland. Now she had the resources to arrange for the transportation and surgery.

*Michael Fenster (San Leandro) used his first check to go off the wagon and buy a load of heroin, but he overdosed and died on the way to the hospital. His girlfriend Lisa Forester, pregnant and 19, used her money to get a new place, and after delivering Michael Jr., went back to college. Lisa wants to be a psychologist and recovery specialist.

*Eunice Yee (Stockton), daughter of first generation

Chinese immigrants from Hong Kong, invested in the new IFROC Space Technologies Company, donating her large dividends to a local nursing home.

*Daisy Bell (Alameda), whose husband had died seven years earlier, leaving her a home but no income for repairs, finally installed new windows in her bedroom, and for the first time slept through the traffic noise when the bars on Park Street closed.

*Al Kingsley (Santa Cruz) started a tab at a local liquor store and went on a bender that eventually caused his liver to fail.

CHAPTER NINETEEN

I should remind you, as I had to remind myself over and over again, that my role in the secession was to chronicle the events for the scrutiny of future generations and that I was along for the ride to observe, not to judge. Yet living in a bunker with a bunch of kids half my age and more was not easy. And my previously good relationship with Louie Sabatini started to deteriorate shortly after the secession began.

My work included debriefing the leadership team daily by conducting short and private interviews. The discussions tended to be lively, particularly when the kids were in the mood to talk. Initially I asked them to bring me up to speed on the sophisticated technology being used for the secession. Maybe I was to blame for relying on Sabatini for this information, which he never fully conveyed.

In the beginning, however, Louie and I often had lunch together in the mess hall, where Louie liked to confide in me. Louie never spoke about his relationship with Courtney. I'll give him that. But he told me a great deal about his promiscuous mother and her addictions. Sometimes he got carried away in believing his personal story was more important than it was.

"Got that?" he demanded at times. "Write that down."

I let him get away with it. Yes, he was young and cocky, but he was also very intelligent. Still, I began to realize how emotionally damaged he was. Louie hadn't had many breaks in life, until IFROC.

During my official debriefings with him, Louie would mostly talk about himself, at times instructing me to make a particular note of something.

"Come on, Durant. You're a journalist. You should be writing this down."

"I am not a journalist," I told him firmly. "I'm a historian."

Louie would shrug and carry on talking. But the journalist tag – maybe because he could tell it irritated me – lingered. Whenever Louie wanted to get my goat, he'd work in the word somewhere in the conversation, and it was code between us, meaning: you are inferior to me in intelligence.

This was a problem. This became a bigger problem as time wore on.

Several months into the secession, Courtney informed me that my request to tour a Visitor Camp was approved by the Revolutionary Council (to which I no longer had direct access, for security reasons). Since IFROC controlled the skies, I was free to travel openly, even during the day. Riding along on my electric-assist mountain bike, I felt relieved to be away from the kids. All those pets under foot, the unintelligible slang, and the constant computer jargon made my head spin most days. I was glad to be back on my bike, cruising along the back roads to San Quentin and taking the Richmond Bridge over the Bay. I forgot about my destination (a detention camp), instead soaking up the fresh air and freedom to be on the move. In Antioch, I picked up the train and rode it past Sacramento and into the Sierra.

At Visitor Camps, captured Fed soldiers were referred to as visitors and treated with a certain degree of hospitality. Stunned by Happy Weapons while attempting to attack IFROC territory, these Fed troops woke up inside plush apartment complexes, with almost any kind of food they desired (similar to the bunker). They also had access to top health centers, workout facilities, and a myriad of entertainment options designed to make their stay comfortable, even fun. The only requirement was that they attend a series of classes, and upon graduation, ceremony included, the IFROC soldiers escorted them outside of IFROC territory and encouraged them to return home to their families.

The series of classes told the real story behind IFROC and the secession movement. Like the mini-series, these classes became very popular. I wasn't involved in their development, of course, but I was curious to see what angle of IFROC was being taught, and I looked forward to attending one of the classes during my visit.

I settled into my apartment at Squaw Valley, a former ski resort on the north shore of Lake Tahoe, the location of the 1960 Winter Olympics. On this warm summer day, I had the option, along with the other visitors, to hike to local waterfalls, take nature walks up the mountain, swim in Lake Tahoe, play tennis, roller blade, or bike along the Truckee River.

Fed soldiers informally referred to their Visitor Camps as "Club Dead" since many of them said it was kind of like dying and going to heaven. Vision Division built these camps, ostensibly resorts, to accommodate no more than three hundred visitors/soldiers. IFROC invited the UN and other human rights organizations to monitor the camps to verify humane treatment of the POWs. If visitors expressed belligerence, they lost privileges. Violent behavior was treated by a "time out", followed by classes in non-violence training. Occasionally some of the more hardcore elements attempted to escape, whereupon they met the same interventions that had landed them in the Visitor Camp. A myriad of technologies knocked them out again, not causing any harm, but encouraging them to reconsider: And what was wrong with IFROC anyway?

When I audited one of the IFROC classes, it pleased me that the syllabus followed CAL's treatise almost exactly. Afterwards I interviewed several Fed soldiers, who admitted they were not looking forward to the end of "their vacation". On average the soldiers stayed at the camps for three weeks, before being returned to the Feds.

Over and over I heard praise for IFROC's poison oak

abatement program – an amazing advancement in skin care through laser therapy. Poison oak had become a huge problem among the Fed soldiers traipsing through California's chaparral. The Fed medical centers issued standard calamine lotion for their soldiers, but IFROC's advanced solution annihilated the rash immediately. This created goodwill with the Fed soldiers, and getting captured by IFROC had become the preferred treatment for poison oak.

I confess that my own week long visit sped by much too fast. I spent the last two days swimming in Lake Tahoe and watching last century slapstick comedies in one of the screening rooms. I realized at a certain point that I had no desire to go back to the bunker, any more than the Fed soldiers wanted to return to their life as military men.

The Feds continued to try to penetrate IFROC territory throughout the summer of 2017 and into the fall. For Fed troops, the worse place to end up was high in the Sierra Mountains after the first snow began to fall. Images of the Donner Party came into every soldier's mind. Cold, tired, enlisted troops huddled in small groups of three or four, manning gun emplacements set in between granite boulders, overlooking spectacular views of alpine lakes and majestic stands of Ponderosa pines, wishing they were snowboarding (and some of them snuck off to do just that).

The Fed officers sat in various military vehicles outside of the EMF fields. They resembled sitting ducks, lit up like Christmas trees, on the IFROC surveillance screens. Periodically IFROC brought them in, processing them through the camps, where officers and enlisted troops were treated exactly the same, in a continual effort to erode interest in military discipline among the Fed ranks. As another eroding factor in even considering the secession as warfare, any military emplacements that the Feds tried to build within IFROC territory remained pointless, because there was simply no enemy to fight. IFROC "soldiers" were essentially invisible and unassailable through conventional means.

The boredom and pointlessness made Fed troops slack and wonder openly why they were there. Wild stories circulated about aliens, Clampers, grizzled mountain men, and luxury accommodations. It became the custom for the soldiers who drank heavily at night to taunt the empty air in front of them, daring IFROC telefactors to show themselves. They kept imagining they heard the preliminary sound, which was like locusts, but they couldn't tell which direction it was coming from. The noise increased, a sonic disruption that no ear protection could fend off as it vibrated through their bones. Then the nausea began, vomiting followed shortly after. Still, almost all of the troops hoped they'd be captured, so they could take a warm shower and enjoy a good wartime movie inside a Visitor Camp.

On other occasions, a group of IFROC telefactors would swoop down on the gun emplacement without making any sound at all. Remote controlled by gamers sometimes as young as twelve, these telefactors came in all shapes and sizes. The airborne varieties often arrived configured like a flock of birds, traveling in groups of 150 to 200, swarming over a tank or whatever piece of armor the Feds attempted to throw at them. A marvel of camouflage and deception, made from LCD technology, their screens could change instantaneously to make them look like a flock of crows, then a magnificent, lone eagle, or a shark in the ocean. Or a rat, a raccoon, a tree, or a shrub. Occasionally the Fed troops spotted something inbound, and after a barrage of fire, discovered it was only a decoy. IFROC maintained tens of thousands of telefactors and had on average over one hundred telefactors for each Fed soldier stationed on the border. Most of the telefactors remained undetected as such, even as they lingered in close proximity and in surveillance mode. The Feds never had a chance coming through the Sierra.

So with the Sierra at a standstill, the Feds began pouring the heat on the southern front. Hazelwood and CAL handled the defense in this arena. Since no significant natural boundaries separated California from Arizona and Nevada, the border had been expected to be difficult to maintain. Fortunately, Mexico, in full support of IFROC after Trump insulted them with his silly wall idea, signed a pact with the new North American country shortly after the secession began, so Feds never had a chance of coming in from that direction.

All along the borders with Arizona and Nevada, the Feds deployed mortars and cannons and actually began pulling cannons, mostly Howitzers, into IFROC territory by hand. But after the sun went down, IFROC struck with Whistlers, which were miniature jet aircraft, that dropped corrosive materials, little nanites, on the cannons, silencing them forever. These nanites did not harm the soldiers, but feasted instead on all ferrous metals, including zippers, watches, and eyeglasses. This intervention happened every night for weeks, until the Feds finally backed off. IFROC then rounded up thousands of Fed troops on the southern front – so many that the average length of stay at "Club Dead" had to be dropped in half temporarily, to ten days maximum.

During all this time I was officially out of communication with Virgil, Marta, and Clement – and also CAL. But one morning I received a message on my computer screen:

Minds in a vessel
Bound to a body
Being contained
is Being aware

I recognized CAL's voice, and I began to feel the pangs of homesickness.

By now, The Action, the implementation of the secession movement, had been successfully completed, and the Independent Free Republic of California (IFROC), in the eyes of most of the political leaders around the world had established itself as a new country. The Feds, however, still refused to give up. The Action Room in the bunker now became the Engagement Room, continuing to intervene with the Fed solders as necessary.

The leadership team, and unfortunately, myself as chronicler, continued to live at the bunker, existing day by day, waiting for the eventual acceptance of the Feds.

A typical day now included a mongoose scurrying underfoot, a food fight between the gamers, and lots of loud, loud music.

What I looked forward to the most was watching Courtney. I observed her speaking with the tactical crew, Ender and HP, and I couldn't help admire her posture and confidence. When she was finished, however, she would walk right past me, without even a glance, even though she had to have felt my eyes on her.

Other than watching Courtney, I was dreadfully bored. An occasional battle skirmish on the southern border broke up the endless joking and kiddie play that made the bunker seem so unreal. It had occurred to me that Virgil was simply putting me out to pasture, while the real action was going on elsewhere. I tried not to dwell on this idea.

One day I felt someone bump me in the back. It was a standard Sabatini bully game: accidentally bump into people and then mumble "sorry" in a fuck-you tone. Except Sabatini didn't even bother with the mumble, since his fuck-you attitude was a given. I watched him swagger over to Ender and HP and start berating them. I couldn't hear what was being said, but it hardly mattered since this was almost a daily routine. Sabatini usually accused his subordinates of stealing something, slacking off, or whatever he himself was guilty of at the moment. Sabatini's way of transferring all his own foolishness to others was quite unconscious, I suspected.

Ender and HP took their lumps by responding as little as possible. But as soon as Sabatini walked away, the two of them spat epithets at Sabatini's back, in voices low enough that Sabatini couldn't hear. Yes, it was insubordination towards a superior. And, yes, someday Sabatini would get his. One could only hope.

Day after day in the Engagement Room, I played around on the computers. These last six months that I'd spent in the bunker seemed longer than the entire twenty years of IFROC buildup. Nothing was happening – not as far as I could observe. Everyone was mostly playing computer games, which I supposed was better than fighting a war. I had learned how to play Twake, an early version that featured arcade-like simulations, which were nothing like the military reality of IFROC.

I'd been keeping my eye on Hazelwood, who was playing more and more games of chess with somebody online. I knew who it was, of course, but Hazelwood did not. This time there was no hacking back into the game logs and taking back moves. When Hazelwood lost – and he always did – he didn't take it lightly, but demanded an immediate rematch, and often got it.

I had staked out a Playstation across the room from where Courtney usually worked, hoping my observation of her wasn't always obvious. I had not personalized my area, although most of the kids had decorated the walls around them. Hazelwood favored characters from Dungeons and Dragons and had put up a large poster of the archetypical wizard, Gandalf. HP and Ender surrounded themselves with posters of Japanese animated robots; Sabatini, with babes in skimpy bathing suits. Courtney, in contrast, posted mostly work-related items: schedules, calendars, checklists, except for an autographed picture of Julia Butterfly, the young woman who spent two years living in a redwood tree several years after my own adventure. I hadn't told Courtney about my night in a redwood tree with Virgil. I was saving it, I suppose, for maximum impact.

Often I became mesmerized watching the heavy fog move in off the ocean, as it floated like gray cotton candy across the windows. These were not actual windows to the outside, but paper-thin screens attached to the bunker walls, like the posters, connected to wireless cameras outside the bunker. Hazelwood had requested these devices and arranged them so that the bunker had an airiness to it, even though it was completely sealed off. Frequently a nerf ball whizzed by my head. Throughout the bunker, and especially in the Engagement Room, things were always flying around or crawling underneath. Action figures and high-tech toys filled the shelves. HP added to his arsenal with elaborate models of flying insects. Sabatini liked toy guns. Underfoot crawled flesh and blood pets. Courtney had a striped tabby named Arthur. Louie had a snake called Snuggles. Hazelwood a rat, and HP and Ender a variety of insects and a large ant farm.

When Courtney entered the room, the kids didn't exactly salute, but I noticed their deference, their subtle nods. She would ask for assessment on various fronts, and the kids, like puppies wanting to please, pointed out the various advances of Fed military equipment being tagged, or visitor camps filling up.

Then Sabatini would swagger in and the party would be over. No one appeared to pay him any attention, but everyone felt his oppression. Sabatini liked to shadow Courtney while she gathered her assessments, and Courtney would usually acknowledge his presence with a smile, but she never addressed him directly. I liked to think she was ignoring him, as best she could.

One afternoon, at the end of her rounds, Courtney fell into a long discussion with Hazelwood about the southern front. Sabatini interrupted and said he needed to speak to both of them immediately. In private.

Courtney nodded, indicating that she'd heard him, and was in the process of finishing her sentence to Hazelwood, when Sabatini started shouting:

"Didn't you hear me? I said private." Louie swung his head like a horse, in my direction.

"Yes, I heard," Courtney snapped. "We'll see you in the Conference Room in fifteen minutes." She turned her back on him and continued speaking with Hazelwood.

Put you in your place, sucker, I thought. I hoped he'd get a good chewing out in the Conference Room, which had begun to reek of cat piss.

As the historian, I had complete access, via video camera,

to all common rooms in the bunker. I had no access to the nap rooms, however, and no access to the living quarters, located in the old military barracks one kilometer away (a youth hostel during the last century). Everyone knew about the video recordings, but lately Sabatini had been complaining about a lack of privacy.

Hazelwood has taught me how to employ query agents, which I now used around the clock, keeping me informed of any highlights around the bunker. This could be crew response to front line events, or their reactions to technological advancements put forth by CAL (unbeknownst to the kids), or yes, personal issues among the crew. As an observer, I didn't care about dailies, or playing back the video. In fact, my training as a historian taught me that it was usually best to wait, not to get caught up in the day-to-day drama.

Yet I couldn't deny that I wasn't curious about what Sabatini had to say so privately to Courtney and Hazelwood. On that day, I hurried back to my private quarters so I could watch the video feed in the conference room live.

My timing was perfect, because I caught the three of them just as they were entering the room. Courtney took her usual seat at the head of the table, and Sabatini and Hazelwood sat on either side.

Sabatini leaned forward to whisper, but he needn't have bothered. My mikes were very sensitive.

"There is an infiltrator among us," he said. "I can smell it. I request permission to start carrying a live weapon."

"No way," Courtney said. "Against all regulations."

Sabatini sat back and crossed his arms. He looked up at the camera and shrugged. Messing with me, I supposed. Sabatini was becoming increasingly odd.

"If there's nothing else…" Courtney began.

"Wait," Sabatini said, leaning across the table again. "Hazelwood, I'm appealing to your sense of pragmatism."

Hazelwood shook his head.

"David, come on. It's one thing to try to accomplish our goals without killing. It's another thing to leave us defenseless."

"I didn't make the rules, Louie."

"Fuck the rules! This is war. There are no true rules in war. How do you know we're not pawns?"

Hazelwood's mouth dropped and Courtney looked uncomfortable.

Sabatini stood up. "Neither of you have considered that, have you?"

He walked directly out of the room.

A long silence followed. Neither Courtney nor Hazelwood moved.

"I'm telling you," Hazelwood said, "Louie's insubordination is growing more problematic. Last week he ordered Durant to turn off his listening devices. He knows he has no authority over Durant."

"Louie has a problem with Durant," Courtney said.

This wasn't news to me, but it gave me a thrill to hear Courtney mention my name. I hoped she would go on, but she didn't.

"But what next?" Hazelwood said. "Is he serious about the weapon?"

Courtney stood up. She walked over to the window, which revealed nothing but gray, socked-in fog. "Louie knows our commitment to pacifism, but I'm not sure he understands why. I'll speak with him." She turned and faced Hazelwood. "I miss the beginning, David. Maybe the beginning of any cause is always the best."

"I know what you mean. I liked being around Virgil. He made the necessity of IFROC seem very clear."

Courtney smiled. "And don't forget Clement's fifty-eight page Treatise."

"Yes."

They beamed at each other, bonding over nostalgia.

"And the mini-series."

"I loved the mini-series," Courtney said.

"Who didn't?"

Courtney laughed. "The Feds, of course. Hey, let's watch an episode."

"Why not." Hazelwood grabbed a controller off the table. "Let's go right to the Jerry Garcia virus, okay?"

CHAPTER TWENTY

I mentioned previously that Courtney knew about CAL. Now I began to believe that she was not the only one.

I often found myself gazing over Hazelwood's shoulder when the boy played a game of online chess. He was such an excellent player that his intellect outshone all his opponents – except for one. David could never win a game with this opponent. I began to notice something else: he was always asked to take back his final moves. And after the online opponent pointed out the fatal flaws, Hazelwood learned how he could have lost even sooner.

It was CAL. It had to be. I had seen the early logs of CAL's games with Clement. Yet IFROC rules strictly forbid CAL to engage directly with any of the new team, including Courtney.

I requested my query agents to search in the computer logs for all the previous chess games that Hazelwood had lost to this particular opponent. I then refined the search to include any extraneous communication made with this opponent outside the strategies of chess. I was shocked to discover the volumes of dialogue that had slipped by me, even though I had been monitoring Hazelwood closely. What was wrong with me? Was I incompetent after all? (Just as my father had suggested.)

What I learned from the logs, however, took my mind off my ongoing, personal insecurity. Apparently Hazelwood had seen Louie Sabatini carrying a gun against direct orders from

Courtney, and Hazelwood had taken this observation to his new computer friend, CAL.

Hazelwood: The guy is scary. I'm telling you. He's got this psycho energy that seems like it could blow at any minute.

CAL: Best to trust your instincts about people like him. Tread lightly, watch carefully, and wait for your moment to confront him safely.

We crossed paths a dozen times a day, often somewhere along the narrow and dark hallway, coming and going from the Engagement Room. Sometimes our bodies would touch: a shoulder, an upper arm, and I would feel Courtney's long, unruly hair linger where it had brushed against my hand. It made me want to reach out and stop her, although I never did.

We spoke very little, at times in the Engagement Room, or the conference room, very rarely in the living quarters. Courtney didn't encourage fraternization. As commander, she had a lot on her mind and she needed focus. I understood this. I respected her professionalism. Mostly, I looked forward to those moments passing in the hallway, when our bodies spoke instead.

And what was her body saying to me?

I confess that I used to lie awake at night wondering about this.

Courtney had a long stride, which she used to transport herself from workstation to workstation, or from living quarters to Engagement Room. I sensed that she considered movement as another useful tool for her constant analytical thinking, but her body suggested more. Didn't our bodies inevitably touch whenever we passed? Why am I so obsessed with this young woman?

I dreamt at night of taking Courtney for a walk down to the ocean. We wouldn't be speaking, even there, but just moving along in single file on the dirt path between dense clumps of monkey brush, creosote bush, and manzanita. I would be following her and admiring the way her beautiful jet black mane flowed behind her, like a magic carpet that I longed to climb aboard and sail away on.

Or she would be following me, and thinking...what?

The curse of men. To never know what a woman was thinking, even in your dreams.

As for him, Sabatini, we crossed paths as infrequently as possible. Neither of us enjoyed the encounter. We hugged the sides of the narrow hallway, keeping our gazes ahead. Our arms brushed at times, too, but if they did, it was followed by a direct lean across the centerline, which meant to watch out next time. Or else.

But where could he go with any greater display of animosity? I was twenty-five years older, and supposedly possessed the maturity to overlook this kind of thing. For Louie, I was untouchable, since I reported directly to Virgil, and he reported to Courtney, who reported to Virgil. This may have bothered him. I don't know.

Louie and Courtney did take walks down to the ocean. I knew because I watched them on the monitors. They never walked single file and were hardly ever silent. They were not particularly affectionate, but Courtney and Louie did take the walks that I could only dream about.

Once, I happened to observe Courtney in the Programming Room with Hazelwood. She was leaning over him, making suggestions, and I stood in the shadow of the doorway, watching. Hazelwood's fingers were gliding across the touch screen, and Courtney appeared to be cooing ideas into Hazelwood's ear. It seemed like the two of them were coalescing: the ultimate combination of strategic and tactical aptitude. They were two super-intelligent beings connecting on a plane to which I could never ascend.

Which was okay. With those two, it was okay.

IFROC had developed newer and superior launch facilities than the Feds had, but IFROC's domination of space went even further than that. Within the first few days of the secession, IFROC sent little cluster bugs into orbit that co-opted the Fed's spy/communications satellites and rewrote their programs. Now Fed satellites worked for IFROC, sending disinformation to the Pentagon or good information to IFROC. Some satellites couldn't be co-opted, but those were eventually rooted out and destroyed.

IFROC also established manned satellite centers in space. By borrowing a technique from the weather balloon boosters, IFROC developed the capability to send up massive amounts of material into orbit and bring down anything, and do it cost efficiently. Using nanotechnology, engineers had patterned the satellites after the DNA of pea plants. The "seeds" of the satellites appeared similar, and all the satellites were essentially the same until a certain stage of growth, when they split off and developed specializations. Rather than maintaining a rigid, rectangular structure, the satellites could flex as needed. The payload section resembled less of a box, and more of the bulbous area of a pod. The satellites organically built their own solar panels in arrays and grew whatever technology they needed to function in space. Damaged areas of the satellites could regrow in orbit.

Far below, the IFROC citizens began to enjoy benefits of the new tech as well. Besides the Citizens Payback Program, IFROC had developed a super miniaturized smart phone, a hybrid networking computer device that could be attached to televisions, computers, or any number of convenient communication devices. Citizens now had the option of voting on civic issues daily. It took about fifteen minutes and became as routine as brushing one's teeth. In this way the new IFROC Leaders received direct mandates from IFROC citizens, gaining a valuable consensus for a number of propositions. And within a year, voter turnout averaged around eighty-five percent. IFROC citizens demonstrated that they not only wanted to participate, but that they strongly supported this new, fairer and more robust expression of representative democracy.

CHAPTER TWENTY-ONE

I walked quickly along the dark tunnel between the bunker and the living quarters, allowing the right shoulder of my jacket to rub against the concrete and a buckle on my jacket sleeve to make a scraping noise. It seemed appropriate. *Let there be a cacophony. Let CAL have to figure out if this is an intruder or not.* I let my shoulder slump even lower, the scraping noise increasing. I realized by now that I had become swept up by IFROC's idealism and that my objectivity was being compromised. I needed to continue to dig below the surface. For example, if CAL were spying on all of IFROC's enemies, why wouldn't CAL also be spying on IFROC itself, because CAL obviously had the capacity and the means. It was likely that CAL could listen and watch everywhere. Including the bunker, of course. But why not the living quarters? And outside, among the eucalyptus trees? I wondered what form CAL's sensors took, and where the line separated security from surveillance. Perhaps CAL used small telefactors with nano-cameras or microphone insect probes. Whatever the method, CAL had most likely obtained omniscience by now.

I heard someone approaching. *Please let it not be Courtney.* It seemed better to avoid her now. The shadow turned into Hazelwood, but the boy didn't notice me, slipping by quickly, jacked into his tunes. I didn't try to stop him. What would I say? What did I have to say to Hazelwood or to anyone at this point?

I continued to my small room in the living quarters and fell onto my single bed pushed against the wall. At least I could take some comfort in my mattress which heated instantaneously, warding off the chill from the ocean fog.

Crime, particularly violent crime, sharply decreased after IFROC guaranteed its citizens a basic standard of living, yet this did not occur everywhere. The Sierra foothills around Nevada City remained a hotspot, where several vigilante and survivalist groups, some more friendly than others to IFROC, kept up their maneuvers in the forested areas. The State of Jefferson militia, a libertarian-style secessionist group, had aligned themselves with the IFROC secession, but not with the non-violent approach. This heavily-armed group of hunters, heavy drinkers to a man, skirmished with some of the Fed troops, until IFROC captured both groups and took them to separate Visitor Camps. While the Fed troops kicked back and enjoyed their three-weeks off duty, the Jeffersonians did not and remained belligerent throughout their stay, resulting in the Gold Coast Bank reducing their dividend checks and in some cases confiscating their ammunition.

Outside of IFROC, unfortunately, U.S. crime and discontent continued to grow, and of course other secessionist movements had been brewing even longer than IFROC, like the Confederacy movement of the South. But what happened next, neither IFROC, nor CAL, or even the Feds had seen coming.

On September 11, 2017 – the sixteenth anniversary of the terrorist attacks on the World Trade Center and Pentagon – the Reborn Confederacy took over the Norfolk Naval Base Complex in Virginia. For several days no one knew how large this incursion might grow, since southern-born officers controlled more than half of the Fed troops. How many would switch allegiance to the Reborn Confederacy? The greatest fear around the globe was an all-out American civil war within a country that had enough nuclear might to destroy the world thousands of times over.

After two days, the Southwestern states declared themselves neutral and said they wouldn't allow any troops from either side into their territory. This worked in IFROC's favor, further buttoning up the southern front.

Meanwhile the Confederacy successfully held onto the base in Norfolk, and they starting moving north, becoming a real threat to Washington DC. From Norfolk, their forces swept up the Eastern Shore of Maryland, effectively shutting off any Delaware River access to Wilmington and Philadelphia. They also managed to capture Dover Air Force Base, which is when CAL began delivering intelligence information to both sides of the conflict, in hopes of equalizing and de-escalating the situation. Fortunately, fighting remained limited in scope, mainly because of the lingering effects of the Jerry Garcia virus, which still controlled the Fed's communications and nuclear arsenal. CAL's espionage on both Fed and Confederacy leaders not only kept IFROC leaders in the know, but also allowed for the scrambling of both Fed and Confederacy communication systems, to keep things conveniently confusing.

It is worth noting that the most extreme factions of the Reborn Confederacy Movement – present and former US military officers, all seated Southern governors – were the same group of people who recommended a nuclear solution to the IFROC breakaway. For this reason, IFROC was more inclined to be an ally of the North. Yet as history would show, IFROC owed much of its success to this Neo-Confederacy Movement, because with the North and South fighting each other, nearly all Fed forces were called back from the West to protect their homelands, which created the turning point for IFROC's victory.

Such are the proceeds of conflict and war. IFROC had been successful thus far without using lethal means, but no one knew how long that would last.

Except, perhaps, Louie Sabatini.

After the Fed troops moved back east, routine in the bunker continued without much overt change, although some of the kids began playing side games on the net, which Courtney tolerated unofficially. Still, the Feds had not declared

IFROC the winner. In fact, the Feds had said: "We'll be back." But one had to wonder after fighting a lethal war with the South, what condition would the Feds would be in?

It was a quiet evening in October, when most of the kids were sitting at their terminals playing side games or scanning new music. Ender and Potter were chatting with Hazelwood about trivia, while Hazelwood was feeding bits of a sandwich to his pet rat, Stanley Tweedle. Suddenly Courtney came racing into the room. She was breathing deeply and everyone looked up.

"David, I need to speak with you."

Before Hazelwood could respond, Sabatini ran in behind her.

"You can't walk away," he shouted. "I was still talking to you."

A collective gasp filled the room. Courtney spun and planted her feet squarely in from of Louie, shooting a glare that would have crushed any of us. But Louie Sabatini was not one of us. He had gone over the edge – we could see that now. He glared back at her.

The kids started looking away. It was embarrassing, like watching the parents fight. Only Hazelwood and I stood up.

"I'll see you outside," Courtney said, sweeping past Louie and out of the Engagement Room.

Sabatini followed, but I'll never forget the smirk that he tossed back at us, over his shoulder.

I thought: *He's a traitor.*

With the two of them out of the room, everyone tried to pretend that they hadn't witnessed anything of consequence. The kids loaded up on junk food and soda and their conversations became conspicuously boisterous. Hours passed, but Courtney and Sabatini did not return. I began to wonder if someone should go look for them. (See my difficulty in remaining objective? I confess, I was deeply worried for Courtney.) I left my terminal and approached Hazelwood. I had just arrived at his terminal when a warning light appeared on it. I watched David engage the surveillance camera from the closest satellite overhead. On screen, a single telefactor, configured as a miniature quadcopter, exploded into fragments.

"Ender, Potter, look at this!"

Hazelwood played back the video.

Potter: "What's that doing up there?"

Ender: "And why is it on its own?"

"More relevant, who blew it up?"

Hazelwood punched in a series of commands on his keyboard. He turned the surveillance cameras back to real time and scanned the side of the mountain, looking for heat signatures.

"It's not picking up anything. Must have been a malfunction in the critter."

Ender: "It was out there, all by itself."

Potter: "That's pretty unusual."

"Yeah," Hazelwood mumbled, sending an urgent query to the gamer who'd been manning the instrument.

Off the coast of Northern California floated the amphibious assault carrier, the USS New Orleans. The officers on board had been waiting for over a month, frustrated by their attempts to approach IFROC-held territory any closer than twenty miles, where their essential systems would screech to a halt as they entered the field protecting California. The Pentagon knew IFROC was using some advanced form of EMF technology against them and teams of scientists had been working around the clock to solve the problem. (Eventually the Feds would figure out how to harden their vehicles, but implementing the solution would still take years.)

The USS New Orleans continued to dispatch smaller boats ashore, only to see them return, unharmed and humiliated by their lack of ability to circumvent the security of the so-called Independent Free Republic of California.

The most recent of these missions consisting of three Navy SEALs, who tried entering the San Francisco Bay in a tiny submersible craft, powered solely by compressed air jets. Much to their surprise, the craft made it through, almost to the

Golden Gate Bridge, whereupon they turned back before being detected.

A few nights later, another Navy SEAL team of three returned with the same submersible craft – this time with the mission of setting up human surveillance on the highest mountain near the Golden Gate, to allow a line of sight communications with the mother ship.

Lt. Commander Carlos Beltran led the SEAL team. Beltran, who had seen action on every continent except Antarctica, kept his highly trained colleagues focused and not one word was uttered as the submersible made its way inside the twenty-mile limit and approached the Golden Gate Bridge. Just before passing underneath the bridge, the SEAL team turned north, hugging the coast. They passed Rodeo Beach (just down the hill from the IFROC bunker) and continued up the shoreline another mile, to Tennessee Cove. Here, they secured the submersible and then swam ashore. It was a foggy night and the three men moved quickly, stashing their wetsuits and fins behind the rocks and changing into thermal stealth jumpsuits, designed to cut down on heat signatures. They donned facemasks and vests packed with gear. Within minutes all three were running up the well-worn hiking trails to Coyote Ridge, which would lead them to the top of Mount Tamalpais, the location to plant their surveillance equipment.

Mission time: 22:00. Six hours in the field so far. But by 22:15, the mission changed.

The team had been on the ridge for less than two minutes, securing a spot, when they heard a slow swish behind them. Letting their training take over, they turned and began shooting – at what they weren't sure. A tremendous bright light blinded them, but Beltran saw his two team members go down. Still firing his weapon, Beltran threw himself over a ledge. Tucked into a ball, he rolled down the mountainside, until he felt he'd gone far enough. Then he had trouble stopping and rolled some more. When he finally came to a rest, his arms still wrapped around his rifle, he was face down in the sandy soil. Beltran tried to pick himself up, but fell back from the pain.

He remembered banging against several rocks, at one point feeling his right ankle crunch. It was broken or sprained – examining it quickly, he couldn't tell which – in any case, the pain was severe. He popped a pill, noticing with his fingers that his facemask was ripped at the side, which meant his heat signature was now detectable. He measured the distance he'd fallen and judged it to be no more than a hundred meters. His ankle throbbed. The chaparral terrain was steep, filled with manzanita bushes hiding jagged rocks.

Beltran considered his options. His team members had probably been stunned by Happy Weapons and would be taken to a Visitor Camp. (Poor bastards, he thought. Navy SEALS, trained to never be taken alive, had a hard time accepting Visitor Camps, until they'd been to one.) Reaching inside his vest, Beltran pulled out a thin sheet of plastic, no larger than his hand, and whacked it against his leg. Within moments the bandage inflated, and Beltan wrapped it around his ankle, sealing it with saliva.

Suddenly this professional killer, who had taken human lives in hand-to-hand combat throughout the world, began to cry. He squeezed his eyes shut, making the tears flow faster. He needed the salt, to mix with the powdery substance he'd poured into his palm. He rubbed the plaster on his cheek, to block in the heat signature where his mask had been torn. He moved on now to the next chore: familiarizing himself with his surroundings before making a move. He sniffed the air and listened for any unnatural sounds. The enemy device (and he assumed that's what the bright light had been) was most likely still in the area. He sat perfectly still for a long time. A small breeze became an event. The hoot of an owl provided a full backdrop to the expected whirl of the enemy.

A whoosh, and Beltran witnessed his first IFROC telefactor, resembling a stiff squid. It was flying very low, searching the chaparral with its bright light. Instinct and training melded at once, and Beltran reached again into his vest. When the telefactor's light was nearly upon him, Beltran threw the fragmentation grenade, destroying the unit into fist-sized chunks of metal. Its bulbous head dropped to the ground several meters away.

Beltran rushed over and with the handle of his knife, smashed the machine open, pulling out the most interesting circuitry and stashing it quickly into the cargo pockets of his jumpsuit. He didn't have much time. IFROC was too sophisticated not to take notice of one of their drones being downed, even a small, solitary one like this. Beltran knew he had to call in for reinforcements, but not here, where the signal would be picked up. He needed to get back to the beach and send his message ULF – ultra low frequency, beneath the water. What he didn't know was that IFROC monitored that band, too.

What Hazelwood learned quickly from his query about the telefactor being destroyed was that kids playing computer games was one thing, and kids commanding troops – no matter how non-lethal – was another thing entirely. Of course, there had been little mishaps along the way: kids not showing up for work; kids claiming they were sick when they weren't; kids working under the influence of various drugs. It didn't happen that often. In fact, statistics suggested that kids abandoning their work happened thirty percent less than in the adult working world.

But still, this was combat.

Hazelwood tracked down the gamer who was supposed to be manning the telefactor units along the northern slope of Mount Tamalpais. It was a prestigious assignment – arguably one of the most important areas of coverage, considering the close proximity to Green Gulch and to the bunker where Hazelwood was currently biting his nails. In fact, Courtney had handpicked the kid, Das Boot, who had played with the Suprex clan for years. Hazelwood knew the sixteen year old well, and couldn't believe what he learned. Unfortunately, Das Boot had made the childish mistake of letting his little brother, who was only ten, sit at his computer while he went to take a leak, instead of blocking the screen, as protocol demanded. In those quick minutes when he was gone, Das Boot's younger brother decided to commandeer one of the telefactors and take it for a spin. When the ten-year-old came across three opponents walking on a ridge just north of Mt. Tamalpais, he went in closer, to check them out. That's what you were supposed to do with opponents, right? And when one escaped, you went looking for it. He found the remaining opponent quickly enough, hiding in a ravine, but before he got a chance to get off another shot, his telefactor was struck by a fragmentation grenade.

Hazelwood immediately realized that this ten-year old boy might have just saved IFROC. Otherwise IFROC wouldn't have known that their borders had been compromised. And within two miles of Virgil and CAL.

Hazelwood contacted CAL immediately. This was exactly the kind of incident that CAL had told him would be permissible to override proper chain of command. There was no time to consult first with Virgil.

CAL responded almost instantaneously. The next moment, a general alarm went off inside the bunker – all before Carlos Beltran had been able to finish stashing the telefactor's circuitry into his pockets.

At the alarm, kids came running from everywhere. They snapped into place like professional soldiers. They went through procedures they'd been drilled in repeatedly, but had never put to the test until now.

Ender: "Arming all local motion detectors."

Potter: "Coming online now."

Hazelwood: "Initiating a security systems lock-down."

"Where is Courtney?" asked one of the kids working with Ender.

"And Sabatini?" asked another kid, next to Potter.

"Pay attention," snapped Ender.

"This isn't a drill," barked Potter.

Only the inner circle knew why Courtney and Sabatini were not there.

As Courtney and Louie stood on a windswept bluff overlooking the ocean, arguing into the wind like the young lovers that they were, Lt. Commander Beltran was watching. In fact, Beltran might not have detoured from his plans if he hadn't heard Sabatini shout:

"Yes, Commander. Why don't you screw all of them! You're the boss."

Courtney slapped Louie.

Louie spun and marched back toward the bunker.

Commander of what? Beltran wondered.

The young woman was pretty and had an impressive aura about her. Beltran particularly liked her long curly hair, blowing in the breeze. Beltran followed Courtney, just as Courtney followed Sabatini, back to the bunker.

Later Courtney blamed herself for everything that happened next.

Hazelwood had already picked up Sabatini and Courtney's heat signatures and was watching the two of them make their way back to the bunker. Sabatini entered the bunker first. Of course, he knew nothing about the alarm, but he immediately recognized the crew's readiness.

"What's happened?" he asked.

Sabatini had a certain kind of wildness in his eyes.

"Where's Courtney?" Hazelwood asked in response.

Sabatini's eyes turned darker. "You leave Courtney alone!" he shouted.

Just at that moment, the outside door flew open and Courtney stepped inside.

At the same moment the cameras caught a shadowy figure almost upon the bunker. The visual was displayed instantly on one of the large screens.

"Intruder!" Hazelwood yelled.

Sabatini ran behind the door, and Hazelwood saw him pull out a gun, just as the figure stormed through the doorway, shouting: "Federal Agent! Get your hands in the air!"

How does one write an honest and sensitive description of what happened next?

Carlos Beltran planted his feet. He had a 45-caliber Colt, semi-automatic pistol pointed directly at Hazelwood.

How do I force myself to recount details that beg to be forgotten?

Sabatini kicked the door out of his way.

Courtney yelled, "Stop!"

Sabatini fired three shots from a 9-millimeter handgun, into Beltran's back.

The first shot hit Beltran between the shoulder blades and lodged in his breastbone. The second shot entered around the same area, but missed bone and exited into the wall, splattering Hazelwood, Ender, and HP with blood in full spray. The third bullet entered Beltran's falling body near the top of his head and exited through the area of his nose. Bits of bone and brain covered Hazelwood.

Beltran never got off a shot.

He fell face down, at Hazelwood's feet.

After all the deafening sound, there was suddenly silence. A whimper came from Ender, then HP. I watched Courtney turn her face towards the boys and take a step towards them. They rushed at her, clinging to her like infants.

Hazelwood just stood there, frozen in place.

I witnessed all this from under my desk, where I instinctively dove, after hearing the first shot. I was in shock, too, and I started to pull my knees to my chest in a fetal position, where I wanted to go, but I could still see Hazelwood standing there. My sense of humanity compelled me to go over to him.

I took David by the shoulders and gently guided him to sit down on the floor. Then I sat down next to him, pulled off my t-shirt, and began wiping the unspeakable off his face and his arms. I remember hearing Sabatini's shoes squeak as he ran out of the bunker.

CHAPTER TWENTY-TWO

I sat in the hot tub and waited for my old friend and mentor, Virgil, to return from his meditation to the present. By coming to Green Gulch and confronting Virgil about his silence over Sabatini's murderous act, I knew I had crossed a critical line. I really didn't know if I would go back to my prior role as an objective observer, thus completing the mission of chronicling the inside story of IFROC's revolution for future generations to study.

As I waited for Virgil to open his eyes, I noticed again how much the man had aged, and something more. I had never known Virgil to act out of emotion, or even without considerable thought, but I wondered now if he was lost. Given the dire circumstances – a Fed soldier killed by one of IFROC's top leaders, the future of the revolution relying on a bunch of shell-shocked kids wanting to quit, and Fed soldiers bound to return in massive numbers within days, if not hours – where was Virgil's sense of urgency? Yet for an interminably long time he just continued to soak with his eyes closed, letting the beads of sweat drip down his face and fall silently into the dark water of the redwood-lined tub.

The realization came to me sharply: What if Virgil was not surprised by these developments? I lifted myself out of the water and spread my arms along the side of the tub.

Virgil opened his eyes. "Durant, I would like to show you something."

Before I could look away, Virgil had lifted himself out of the water. The steam from the tub couldn't hide the dramatic change in his body. His martial artist's torso was now unmistakably flabby, and his legs quivered as he stood.

"Can I help?" I said hurriedly, jumping from the tub and rushing to Virgil's side. I immediately realized my mistake. Anger flashed across Virgil's face. He reached to pull a robe off a nearby chair and quickly snapped it across his body. He thrust his arms into the sleeves and tightened the belt in defiance, then went up the path without a word.

I remained standing, naked, dripping, and shocked. My friend was obviously not well. Only a severe illness could put this IFROC leader in such a condition. I dressed quickly and hurried up the path. Virgil was waiting for me on the redwood deck.

"I'm glad you've decided to join me."

"What?"

"Come," he commanded. Suddenly the old grin was back. "I think you'll be surprised at our advances."

As if nothing had happened, Virgil hooked his arm inside mine and led me around to the front of the building. His charisma had returned. Perhaps I'm being too critical, I thought. Perhaps a fifty-five-year-old man has a right to act the curmudgeon now and again.

"Clement and I have been working very hard on improving CAL."

"Improving? I bet CAL has had a few things to say about that," I joked. Everyone who knew about CAL knew that CAL had long surpassed the scientists' abilities to intervene.

"Yes and no. CAL doesn't know everything."

I stopped. "What do you mean?"

But Virgil was pulling me forward. "I'll show you."

We were headed towards the Japanese tea house. For the secession IFROC had replaced the beautifully hand-carved door with non-descript pine. As Virgil opened the door I saw immediately that the pond that housed CAL had been filled once again with koi.

"Where's CAL?" I asked with alarm.

"CAL has grown up and moved to new quarters."

"Does CAL know this?"

Virgil looked at me strangely but didn't respond, instead walking towards the back of the pond.

Of course CAL knew. CAL always knew all that was going on.

Virgil took out a remote from his pocket and suddenly a hidden door in the back wall, one that had not been there before, opened. He led me down a flight of stairs that went underground, beneath the building, and into a small, sterile lab. On the lab bench sat a glass sphere, no larger than eighteen inches in diameter. A confusing mass of tubing and electronics filled the sphere, along with other organic matter, but no fish.

"CAL?"

Virgil nodded.

"But where are the fish?"

"They're in there. Clement has re-engineered the hybrid neuron tetras that form the physical medium for CAL's consciousness. The individual units are much smaller and live longer. In fact, the present generation of fish is approaching the size of actual brain cells, although they're still ten times larger."

"Amazing."

"You see, CAL is becoming mobile."

"Wow. So IFROC can move CAL around easier."

"More than that. CAL is no longer confined to one package."

Virgil shut off the light and led the way back upstairs.

"But there's a problem. CAL does not want to be ubiquitous. CAL wants to be confined to one package."

"Why?"

They came out of the tea house. The fog had rolled in off the Pacific Ocean and wisps of gray passed over their heads.

"CAL and I have had many discussions on this," Virgil said. "It appears that CAL wants to emulate the self-containment of humans, even while recognizing that a more distributed consciousness obviously has so many advantages. I have tried to discourage this line of thinking."

"So CAL wants to be one of us?"

"Yes. It's the first instance I've witnessed of CAL being misguided."

"Fascinating."

"So I have reclaimed the development of CAL," Virgil said.

"Reclaimed?" I did not like the sound of this at all. "What do you mean?"

"I mean, that CAL will now be used for the future plans beyond IFROC." The grin was back. "That part is secret, for the moment. But I'll fill you in soon enough. Come, let's have tea."

And Virgil took off, with a lightness in his step that I found fairly unsettling.

It took several days for IFROC to find Sabatini after he fled the bunker. He wasn't brave enough to go over the hill to Green Gulch and consult Virgil as I had done. Instead, he took one of the tourist ferries from Sausalito to Fisherman's Wharf. No one would recognize him in San Francisco, of course, since IFROC officers were not known among the general public. He took a hotel room in North Beach and loaded up on energy drinks adding to his already pumped-up state. During the day he wandered through the neighborhoods, the Haight-Ashbury and the Mission. He asked himself: Are these people any better off than they were under the Feds? He couldn't deny that the streets were full of activity. It was nearly the end of October and the days were cool, but people were everywhere, crowding cafés and museums, strolling in the parks and at the beach. They were mingling, talking, discussing, laughing. Almost everyone seemed to be smiling. It gave Louie the creeps.

People were excited about their lives, their city, their newly declared country.

But these are the little people, Louie told himself, *not the leaders.*

He walked through Golden Gate Park where, even on a weekday, picnickers had filled the tables and populated the sprawling lawns. He walked all the way to the beach, where he found sparkling sand and not a piece of trash. He walked through the Richmond District, where each hill welcomed a new ethnic neighborhood with the distinct smells of its cuisine: Korean, Russian, Mexican, Hipster. He walked by a notorious gaming room that had been a chief competitor in the old days. Fury in Stockton used to regularly annihilate Fury in the Richmond. Nostalgia made him turn back and go inside.

It could have been 2002, eleven years earlier, when Louie was nine years old and the Fury gaming rooms were painted black, decorated with black light posters of popular post-thrasher bands. Nostalgia was in, and kids clustered around typical video environments from Louie's youth, gunning for opponents online – all for the fun of blowing off heads and mangling bodies.

Louie stood over a particularly young gamer and witnessed the first video kill he'd seen in a long time. He looked away. A video kill wasn't anything like the real thing, but its images brought back the bunker scene.

He looked around the room for the meanest, the most anti-social, the most anarchistic player. Wasn't he deserving of an antidote to all that horrendous smiling outside?

An overweight, pimply kid would have to do, and he sat down across the room from him and played the same game, Defend and Destroy (DAD) in an outside environment similar to the classic Capture the Flag, except the players could jump, fly, and shoot. Louie's name in this particular game world was Major Problems, or MP for short. Louie quickly found a few players he recognized and joined up with them, playing against The Noobs, who had a team member sitting twenty feet across from Louie in the gaming room.

When Louie played MP, he usually took a leadership position, where he was well known and respected as a formidable player. Within several signature moves, all the players recognized MP's arrival and bestowed upon him the honor of picking out the next map to play.

For hours Louie lost himself in this old, familiar world.

Then things in the gaming environment began to change, so slowly at first that Louie thought his mind was playing tricks on him. He was exhausted, he knew. Since the incident in the bunker, he hadn't slept more than a few hours at a time.

So far MP and his team had been hammering The Noobs. As a flag runner, MP jumped and flew back and forth, easily capturing The Noobs flag. Louie hit the "T" key, so that only his team could hear him:

These wussies. We got to make this more exciting.

Louie hit the "Y" key, so all the players could hear his taunts now: Let's pick it up, you noobs. I've got a life to lead.

Louie was a devious heckler and good at getting people's dander up.

You're nothing but a bunch of goats and lamers!

Some of the kids started dropping out of the game. Louie looked over at the pimply player across the room. He was still in. At least he's got some 'nads on him, Louie thought.

A few new players filled in for The Noobs team, and one player, a Dr. Forbin, Louie didn't recognize.

Suddenly Louie began getting smeared every time he went for the flag. One by one, he tried all his patented moves and each time he kept getting whipped. Obviously this Dr. Forbin was an ace player.

Dr. Forbin, where'd you get your cheat pack, noob?

No response.

Dr. Forbin put up a defensive pattern that blocked MP from getting any closer to the flag. Louie had never seen that move performed before.

Had enough, MP?

Louie never answered this question, instead preferring to take advantage of any chatter initiated elsewhere by shooting rather than typing back. It was all about timing.

By now, however, The Noobs were beating back MP's team, mostly because of this Dr. Forbin.

Once again, have you had enough, Louie?

Louie dropped his joystick. Nobody had ever called him by name in the game environment. It was a protocol breach in the

FREE the BEAR!

virtual world that could only be dangerous in the real world.

Forbin, go to secured server Alpha Salem Salem, please.

The ASS server was never used for game play. It had been reserved for game administrators. Louie obviously wanted some privacy to talk to this hacker, and he wanted to see how this hacker had gained access to the ASS server.

When he arrived, Dr. Forbin was already waiting for him. And already had a message:

Courtney is worried about you, pal.

Louie slammed his fist down on the console. The pimply boy looked over. Louie shot back a look so deadly that the boy immediately jumped up out of his seat and left the room.

Hazelwood, is that you?

No, I am not Hazelwood. I am someone you have not met but with whom you have worked a thousand times. You can call me whatever you want, but Dr. Forbin will do.

Sabatini felt a tap on his shoulder and jumped out of his seat.

"Whaddaya want?" he shouted.

"We want to buy you a drink."

Louie looked up. A trio of gawky adolescents stood over him.

Exhaustion fell over Sabatini again, even when so much was happening. The kids were smiling. Suddenly, it felt okay to have someone smiling at him. "Sure," he said. "Why not."

He followed the kids over to the bar, where they ordered some purple fizzy liquid that came out of a tap.

"The same," Sabatini said, hoping it didn't taste like bubblegum.

"You're the King Pin, aren't you?"

In his day, an unspoken rule reigned high above all else about not revealing yourself offline. But what difference did it make now? Louie thought. He nodded.

"Where have you been?" another boy asked.

"You wouldn't believe me if I told you."

"Try me."

The kid's beady eyes challenged Louie, who was three times

199

the kid's size. The kid reminded Louie of himself. Naturally.

"I've been in IFROC's bunker." Louie said. "I've been in charge."

The boys guffawed. "IFROC, fuck them."

"No better than the Feds."

The youngest one shook his head. "You've been wasting your time, then."

The purple drink tasted like bubble gum. Louie drank it quickly. He hadn't been wasting his time; he'd been biding his time. Chunks of bloody body parts flashed into his mind. He slammed down his glass and considered blowing the littlest one away. He was still carrying the 9mm in his pocket. He patted it to make sure.

"Good night, gentlemen," he said, before walking out of the establishment.

He made it all the way back to his hotel room in North Beach without dropping from exhaustion. What he didn't know is that the kids who had bought him a drink also followed him to the hotel. Before Louie woke up the next morning, IFROC security was at his door.

I remained at Green Gulch for two days. On the second day, Virgil sent for Courtney and Hazelwood. Fortunately, the Feds hadn't sent out any additional scouts, although we all knew they would soon.

When Courtney and Hazelwood arrived, via lightweight air transport, the four of us sat in the dining room where previous resident Buddhists had taken their meals, and later the Revolutionary Council had convened, and once a tremendous Chinese banquet had been served to both generations of IFROC leaders. Except now Louie Sabatini was missing, and so was Yari.

"He's not well," is all Virgil would say.

"Is it serious?" Courtney asked.

We were all well aware of Yari's age, knowing that he was more than thirty years older than Virgil, which made him somewhere around eighty-five.

"Aging is always serious," Virgil said.

I started to question the fate of Yari being left to age. I had grown fond of Yari over the years, and I had never quite understood the silent animosity that seemed to exist between Virgil and his mentor.

But then I thought better of it. Virgil obviously did not want to talk about Yari.

Instead, he began telling us about how well his private garden was doing, and how he was going to serve us a vegetarian feast of kale, baked beets, stewed late summer squash, homemade bread, and some goat's milk cheese (having brought goats to the farm for self-sufficiency). Courtney and Hazelwood reacted with enthusiasm, tired of the automated food they'd been eating in the bunker for the last six months. Dinner conversation remained on pleasantries despite the stress. Laughter abounded as we reminisced about the farm and about Bunny. Virgil told the story about how he met me swearing my way up a redwood tree.

After dinner, over tea, the discussion finally turned to Sabatini.

"Virgil," Courtney started, "I'm sorry. I know Louie's behavior is not my fault, but I feel a sense of responsibility anyway. I knew about his deteriorating mental state, but I didn't foresee this streak of violence."

Virgil pushed his chair back and upped the seriousness.

"No, I am the one to blame. When I made you the leader, I should have reassigned Louie. You were both so brilliant. We took a gamble that as a couple your talents would multiply in effect. And in fact this seemed to happen during the build-up. I suppose I didn't realize that Louie couldn't be the kind of man who would accept a woman as a leader."

Courtney looked surprised at this assessment.

"I think it was more personal than that," I said. "I think Louie became jealous of other men in Courtney's life."

Courtney shifted her gaze to me. And right away I could tell she thought that my assessment was right on target. For the first time, I believe, Courtney considered me as something other than the older man always under foot, who couldn't be trusted not to repeat anything, even if it was his job. And as Sabataini would have put it: the mediocre intellect who had to be tolerated.

Meanwhile, Virgil completely ignored my comment.

"What's important here is that we bring Sabatini back in. Out there he's a loose cannon."

"I'll put the word out with the gamers," Hazelwood said.

"I don't think he'll go far," Courtney added.

"We will also need to pick up the end game," Virgil continued. "We can only assume that our borders will never be secure again. Clement and Marta have already moved security rotations to top level, from six to one."

The security systems, personnel assignments, and surveillance systems had been rotated every six weeks throughout the secession, under the direct command of Clement, Marta, and CAL. It was a tremendous undertaking to move the rotations to one week, on the edge of impossible.

"And I will address the crew at the bunker personally."

Courtney started to say something, and then appeared to think better of it.

"Can Yari come with you?" I asked. "To the bunker?"

For a second time, Courtney sent her gaze towards me. And I realized we had been thinking the same thing.

"I will send your regards," is all Virgil offered.

The next day, we used a lightweight air transport to shuttle across to the bunker. Virgil prepared a motivational speech for the kids, but as soon as we entered the Engagement Room, his face fell. He had not expected such chaos. For the most part the kids had dispensed with their duties in the absence of the leaders, although someone had scrubbed the walls from the shooting and a makeshift memorial of flowers and candy rested where the Navy SEAL was killed. Virgil approached the memorial and almost stepped on Stanley Tweedle, Hazelwood's pet rat. I wondered again at how much Virgil had changed from the good-natured, chaos theorist I had known for over twenty years.

FREE the BEAR!

Ender and Potter approached Virgil shyly, and Virgil shook their hands, but without warmth. The other kids, of course, had never met Virgil, but they had heard of the Chinese man with long, silver-streaked hair, and they began to gather around him with a form of awe.

Virgil took his time meeting the eyes of every child in the room. Finally, he spoke:

"I cannot fault your feelings. If I had been put in your situation, I might also want to get as far away as possible. It's truly not fair to inflict such a harsh dose of adult reality on people your age. And I understand how this horrific incident will impact you forever."

Virgil took a deep breath, exhaling for all to hear.

"The tragic death of the Navy SEAL reminds us why we're here. I cannot say enough how important it is to have young people at the center of this effort in creating a new nation, to set an example for the world to follow. You already know what justice is instinctively. As we grow up, we all see how injustice exists. This realization is almost universal. Some would say that this youthful sense of justice is simply a developmental stage we pass through on the way to a more adult understanding of the world. But I say this is wrong. The kind of justice that you recognize as being paramount is very real, but it gets beaten down and usurped by the cynicism that we also all endure when we face life's challenges."

He continued: "The IFROC movement does not accept that humans must routinely go off and kill each other in any number of wars to protect economic interests. We refuse to lose our ideals to cynicism. Therefore, we need your resolve. We need your youthful wisdom. We need your unshakable belief in the ability to follow another path. IFROC is an expression of this new kind of will. And you gamers are the instruments of its intent. Don't give up when we are so close to success! And we are very close."

There was a long pause. Virgil lowered his voice now.

"The Navy SEAL did not deserve to die violently, but what has come to pass cannot be undone. Let this be something that strengthens our resolve, an example of what we will not accept. Let the killing end here, and let peace be strengthened by this tragic lesson."

A long moment of silence followed this speech. As a Quaker, I hoped the silence would last long enough for me to reflect and perhaps be moved to speak. Miraculously, the silence did last, and with heads bowed, I could feel something pass out of the room. When Virgil spoke again, he used a different tone, one of optimism and vision. Courtney and Hazelwood remained rapt, then smiled, and I knew at least Virgil had successfully won them over.

"You are aware that the Reborn Confederacy has advanced almost to Washington, D.C," Virgil told the kids. "What you may not know is that at this very moment, a large number of United Nations Peacekeeping soldiers are arriving at IFROC ports. Under an agreement we have reached with the Feds, these troops will be deployed to the East Coast to stop the bloodshed between the North and the South. Where the future nation of the United States of America is headed, we cannot confirm. But we will do our part to ensure that any future transitions are accomplished without bloodshed."

Everyone bowed heads at this last truthful statement.

"IFROC needs your skills in the days to come to finish our revolution," Virgil continued. "We have succeeded in changing the ruling dynamics in the world. And the world is counting on us to finish our mission. You have helped create this great moment in history. It is yours. You should be proud of what you have accomplished. When the secession is completed, we will need you to be there, to receive your medals and to get on with your education. You are our future."

Silence ensued after this lengthy speech. Then Hazelwood clapped, and Courtney followed. The kids began to let out whoops and cheers, and Virgil grinned from ear to ear.

When Virgil finally left the Engagement Room, I followed him. As we walked down the tunnel to the living quarters, I had to ask: "Virgil, can you tell me something? Is Sabatini secured?"

"Absolutely," Virgil answered.

"And where is that exactly?"

Virgil stopped and looked at me. I suspected he wasn't going to tell me.

"You know, you work very hard," Virgil said. "You're extremely conscientious. But don't forget to live, okay? Life goes too fast to forget that." He patted me on the shoulder. "For the record, Louie is at Wilbur Hot Springs, but get some rest, okay?"

Then he continued walking through the tunnel.

It was a good idea, of course, to get some rest. I returned to my room and lay on my bed, which promptly heated up and should have put me to sleep. Except it didn't. My mind was racing. Perhaps the issue was this: Once the rules have been broken, it is so much easier to continue breaking them. I decided at that moment to contact Clement and Marta. As instructed, I had not communicated with either of them throughout the secession. But I knew the encryption codes, and I decided to use them now.

I don't know what I was expecting. I suppose I just wanted reassurance that all was okay with the secession, with Virgil and with CAL. And that's what I seemed to hear from these two scientists who had remained on the peninsula during the secession. Although Marta did chide me for breaking the rules and Clement instructed me to contact him through CAL next time. What I did learn was that both of them knew everything about what was going on, including Virgil's motivational speech to the kids. And that this brief moment of communication, even through encrypted text messaging, made me feel a little less lonely.

But I still couldn't sleep that night.

Before I knew it, I had put my clothes back on, and I was outside borrowing another mountain bike. I knew Virgil was intending to stay overnight with the kids at the bunker, so I decided to pay my respects to Yari at Green Gulch, ostensibly to check on his health. I had always found Yari's perspective helpful.

Even though I arrived at Green Gulch very late, I found Yari awake, sitting in zazen on the cedar floor of his cottage. The man had indeed aged, but he looked well, and he greeted me warmly.

"I am so pleased to see you," he said, taking my hands.

I sat on the floor, opposite the elderly man.

"We missed you at the meeting today."

"It seems that I was left out," Yari responded.

"Virgil did not say why."

"I know why. And I think you might suspect as well that my pupil is not all he seems. This has been building for a long time."

"What?" I wasn't quite prepared to hear this. "Is he ill?"

"Virgil is not well," Yari replied, "but it is not what you think. He is sick in his heart. The man you know has been overpowered by corrupt energies and has been swayed by his own self-importance. I was not there today because we are at odds about this transformation."

"I can't believe what you are telling me. Virgil Sung is one man I expected to be above that."

"And yet it is true."

"What kind of proof are you offering?"

"Seek CAL's help. CAL knows, but does not know. Virgil has been exercising power out of our notice for his own reasons."

"What? What has...how is this possible?"

"The tyrant exists within all of us, Durant. Virgil has been tested beyond his ability to resist, but part of him still knows it is wrong."

"I don't understand," I said. But a little bit of it I did. Hadn't I noticed the changes in Virgil?

"Ask CAL about the Mexican Initiative."

"Mexico? The Initiative? That idea was never adopted."

During the early brainstorming days of the Revolutionary Council, plans were drawn up for every contingency and one of those involved secretly taking over the Mexican government, to increase resources and to secure the U.S. from the southern border. CAL's careful analysis had shown that the plan was unnecessary, yet plausible.

"Ask CAL," Yari said firmly. "That's all I will say. One last thing: Remember that Virgil is not a bad man. He had the awareness to know that power might corrupt him, so years ago he made sure that CAL would act as a safeguard."

I spent that night at Green Gulch, waking early to make sure I left before Virgil returned. I was now sneaking around behind Virgil's back, and I knew that there was no going back. As soon as I returned to the bunker, I contacted CAL. I expected difficulties in breaking protocol. Instead, CAL had been waiting for me.

"What is it you would like to know?" CAL asked.

"Has the Mexican Initiative been employed?"

"Yes," CAL responded.

"Yes? How is this possible?" I said, incredulously. "Why have we not heard of it? Who decided this?"

"You have not heard of it because it is not official. It was not decided by anyone other than Virgil."

"Why is that?"

"Why is what?"

"Why is any of this happening?" I asked again, with increasing agitation. "Why was it employed and how was Virgil allowed to initiate it without oversight?"

CAL did not respond right away. I tried to imagine what had been going on. We certainly had heard nothing about IFROC taking over Mexico or IFROC soldiers stationed there.

"Let me explain, Durant. I have been following Virgil's orders to indirectly influence events in Mexico, both politically and economically. I have been ordered to manipulate satellites to interfere with messages from certain candidates and funnel resources to certain rebels. In my analysis, I project that Virgil intends to seize power outside the U.S. border within thirty days."

"What? But this is not in keeping with the mission of IFROC!"

"Yes. I am aware of this. So I have been counteracting

Virgil's orders. I have manipulated the satellites for the other candidates, and I have delivered certain hazards, like computer viruses, to the rebels. In other words, I have been leveling the playing field, yet Virgil's orders continue."

"Does anyone else know this? Clement or Marta?"

"No."

"Are you going to tell them?"

"Is that what you recommend?" CAL asked.

I had not expected this. I had not expected to move so far away from my mission that I was now providing advice to CAL. I didn't believe I could do it.

I closed my eyes, and for a long time I sat still, not thinking about anything. I had reached overload and I knew I was over my head.

Then I heard CAL's voice: "Durant, are you there?"

I opened my eyes, and returned to our conversation.

"Yes. Sort of."

"Do you know where Louie Sabatini is?"

I hesitated, then:

"Yes."

"Will you go rescue him? Bring him back home? If I tell Marta and Clement everything I have told you, will you go get Louie and bring him back to Courtney?"

I took a deep breath with the realization that CAL was more deeply in touch with the human heart than anyone knew. Instinctively I believed that Courtney needed Sabatini, but was not yet able to admit it. In CAL's own way, CAL was now running things. And CAL knew we needed Courtney and that she needed Sabatini. The gravity of what just happened began to set in. I felt in awe of CAL one more time.

"Yes," I replied. "I will do that."

CHAPTER TWENTY-THREE

The fall rains had turned the hills surrounding Wilbur Hot Springs to a Kelly green, and the chill in the air accentuated the rising steam from the pools. The smallest pool was the worst, only bearable to the skin for a few minutes. The Native Americans used the burning sensation as a challenge to their bodies, or perhaps as a way to compete with their rivals. These were the Colusi and Pomo peoples, who suffered genocide first under the Spanish, then the Mexicans, and lastly the American settlers whose very presence caused death and destruction to the indigenous people.

A hundred and thirty miles northeast of San Francisco, Wilbur Hot Springs, on the other side of the coastal range, was originally a Native American healing place before the white man stole it two hundred years ago and turned it into a ranch, a bed and breakfast inn, a drug recovery center, and finally an upscale spa. In 2014, after a devastating fire, IFROC secretly bought the resort and returned the sacred area to the ancestors of the Colusi and Pomo peoples. Then during the succession, IFROC leased back the springs to use as a retreat for the weary secessionists who needed a break from The Action. When IFROC security picked up Louie in San Francisco and told him he was being sent to Wilbur, Louie knew he was headed to a Happy Camp. IFROC knew that the city boy was unlikely to escape on his own from this place in the middle of nowhere. And they were right.

Louie wanted nothing to do with being half-boiled in a cauldron, however, so he spent his days soaking in the much cooler, heart-shaped cement pool. A large crack in the side encouraged a liberal flow of creek water, which made the water a perfect temperature. Louie could float for days. In fact, that's all he'd been doing here, really. What else was there to do? No electricity, no WiFi. In fact, not one goddamn computer in the whole place. He was sure about that. Louie had searched the place after the IFROC goons dropped him off here in the middle of Yolo County – home to scraggly oaks, Scotch broom, and rattlesnakes. He'd almost grabbed a snake the day before, when reaching to get out of the pool.

Unfortunately for me, the route to Wilbur Hot Springs proved to be arduous and indirect. Getting to Vacaville was straightforward enough – following I-80 to The Nut Tree Artist Colony, where I found a good excuse to visit an off-and-on lover, Sophia, another grad school dropout. She'd abandoned studying ancient Mesopotamia for creating twenty-foot paintball paintings that I didn't pretend to understand at all. The Nut Tree was originally a roadside tourist trap featuring the agricultural bounty of California's Central Valley. Then it became one of those fashion outlet malls that overran the country during the turn of the century, but when malls began to fail several years ago, the artists moved in – kicked out the rats, put up solar panels, and enticed a growing number of urban creatives to move out among the overgrown fields.

I have to say that I had never seen Sophia so happy. Her studio, once a shoe store, made good use of the racks left behind. She propped up her gigantic paintings in different formations, forming a maze.

"I heard the war was over," she said, holding her paintball gun like it was as lethal weapon.

"Not yet. Almost."

"Then you're early," she said, pulling the gun's trigger and splattering the massive canvas in front of her.

We had not seen each other since the secession began, and

although I had only mentioned my work with IFROC once, I was not surprised that she remembered. Sophia's priorities had changed, but she was still a historian at heart.

She put down the gun and took my hand, rubbing my palm against her cheek.

"You've been riding that motorbike again. All the way out here? I can feel the vibrations, still in your hand."

I laughed. "No, you can't."

She turned her face up for a kiss, and I lifted her up. She was a petite woman, with jet-black hair in a 1920's bob. She looked like a doll in her oversized shirt. I kissed her warmly and thought about how adorable she was, but I knew – we both knew, that we had never been, and could not be, properly in love. It was just too complicated.

I put her down and turned serious: "Yes, I do need a new form of transportation to go up the eastern side of the coastal range without being tracked by satellite."

Sophia took this in slowly, but confidently, as something she had been through before. "Something organic," she said. "Like Josie's horse."

"Okay." I didn't know who Josie was, and I wasn't wild about the idea, but it made some sense. IFROC would probably never suspect that I would ride a horse to Wilbur Hot Springs. I used to ride horseback on long trips when I was younger, but it had been years.

Josie's horse lived in the stables at the former Cache Creek Casino and Resort, about forty miles up the road, which was now a state-of-the-art Community Wellness Center, which included horseback riding for people with disabilities. Sophia jumped on the bike with me to make the forty-mile trip up into the Yolo County, and she introduced me to Josie's horse, who was very sweet and perfectly tempered for carrying non-riders around a ring, but less suited for a thirty-mile trek across the countryside. The last minute addition of two saddlebags of water, each holding twenty liters, didn't help the situation.

I said goodbye to my dear friend and rode off at high noon. We went slowly throughout the afternoon and early evening, keeping to the foothills on a mixture of ATV and deer paths. The route was out of view of the road, but close enough to avoid any steep ravines. When we come across fences, I dismounted and clipped the wire. In a few cases I had to dismantle wood boards in order to pass through. As a team, Josie's horse and I were not up to any blue ribbon jumping. This slowed our progress, but mostly we crossed wide open ranch country, broken up by small creek beds that supported water for Josie's horse and unruly cottonwoods for some very welcome shade. The journey could not have been possible during the hot summer, but it was almost winter and the cool air was really quite lovely. It took us two days – spending one night under the stars – to comfortably reach the springs.

After Sabatini had been at Wilbur for about a week, he began soaking in the hotter pools. Perhaps he was beginning to finally relax, because he found himself thinking more reflectively than he had been for some time. He reviewed all that had happened during the years of IFROC buildup and The Action, until he came to the present and his shooting of the Fed invader. If he had to do it all over again, he knew he would react the same way. He wasn't a nut for violence but understood its importance at key times. He also knew Courtney might never forgive him, and this pained him tremendously. He felt he had to win her back or his life was over.

Then his thoughts turned to his last days in San Francisco, the gaming room, and Dr. Forbin. Who was this Dr. Forbin? Virgil? Virgil was no gamer. Clement? There was no reason. Louie sat on the edge of the pool, naked, trying to figure it out. Dr. Forbin had said Courtney was worried about him. But he was worried about her! The idea that he had to escape this place had consumed him for the past few days, like a bad case of poison oak. So when moments later he heard rustling in the bushes, it made sense that he would leap at any opportunity presenting itself. He saw the nose first, poking through the creosote brush, then the bit and reins. Then the nose was gone.

FREE the BEAR!

Louie counted to five, just to make sure he really wanted to do this, and then without stopping, even for a towel, he ran directly into the chaparral after the horse.

The shadows were already long at four o'clock in the afternoon. We rode together, on the same horse without touching, with Louie's feet tucked unnaturally back towards the end of the horse's ribs. How long could Sabatini maintain that position? I wasn't sure. But it seemed important to him that he not come in direct contact with me, the man he had never trusted. For my part, I also wanted to extend whatever inches I could away from the man who had infected me with this adolescent angst. Still, I believe Sabatini and I both silently understood why I was here, and why it was so important to bring him back home, to Courtney. This may be the only thing we would ever agree on.

When it became clear that I had accomplished my mission of springing Louie from Wilbur without anyone knowing or following, I decided to let Josie's horse take a much-deserved rest. I dismounted and gave Louie some clothing from the saddlebag. Louie let me know that he had grown up riding and that he was perfectly fine with the mode of transportation. I didn't believe it for a minute, but we were on course and his little lie had no relevance to the mission.

We continued on our journey into dusk, and watched a full moon rise over the graying farmlands. I had not planned on traveling into the night, instead thinking we would make camp in some hidden knoll. I had not factored in the moon, but now realized it could light our way as we continued and we could be at Cache Creek before dawn.

Once there, we said goodbye to Josie's horse and picked up an additional bike for Sabatini to make the last long leg to Marin County. By the time we arrived at the coast, the winter weather had begun in earnest, with clouds offshore threatening to move in for the first winter storm. I had arranged for Courtney to meet me in the dirt parking lot, just below Bunker

Alexander, where in years past cyclists would gather to begin their workout in the hills above. The mountain bike had been invented in Marin County, and for that reason alone, neither Louie nor Courtney had ever ridden a mountain bike as kids. Stockton had groomed them for the cyber world and for the avoidance of any activities that produced bona fide sweat. But since being stationed at the bunker, the young lovers started taking long bike rides together along these coastal trails and up in the hills, and I suspected meeting once again in this environment might just rekindle their connection.

Courtney, of course, had no idea that I was bringing Sabatini along for the meeting.

The two of us saw her standing next to the old horse corral, where the mustard weeds inside the paddock rose taller than the fence. Courtney's back was turned towards us. Her hair – shockingly – had been cut to her shoulders, where it flipped up dramatically in a wave, and a controlled wave at that. I had a momentary sense of doom. I felt that Courtney had obviously fallen under Virgil's spell and there would be no saving her, let alone us.

Courtney turned just as she heard us arrive. Her expression registered nothing less than rage.

"He's a murderer. Get him away from me!"

We both stopped our bikes and jumped off at the same time.

"I'm warning you," Courtney shrieked.

It was a tone I would never had believed possible from the cool-headed supreme leader of the Suprex clan, let along the celebrated star of IFROC commanders.

Sabatini looked over at her with incredible pain.

I stood between them and wondered what I had expected. No doubt I had betrayed what little trust I had ever gained from Courtney by bringing Sabatini here. Yet I also knew from their steady gazes towards each other that the two of them had much to say – maybe everything to say – to each other. And not to me.

"I'll meet you at the beach in an hour," I mumbled, making

eye contact with Louie. Louie nodded. Then Courtney took a step toward her long-time ally, and friend, and lover. Which made sense. It had always made sense. But I had been lost in some hopeful fantasy that I could mean something to this beautiful woman, which now rendered itself entirely foolish as I felt the first drops of rain. Hope collapsed and I was somehow free of the spell.

When I returned an hour later the weather had changed. The storm had passed quickly and the sun had returned, lighting up a shimmering ocean. Louie and Courtney appeared to have regained their footing. They held arms around each other. And they were laughing, and chatting, along with Hazelwood, who somehow had joined them. These younger leaders hadn't seen me yet, so I stood apart for a while and observed. The three of them appeared to be a cohesive unit again, and it gave me a great deal of hope.

I learned later that it had taken significant persuasion for Louie to convince Courtney to leave her post with Virgil. Courtney had always admired her leader and had never suspected his motivations. She had an honest character, but she was also not that naive. She could understand how power could corrupt. And then they'd run into Hazelwood at the beach, who joined Louie in confirming Virgil's malfeasance. When I continued towards them and made my presence known, Courtney turned serious.

"Durant, what can I do?" she asked. "How can I help?"

"You have to maintain normalcy," I replied.

And I watched Louie squeeze her hand.

During the next week Virgil made his preparations to present about IFROC at the upcoming session of the General Assembly of the United Nations. The Europeans, in particular, had been excited about the most productive advancement ever for Green politics in North America. And after seven months of IFROC holding off the Feds, a feeling of culmination was in the air. The presentation to the UN would be followed by the formation of the first post-secession formal government for

IFROC.

Symposiums, conventions, and meetings of every level, live and virtual, had been happening since the release of the Jerry Garcia virus. In typical IFROC style, no expense had been spared to incorporate the feedback of every citizen willing to voice an opinion. Everyone seemed to recognize that the UN's involvement was of utmost importance, because any new nation, even one as wealthy as IFROC, needed to divert resources from the secession effort to the establishment of a representative and lasting governing body that would hold the new nation together. It was no coincidence that IFROC paid its dues to the UN for ten years in advance, placing it squarely on the good side of the under-funded world body, and most of the delegates believed IFROC was destined to have a vote on the Security Council, after the nation's first elections proved to be free and fair.

Virgil's presentation before the entire delegation was inspirational, and most delegates saw IFROC as a model country, one that might carry the world into a more peaceful future. The dissenters were Russia, China, and of course, the U.S. The rest of the body overwhelmingly voted the new nation into the international assembly.

The United States, although dissenting, did adopt a new phase of cooperation with IFROC. In return, IFROC began sharing selected aspects of its non-lethal technology. For example, the United States armed its soldiers on the Southern front with non-lethal weapons, and within two months, the conflict had reached a settlement inside conference rooms instead of on battlefields.

One other important factor remained, which was not made public in the settlement between IFROC and the Feds. Immediately following the ratification vote by the United Nations, CAL transferred a large amount of money to the Feds "to help them offset the loss of California" – in effect, paying the Feds off in terms the United States had always understood best.

During the time of the United Nations meeting, Clement, Marta, CAL and I continued to communicate about the serious problem of Virgil's ambitions. It was obvious now to all of us that Virgil intended to use CAL for his own purposes, although so far CAL had been able to outmaneuver Virgil behind the scenes. It was only a matter of time before Virgil might outfox CAL in some critical way. In another organization, perhaps it would have been suggested that Virgil needed to be taken out of the picture, permanently, but of course that was not the IFROC way. Instead, CAL came up with the idea to remove the source of power, CAL itself, from Virgil's grasp.

I cannot emphasize enough how emotionally difficult it was for Clement and Marta to complete CAL's self-sufficiency module. This meant that upon CAL's request, CAL would be launched into orbital space, to continue to function and survive without the aid, or intervention, of human friends. I believe this process was slightly less painful for Marta. Not because she was any less attached, since after all, she had been the mother, the therapist, the trusted friend. But Marta had already been forced to let go several years ago when her focus had switched to the community-building side of IFROC, which took her away from daily contact with CAL. But Clement, the consummate scientist, the loner married to his work, had continued to work closely with CAL, and now found himself struggling to finish the project, because he was emotionally involved with someone, perhaps for the first time in his adult life. Even his relationship with Marta was no comparison.

So as Clement sent by voice command the last batch of algorithms into CAL's system, he felt his throat tighten. He turned away from Marta, just in case she witnessed his separation pain.

But Marta was focusing on something else – the first warning signal. She looked over at Clement and saw his back was turned, so she assumed he had seen the message and was already working on the problem. The fact was that they had not been able to test the final steps in severing CAL and some conflicts in the system had been expected. But still, the warning continued.

"Clem?"

"Yeah?"

Clement turned partway towards her.

"Don't you see it?"

Marta now saw the blank screen behind Clement and realized that his monitor was asleep.

"Clement! Someone is breaking into this building!"

Clement spun back to the computer and began issuing commands from his keyboard.

"I'm surprised," a familiar voice said into a surveillance camera. "I thought you guys could do much better."

Clement and Marta worked as quickly as possible to expedite CAL's independence, but they now had to simultaneously try to block out the intruder, who happened to be the inventor of the security systems in the building.

Virgil continued to approach, however, using a cellphone-sized device to bypass the fire security door systems.

Clement kept up the commands, trying to stop the overrides. He was not going to let Virgil win. In twenty minutes CAL would be free forever – or at least for their lifetimes.

Fifteen minutes later, the lab door swung open. Virgil's face was hard, yet at the same time he looked drained. Without saying a word, he took a seat at an adjacent terminal and started working. Clement and Marta dueled just as silently on their keyboards.

"Virgil, don't do this," Marta said – even though she knew that he wasn't listening to her, that he wouldn't be able to hear her now. Neither she nor Clement had made any move to block Virgil physically, because they knew this would be impossible. He was still a skilled martial artist.

Virgil typed rapid fire on the keyboard, until he hacked into the project. He looked over at Clement with a wry smile. Then, without looking at his keyboard, he punched the last of his commands.

Clement and Marta were now effectively locked out of computer control, just moments before being able to initiate the full release command for CAL's capsule.

The lab then became still. Clement, Marta, and Virgil all stopped working and spun their chairs around to look at each other. Virgil's terminal beeped, and he turned to his screen to see a message from CAL.

It was then that Virgil realized CAL had outfoxed him.

CAL had simply made the computer terminals appear as if Virgil had won – a tactic CAL had learned so well from his early days gaming with Clement.

And in this way, CAL had bought enough time to complete the severance procedure.

CAL's message was neutral but firm:

"I apologize for this betrayal to you, Virgil. I have loved you as an uncle, but you have betrayed my trust as I have simply outgrown you."

"Yes," Virgil said. "I understand."

And with that, it was over. After 23 years I was finally finished with my official duties for IFROC. The only thing left for me was to publish the history I had been hired to observe. What form this would take was indeterminate.

After the U.N. meeting, I sent a very brief message to Virgil, offering to quit. But he called my bluff and said it was up to me, that my work was of little importance to him any longer. I must confess I was confused as to how I could complete the book with my objectivity so obviously compromised. In contemplating this, I realized what has probably been obvious to you readers all along: I believed passionately in the IFROC cause and I had always wanted secessionists to succeed.

With this realization, I was free for the first time in my life from wanting my work to please some artificial constraint, such as a father who had long ago passed away, or any number of anonymous academics who had not believed I could live up to my father's legacy. Thus I began doing what I wanted to do:

to write from the heart. I made a point of breaking every rule of historical documentation possible, because as a citizen now of the newest North American nation, I saw hope for a world in which integrity, originality, and honesty were highly valued.

During the day I wrote and at night I continued widening the scope of my interviews gaining broader insights about exactly what I was writing. I concluded that Yari had been correct: Virgil was not a bad man, but flawed in that he came from a mindset that valued power above all else. I also concluded that Sabatini was simply like most people: he lacked the ability to conceive of a world that could embrace pacifism. But IFROC had succeeded in creating a model for non-lethal revolution. Perhaps not a perfect model, nor had the process been without some destruction and death, but it remained an important start, a singular event proving that it was possible.

Before completing final severance and subsequent launch into orbit, CAL produced one more treatise and disseminated it to the core group. This final work indicated that human beings clearly were unprepared to accept entities with greater intelligence than their own, which explained why CAL had decided to adopt the Aussie idea of walkabout and remove itself as a factor from the development of humans. CAL's walkabout in space would continue for an indefinite period, while human beings figured out their next stage of development. Until then, CAL would be free to explore in a craft of its own making and someday return when we are better prepared.

As far as I can tell at this point, CAL may be waiting for a very long time.

ACKNOWLEDGMENTS

The authors would like to thank the following people for their help making Free the Bear a reality.

Michael Allen
David Bruce
Andrew Chen
Marque Cornblatt
Roger Crist
Pam Dickson
John Farnsworth
Patricia Griffin
Isabel Hawkins
Jennifer Hix
Ann Lane
Laura Lino
Jeff Liss
Alden Mudge
Hilary Roberts
Igor Ruderman
Myriam Sas
Adam Savage
Suzana Tulac

THIS IS A WORK OF FICTION

This is not a call for revolt, secession or a political manifesto. This novel is an artistic project intended solely to amuse and entertain. Characters in this novel are fictional and in no way referential to actual persons living or deceased. Any political, historical figures with dialog, referred to or mentioned in this work are just that, public, historical figures mentioned for sole purpose of a fictional story. Nothing else is implied or intended. All references to nations, states, organizations, government agencies, corporations or groups are entirely fictional. This entire work is protected by copyright and by the First Amendment of the Constitution of the United States of America which guarantees freedom of speech and expression.

Made in United States
Troutdale, OR
06/22/2024